## About the Author

As a husband to a wonderfully patient wife and a dad to two beautiful teenage girls, Steve Wilkinson thanks his lucky stars that life has dealt him a good hand. Writing had been a passion ever since his favourite author, the late great David Gemmell sadly died way too early. His books and characters helped shape his childhood that still live with him today. Writing feeds his soul, and his family is his strength. Anyone who reads his books and says that they have enjoyed the story is the icing on the cake! He also love cake!

# The Greater Good

**Steve Wilkinson**

# The Greater Good

Olympia Publishers
*London*

**www.olympiapublishers.com**
OLYMPIA PAPERBACK EDITION

A CIP catalogue record for this title is
available from the British Library.

ISBN: 978-1-80074-803-3

This is a work of fiction.
Names, characters, places and incidents originate from the writer's
imagination. Any resemblance to actual persons, living or dead, is
purely coincidental.

First Published in 2023

Olympia Publishers
Tallis House
2 Tallis Street
London
EC4Y 0AB

Printed in Great Britain

# Dedication

I have always been jealous of those who have a true faith. To believe without question and to know without fact, is a gift I have yet to receive. I find myself hoping that any who find a faith are rewarded in their belief in written truth. My path is to follow a faith where God does not live. As I watch the world often burning around me, much to the calls of religion and interpretations of truth, I wonder if those who look to find a place in the next world, could try a little harder to enjoy their time inside this one. We all live on the same planet, regardless of what we believe comes next. It is noble when people actively look to make change. But those who try to save the world must make sure that it is a world where we all need it saved in the same way. Activists should not become terrorists to have another point of view is not a crime. To have another perspective is not wrong. But to blindly refuse to listen is immoral. This book is dedicated to my family, where my faith never needs to be questioned, as my love and belief in them all is real, not written. They are all I will ever need to worship in this world and whatever comes next.

# Acknowledgements

Thanks to my patient loving wife, who has encouraged me to finally share my words with the world.

# Chapter 1

## Beyond Reasonable Doubt

Timeline—3 September 2019
Life Sentences

If a person is found guilty of murder, a court must give them a life sentence.

A life sentence lasts for the rest of a person's life – if they are released from prison and commit another crime they can be sent back to prison at any time.

*Whole life term*

A whole life term means there is no minimum term set by the judge, and the person is never considered for release.

For most of the day, Joshua Wright sat with his head in his hands, staring down at the floor. A few feet away, in the public gallery, three sets of parents sat, listened, and watched as both sides of the case spelt out their closing statements.

Nigel Fetherington QC, for the prosecution, began his closing statement. Mr Fetherington was over 6'5" tall, with a serious, gaunt looking face and a full head of white-grey hair. There was not an ounce of fat on his entire gangly body. Supporting a razor-sharp chin that balanced a tiny wisp of a beard on the end, he gave the impression of a wizard in a three-piece suit, rather than any man of law. Moving to the front of the members of the jury, Mr Fetherington spoke directly to each of them in turn,

"Joshua Wright was in complete control. He knew exactly what he was doing, he never once considered his actions wrong."

"At any point, he could have stopped and taken stock of what he was about to do but chose not to. Each of the three victims did not have a choice. These innocent, young people were coldly killed at the hands of this callous, deluded individual who had not known any of them personally."

"This man claims he was divinely told to commit these horrific murders, for this is what they all must be called. There is no justification in any court in the world that can accept what he was doing was for his God.

"There can be no justification for murder no matter what. There are no words to comfort these poor families here, robbed from those they love the most. Each of these family members need to feel justice has been properly served, which can only come from a severe sentence that allows this man to be locked away for the rest of his life."

"Cold-blooded, unprovoked, seemingly random murder has no place in modern society. The prosecution calls for the honourable judge to take each of these crimes not as three linked deaths but consider each one as gruesome, separate acts of murder, for that is what they are.

"If I were stood before you today, prosecuting this man for just one of these crimes, I would be calling for the bench to make the right sentence of committing this man to a life in prison. But Mr Wright is charged with three accounts of murder.

"All equally disgusting, destroying not just the lives of those he killed by his deeds, but affecting each one of their families and their friends forevermore. All these broken, understandably angry people here today are already serving a life sentence of learning to live without their loved ones. Joshua Wright, without any prior convictions, chose to take life from those who deserved to live."

Nigel Fetherington walked over to stand before the man in the dock. Pointing towards the tall plastic box containing the defendant, he paused for a few moments dramatic effect. Speaking again, this time his voice was angry,

"There are times when a prison is too lenient for such a crime. Joshua's erratic behaviour has shown that he is unsafe to be allowed to know how long he must serve, to be able to walk amongst us all again.

"Some say all men should have a chance to redeem, reflect and repent their wrongs. I have always been one who agrees with this noble path of justice. If condemning Joshua Wright to a long prison sentence, allows him a chance to rehabilitate, then perhaps we should look on sentencing with the hope that he will one day come to realise the pain and regret of his crimes."

"But and I say this as one who has been stood here many times before, I have rarely known a man so completely convinced that his murderous actions were reasonable and the only choice he could make.

"I implore you all to remember, this man has pleaded *guilty* to all these crimes, he does not attempt to pretend that his actions were either wrong or difficult.

Each was intended, each was done without remorse."

*'You are charged with multiple first-degree murders, how do you plead?'*

*'Guilty your honour.'*

"Remember again, these were the words you all heard on the first day of this trial from Mr Wright.

"At no time has this man tried to defend his actions, he is

steadfast in admitting what he has done is good and right. My job as a prosecutor, in this case, has not been to convince you all enough to convict, I have tried to demonstrate that some people are beyond rehabilitation. I do not believe Mr Wright will ever admit to stating what he has done was either wrong or murder, he stands here believing what he has done is just. This leaves me with no choice but to state that a life sentence is, without doubt, the only decision you must make." Nigel Fetherington took a breath.

"The prosecution calls for the hardest sentence you feel is correct for one so lost that he does not see the pain he has caused. Thank you, your honour." "Taking a long look at the man in the dock with cold, steel blue eyes, Nigel Fetherington QC turned and walked away, back to sit on the front bench."

Next came the closing speech of Bill Gregory QC, who stood up for the defence. Mr Gregory was a short, timid looking man, balding with a bulging stomach to match his round head. Standing in front of his chair, he spoke only towards the front bench, whilst leaning hard onto a red leather briefcase on the desk before him.

"Your honour, although there can be no excuse for Mr Wright's conduct after these killings, after listening to the prosecution present their case so well, it is clear I will lose today, and rightly so."

"However, there is only one consideration here today I can ask, and that is to conclude a verdict based on the evidence. Nothing more, nothing less. Joshua Wright has explained to you all that he thought he was told by God to kill these three strangers. Joshua has no idea why they were chosen, why they were randomly selected, or why it was his holy task to kill them. This is a man who, up until a year ago, had never committed any crime. Mr Wright has never even had a parking ticket or ever been under any sort of investigation. Mr Wright is a man who up until last year, we would state as being a model citizen, in a good job, paying his taxes and even helping to feed the homeless in his spare time."

"So, what would make a peaceful man suddenly go from one we would consider good, to someone of pure evil, where he is able to commit such terrible crimes. Mr Wright says God, but most of us believe this to be madness. But he is not looking to be given a sentence based on insanity. Yet, I ask you all here today to question what we think is right."

"We are all quick to dismiss Joshua Wright who says he has been told by God to commit horrific acts, yet we all swear on a Bible to the same God that justice will be served here today. We are both using God to justify our acts, so we cannot dismiss that God plays a large part in deciding the truth."

"To think that this same God would ask a man to kill is without question, one most of us would think to be madness. We always treat those who hear voices from the divine, that go on to commit acts in his name as terrorists or clinically insane. It is very hard to look Mr Wright in the eyes and feel nothing but utter disgust, for what he has done is beyond normal reason. Using God to justify these actions is an easy alibi, for it gives us no real way of proving if Joshua Wright is a liar or someone who is so religious that they will do anything they are told when their *calling* comes."

"As we have told you in this case, Mr Wright was never one to be particularly religious until just two years ago. Joshua attended a church group regularly which is not a crime. Joshua was not part of any strange cult, nor was he known to have a particular religious background. Mr Wright's *calling* came suddenly, with enough power to convince a good man to kill those he did not know nor have any prior links to. This is all very painful, very random, and ultimately, very sad."

"When we use God to justify events there is always a void that is difficult to fill. But God is also used to justify many things in our lives.

"Most weddings are blessed under God. Funerals are finalised to receive the dead under God's watchful eye, and we pray to God to try to change events, usually from the terrible to make them good again. But in this case, Joshua Wright wants us to think the reverse can be endorsed, where God has told him to commit a terrible crime, where innocents have been targeted for His unknown reasons."

"In each of the three crimes, the evidence suggests the acts which led to the death of these wonderful family members was done without any pain to the victims. If Joshua is guilty of these crimes, then each was carried out carefully, so not to cause any terror or suffering."

"When we speak of murder, we tend to think of the terrible pain and suffering for those in their final moments as the realisation of death from another confronts them. But, in this case, from the forensic evidence presented to us, each of the victims was killed without fear or knowledge that death was coming."

"Mr Wright has pleaded guilty. I believe somewhere inside, he is still feeling completely guilty, for the guilt of following his calling will be with him until he too meets the God he claims to serve."

"The defence is not looking to disguise anything the prosecution has told you during this case. All that I ask is that when we sentence, we consider *how* Joshua Wright chose to end the lives of these three random people. There can be no justice for murder. To kill is completely wrong, no matter the motive or cause. But I ask you to look at what has been said during this trial closely, consider the evidence, knowing that the only real pain suffered was by all those here he has robbed from their loved ones."

"If the sentence is to be life and these murders are all pre-meditated as told, we must use this time to allow a chance for this man to come to terms with what he has done."

"Mercifully, there is no violence here to discuss, but murder is murder and for this man to plead so, then justice must be done. The defence gives way to the prosecution and knows that whatever decision comes from the verdict your honour delivers, it is done under the divine court this room is sworn to serve, *under God.*"

"Many of us talk to God in prayer, or silent thought. Many of us hope that he will answer our calls. Those of you who truly believe in God, I leave you with one question."

"Why do you pray if you are not expecting an answer? The answer is hard for us all to accept. Those who hear God are thought to be quite mad, yet those who speak to him are normal."

"We have a priest with us today, who told us earlier that God would never ask such a terrible thing from anyone in his flock. We all nodded our heads as we agreed with the fathers learned and respected knowledge of church law.

"But how does the priest know this information? Did God tell him of these things, if so, why are we not sitting here condemning this priest for hearing God's voice?"

"Those who make a career in the cloth, say they "hear" their calling, but what do they hear? In church law, the 10 commandments tell us clearly, *Thou Shall Not Murder*. This is the foundation to all our lawful principles as good people, forming the very bedrock of mainstream religions."

"If God told Joshua Wright to kill in His name, it goes against the very ethical principles he gave Moses on top of Mount Sinai. But, in all Biblical texts, including this one we have sworn an oath under today, Moses was *just a man*, who heard the voice of God and obeyed his commands."

"It is difficult for us all to accept, but we judge only those we think of as good, that can truly ever hear God's voice. If we condemn Mr Wright today, as we must, then also accept that those who claim to hear God's voice, are either sane or worse, speaking the truth. To judge what God has or has not said is difficult for any jury to uphold."

"The defence rests your honour."

Sitting back down on the front bench, Bill Gregory, began to write a few notes, as he readied himself to accept what could only be a lost cause.

For a moment, there was silence, save for the muffled sound of sobbing from one of the mothers above. Both lawyers put their pens onto the table, ready to listen to the judge both knew well. This was not expected to be a case where anyone would be sitting tomorrow, for the defendant, admitted, confessed and *was* guilty. But justice and procedure still needed to be followed.

Removing his round silver-rimmed spectacles, the red gowned judge, starred into the members of the jury, ready to deliver his final summary of this case.

"Good afternoon ladies and gentlemen of the jury. I will speak to you today on behalf of the crown. Over the past four days, you have heard from both the prosecution and the defence, both presenting you witness statements and evidence that this man, Joshua John Wright, stood here in the dock, did commit the crime of murder on three counts."

"What you have been told by the prosecution is that Mr Wright stands accused of not one, but three murders, a crime that carries a heavy sentence, a crime which seems to have no clear motive, but spurred by voices heard only inside his head. You must consider and debate the seriousness of this crime. You must remove any religious feelings you may well have, for the crime is still murder and as such, must follow the rules of justice in this land."

"We have been told that mercifully none to the victims suffered, but still we must remember that none of these innocent people deserved to die. Here in this country, we follow the word of written law and murder is amongst the highest crimes listed, so if you are to find this man guilty of what he has been charged with committing, then with it I will deliver a sentence that this high crime deserves."

"The defendant has not at any time tried to either deny or defend his guilt for what he has done. Hearing this statement, with the defence also stating that they have heard this free admission of guilt, this should make decisions easy for you all, but I add a word of caution. You each need to ask yourselves that if you believe this man to be guilty of any one of these murders, *beyond a reasonable doubt*, this should guide your verdict. If there is anything to suggest that something is amiss in either the guilty plea or the prosecution's summary, you must come to a just verdict without any debate. We will adjourn now whilst you come to your decision." the judge stated.

Standing, with the rest of the courtroom, he left the room.

Three hours later, the jury delivered their verdict for each murder. All counts were guilty.

For a day, the court was adjourned whilst the Judge, the right honourable, Markus Ponteby QC, considered his closing words and the sentence he needed to pass. Finally, the jury was asked again to gather back inside the courtroom.

Outside, the rain was falling hard, but a brave, determined set of reporters, TV and radio crew stood awaiting results of the sentence passed.

Last year, this had been a huge story, but it had lost momentum whilst it waited to come to trial. Finally, these horrible crimes had come back again into the public eye, after a short manhunt had finally led to the capture, charge, and prosecution of a seemingly normal man a year ago.

This was a crime unusual in its apparent randomness. Three murders, totally unrelated with no motive. The nation was left mystified as to why this man had changed his life to cause these seemingly random murders.

The detective who finally arrested and charged the man with the three murders was none the wiser as to why each of the dead people, all killed within a radius of fifty miles of each other, were randomly selected. If it were not for the fact that each victim died using the same painless way of killing, they could have easily been thought to be separate events. But, due to the fact they were all committed within four weeks of each discovery, this was not a coincidence.

The court was asked to stand as the old judge of thirty-four years' experience walked back into the room. There was a tension and a sense that soon this trial would be concluded.

Sitting at his bench he invited the court to sit again. Turning to the man in the dock, he asked the tall, balding white man in his late forties to stand.

"Thank you, ladies and gentlemen, of the jury. Schedule 21 of the Criminal Justice Act 2003 provides that if the court considers the seriousness of the offence is exceptionally high, the appropriate starting point should be a whole life order. Whilst I am satisfied that the seriousness of this offence is exceptionally high, I must nonetheless consider if this should with it carry a minimum term starting at 30 years."

"Joshua John Wright, for the past four days, the court has listened to compelling evidence of your guilt, which has demonstrated to the members of the jury that you are a murderer. There is no doubt in my mind that you are a murderer, that has led to the death of three innocent young people. The grief of the families both here and at home cannot be overstated. Even in knowing these victims did not suffer, this does not lessen the pain for those that loved them so."

"What prompted you to believe that the voice inside your head was guiding you to kill these people is a matter for speculation, whatever the motive or truth behind your true reasons. Yet, each of these people was targeted intentionally and killed cold-bloodedly, in what in your own words was described as a *holy mission for the greater good*. This case could easily have been trialled as terrorism, for anything done under the name of a God that leads to the death of innocents is often prosecuted as such. But the prosecution has not presented or asked that we treat this crime as terrorism. They have asked I sentence you for multiple counts of first-degree murder, which I must follow."

"While I have had regard to the absence of any other relevant conviction, I have no doubt there can be only one sentence. There is no way to prove your claims of voices inside your head are true and you make no attempt to make any plea of insanity. For the offence of these murders, I sentence you to life imprisonment with a whole life order."

As Judge Ponteby's gavel hit his wooden block, the gallery above could be heard with the family's jubilant calls of "Yes". At the back of the courtroom, journalists scurried through the doors, writing on notepads preparing to inform their various media outlets.

In the dock, the man sentenced to life imprisonment was quietly led away by a policeman through a small door behind. With his head bowed low, he had expected the sentence to be severe. It was the only possible outcome the judge could deliver for such crimes.

Two policemen gestured for the man called Joshua to walk out of the room, along a short corridor to an outside door. In the brilliant sunshine beyond, a crowd of press photographers gathered close to the back of a prison van with its doors wide open. Quickly, the prisoner was pushed up the steps into the back of the caged van, surrounded by the sounds of hundreds of cameras clicking like a field of crickets. As the thick solid doors were slammed shut, the man sat back on the bench seat and closed his eyes allowing his tears to finally flow free, for the voice of God inside his head that had told him to kill each of the three innocent young people was finally gone.

His relief to the sudden silence was completely heaven-sent.

# Chapter 2

## DS Nick Murray

### Timeline—28 February 2018

A year and a half before the court case.

Within the small cul-de-sac, in the village of Netherby, just outside the city of Bath, the chorus of ten ice scrappers across frozen windscreens could be heard. The starlit dark morning was freezing, with a cloudless clear sky. Temperatures of -4 had been shown on smartphone apps before anyone left their houses for the last two weeks, which even at the height of the day, were barely rising above two degrees.

With each pressed scrape, timed to the metronome rhythm of the beating pulse of windscreen wipers, this morning dance of defrosting cars was still the same even with those who had the most modern of cars. In mere minutes, back windows were cleared through heated elements, but only a few cars were given the optional extra and the more important feature of a heated windscreen.

Those who had entered themselves into the new age of environmentally friendly vehicles running off pure electricity, tried to clear their icy screens in the same old-fashioned way. These champions of cleaner fuel, all seemed more concerned than their carbon hungry friends, as leaving an electric car started and standing with its heaters fully on blow to the windscreen, watched helplessly as the battery charged percentage bar on their fully digital dashboards, gave them even less confidence that their clean energy-c vehicle would last the entire day without at least one more top-up.

DS Nick Murray was pleased he had yet to jump on the bandwagon of new power. Many of his colleagues had already become eco-warriors, buying hybrids and fully electric cars that even Greta Thunberg would approve.

Nick had thought the idea quite stupid as most of them were switched over to fossil fuels by the time they reached the petrol stations. With the average commute across the Somerset or Wiltshire countryside sometimes over 100 miles a day, only the smallest of electrically charged cars had any chance of lasting on battery alone.

One of Nick's friends had recently purchased a huge 4x4 SUV, fully electric and carbon-free. The zero-road tax and fuel savings alone had been a real talking point during a morning briefing session, but discovering it needed eight hours to charge for only a forty-mile journey, had changed the arguments somewhat.

The new cost of the SUV alone would have kept Nick's old second-hand diesel car in fuel for twelve years, so as far as he was concerned, the decision to make the right move was not yet feasible.

His colleague had left the briefing angry that day, as many considered his purchase not thought through. It had been a cruel truth that two days later, he had needed to call for help when his SUV battery had given up in the pouring rain, ten miles across the middle of Dartmoor, far from any charger.

Nick had found it difficult not to join his colleagues in teasing the young officer the following day, but as the senior DS in the squad, he had needed to keep a professional lid on it.

Today, he was just happy that his eight-year-old, petrol thirsty two litre Audi TT was purring like a stroked cat, warm and able to last a full four hundred miles on a brimming tank, no matter the cold weather or carbon it needed to burn through.

With the inside of the car sufficiently warm enough to be winning the ice battle of the windscreen frost, Nick happily jumped into the driver's seat, out of the biting cold of the pre-dawn.

For the last ten years, he had always liked to be first into the Bath police station, as to him it showed his team that he was a leader who liked to lead by example.

After a twenty-year career in the Met, Nick and his twenty-year wife, Celia, had moved from London to Netherby, mainly out of a need for his wife to be near to her elderly mother. At the time, Nick had not been keen to move away from their lovely Kent home. After years of getting the dilapidated *old Blacksmiths* to be exactly as they both wanted, it had only been the home they had wanted for just a year.

But, with the loss of Celia's father from a sudden heart attack whilst he was tending Celia's mother after chemotherapy treatments from breast cancer, Nick had decided to sell up to find a house in Somerset, as Celia wanted to help her mother through the treatment in Bath, keeping her away from their home for months at a time.

Finding the house in Netherby was somewhat like the home they had in Kent, but as the old property already had the added benefit of a fully built granny annexe constructed, Celia had managed to sell her mother's home and reluctantly convinced her to move in with them both.

In what Nick thought to be a cruel act of God, his mother-in-law, with her cancer just announced as '*in remission*, had been out on a daily gentle evening walk, as advised by her doctor's only seven months after they had all moved in together. That day, she had become a statistic and victim of a hit and run driver, which Nick had not only been the first on the scene to attend, but he had also led the investigation to find who had killed her.

A drunk driver, whose speeding Friday night journey, had led Nick to support his wife through two years of counselling and helping Celia get through the trauma of it all. Nick had found the man responsible, who turned out to be a Jamaican businessman, arrested him, and been there in the courtroom when he was sentenced to prison for the crime.

The Met's loss had been Avon and Somerset's gain. Bath police had been pleased to receive a seasoned ex-London detective. In just a year he was made DS, becoming a big fish in a small pond, where in London promotion was next to impossible. His posting from London had been made simple, as his ex-boss had given him a glowing report to the Bath Chief constable. Nick loved his new position, although he still missed London and Kent where he had grown up.

With ten years of service working within the Bath branch, alongside two convicted murder cases to his name, DS Nick Murray was well on the career path towards Detective Inspector.

At fifty-five he still had ten plus years left to give the force but hoped this would take on a more managerial role as his bid for retirement and the decent pension beckoned.

Pulling out of his short gravel drive onto the main road, the usually busy A4 at 06.23 was still quite empty. Compared to his days commuting around the M25 and dropping into Lewisham, the journey to and from work was a breeze.

Although he was still very much a Londoner at heart, the

traffic was something he did not miss. Most of his early police life was spent at the scene of car accidents or incidents wherever more crowded roads were causing undue attention to precious police time.

In Bath and the countryside beyond, these types of problems were greatly reduced, which is why his mother-in-law dying in such an event was an even more cruel reminder of his previous life inside the Met.

The soft male voice of the local morning DJ on talk radio spoke about the headlines of the papers today. Nick thought that most DJs of this hour were specially chosen for their gentle light voices, as nobody wanted to hear a loud, brash, 'wake the hell up!' before seven a.m.

Slowly, the DJ was working his way through each of the main fleet street rags, calmly telling his listeners what was happening in the world. No matter what the gravity of the story was, he kept the same soft, level toned manner, barely raising an octave over his usual pitch, *"Yesterday evening a volcano erupted in South America, drowning an entire Chilian village in lava, whilst on the other side of the world, millions are looking at the prospect of starvation as a serious drought seems to be forcing people to migrate. Climate Change champions are linking both events to the same conclusion.*

*"I do not know what to think of these stories really, but I know how cold it is in the UK now, and I for one would be happy with a little of the warm air that volcano must be giving out. Harry over to you in the weather room, what have we got for the weekend, I have two dogs that need walking, are we expecting things to warm up at all?"*

The radio of Nick's car suddenly faded, replaced by the pounding thump of ACDC's "A Shot in the Dark." It was a ringtone that he still loved, reminding him of the heavy metal days of his youth. Pressing the optionally installed phone button on his steering wheel to engage the Bluetooth answering option, the radio was gone. Taking a glance at the screen on the tiny dashboard shelf to see who could be calling him this early, was never a good sign.

As 'A shot in the dark' vanished, a familiar voice came through a crackled phone reception, "Nick are you on your way to the office?" a female voice asked, fading in and out.

Speaking louder than he needed to try to overcome the fading, Nick replied, "Hi Sally, yes I have just left home. What's up?" he asked, knowing the night shift officer on the call desk only ever called if it was necessary or she had been instructed to by a senior.

Sally was just a series of electronic hashes and blips for a second before her voice came back in again at full clear volume,

"...DS Johnson says can you meet him at the scene. The mother is very emotional. We have another team en-route." Sally told him.

Nick pulled the car over to a layby, "Sorry Sally, can you repeat the first bit. The signal is terrible here. I got the bit about meeting Pete on site. Can you repeat the first part of what you said please?" Nick asked, pulling the car to a complete stop.

"Sorry, Boss. Yes. Can you re-route from your commute this morning and head directly to a village called Stockton-on-Avon? I will send you over the address by text now sir." Sally answered.

Within seconds the screen flashed up with a text message of the address, which Nick knew to be about thirty miles away, in the other direction.

Thank God his car was not electric. With over three-hundred miles left in the tank, such diversions were easy to accept without the fear of breaking down.

"Sally, can you give me some idea of what I am walking into?" Nick asked, as he always liked to at least prepare his train of questioning before arriving at a scene.

Sally was quiet for a second. Nick thought she was probably reading what had been sent over to her. With a voice as soft as the morning DJ on the radio station, she replied, "A young male has been found dead in his bed by his mother late last night. Believed to be about sixteen years old. No medical or previous conditions yet known. Popular Schoolboy, from what I am reading. DS Johnson believes he could have been poisoned. It looks like Molly Symonds is already on-site leading the forensics team. Press are aware and already gathering outside the house." Sally told Nick.

Nick thanked the officer and began to programme the sat nav to the postcode Sally had just sent over. Typing in the six digits, the female voice proudly announced that the journey to Stockton-on-Avon was thirty-five miles away. There were no traffic problems ahead and the estimated time of arrival was 7.52 a.m.

Turning his car around, he drove off, following the green road on the central screen display. Within five minutes he was driving past his driveway again and on towards the new Somerset destination.

Stockton-on-Avon was a village he had been to a couple of times before. It was one of the places they had looked to move when he and Celia had first moved down from London.

From his memory, it was a pretty village, built along the banks of the River Avon. Many of the larger properties sat like a scene from Henley Regatta, with jetties and small boarded docks holding rowboats bobbing tethered on the riverside. He could remember that the rest of the village was mainly older stone buildings, built like many chocolate box villages in the area. A huge old church stood with a short spire in the centre of the village, with two local shops and a lovely pub, where they had once eaten lunch. Celia had been very taken by a house near to the church, which had been described on the paperwork as The Old Rectory. When they arrived, it was clear it needed far more work than the photographs from the estate agents had led them to believe, but they had both been taken by the excellent views of the river and the distant Mendips hills.

The old stone house had been amongst their top three properties to see, with a very low price to match. This was going to be their preferred choice until they, fortunately, were informed by the man who had just viewed the property before them, that twice a year the river Avon was known to come up to the doorway and flood the entire garden. Both Nick and Celia had ruled this place out quickly after the heads up.

The only other thing Nick knew of this small village was that it was home to one of the biggest private schools in the area. It was a strange, often unknown fact that the southwest of England, especially in areas around Bath and south Somerset, was home to many of the most prestigious expensive schools in the whole of the UK.

Usually single-sex, most claimed historical roots up to two hundred years, educating students from all over the world. Where Oxford, Cambridge and Eton held the future prime ministers and business chief executives, the private schools of Somerset, Dorset and south west Wiltshire held many of the institutions that would one day supply them with their talented students to come.

All over the region, schools boarding every nationality on earth welcomed students from parents who could afford to pay the huge term fees asked.

Stockton-on-Avon was as far as Nick could recall an all-boys school, known for producing the England Rugby potentials, that mostly went on to the excellent sports university of Bath only forty miles away.

Nick could recall Celia talking about the school over lunch in the local pub with the local estate agent and his young trainee ten years ago. Several names that neither Nick nor his wife had ever heard of were banded towards them, proving this school was used to churning out future stars. Nick nor Celia was particularly interested in rugby, but both had nodded knowingly at the time, trying not to look stupid in front of the estate agent who was a huge rugby fan.

Apart from the school, Nick could not think of anything else that stood out in the area. There had been a serious car accident nearby he had been sent to investigate a few years ago, but apart from this, it was not a place that had ever come up before in his ten-year service here in the Wild West, as Celia called it far too often.

Calling this region the Wild West had always amused Nick. Celia had tried to build up an image that in her late teens and early twenties, Bath and Bristol and of course Glastonbury festival had been among the wildest places to grow up in the UK. Celia spoke of the rampant party scene and city clubs and something she referred to as the "The Dark Clubbing Side" which had hilariously turned out to be nothing more than young farmers secret discos in various barns and hidden buildings where minor narcotics were easily available.

For years she had tried to convince Nick that the West was a wild, untamed region where people knew how to have fun. This was the great untamed frontier where anything and everything was explored, found, and tried. But, as a boy growing up in

South-West London, with a pub almost every hundred yards and a bar, club, or secret rave to suit all flavours of life, believing the South West to be the metropolis of nightlife was a joke. Young farmers were not a patch on the skinhead and punk years Nick had grown up in.

Celia had been genuinely angry with Nick for laughing at her when she described her vibrant wild youth. But, over the years it had become a bit of a joke between the two of them. Celia still insisted on calling the region the Wild West, but Nick would correct her and state it should be called the 'Bumpkin Outback'.

Slowly the sun began to rise over the eastern horizon of the distant Mendip hills. Even with Nick's jesting to Celia, he had to confess that this entire region was beautiful and full of untouched ancient scenery that left the dull grey walled streets of London, featureless to the beauty of the green countryside.

Although they had lived inside the Garden of England in their previous home, there was a little comparison to the remote rawness of the Somerset hills.

As the morning awoke in the skies above him, the sun revealed a landscape, chilled and sparkling like freshly poured champagne. The frost of the night had turned Somerset into a fairyland of crystal, twinkling on every tree, plant, and blade of grass, like a million Christmas lights.

Many houses were now showing signs of life with window lights switched on in bedrooms. Somerset was slowly waking up to the day, but equally many would still be hibernating under warm duvets. The winter this year had been harsh, but for the family, he was driving towards, it had claimed far more than a warm duvet.

The Sat Nav announced that Nick needed to turn off the A4 and head south for two miles. Taking a narrow high hedged Broad, he sighed as the tractor he was following was in no mood to allow him to overtake. Instead, the tractor driver just looked ever forward without a care in the world.

Travelling at thirteen mph, the clock on the Sat Nav added a further three minutes to his destination. There was little he could do as passing the tractor on the narrow road was impossible, daring any car to run the gauntlet of his giant tractor wheels.

In the distance, the bent short spire of a church came into view. He was close now.

As Nick continued to look ahead, he was pleased to see the indicator light of the Tractor come on, turning off left. As he watched the huge red Massey Ferguson leave onto a small private road it made its way towards a five-barred gate, where hundred sheep looked to be hungrily waiting for him. Nick caught sight of a painted wooden sign hanging on a low stone wall at the entrance of the private road: -

*King Alfred's School for Boys. Entrance Beta. 10mph*

This was one of the four entrances into the huge grounds of the school estate. Behind the short drystone wall and across two further fields of sheep, Nick could see a pair of white posted 'H''s placed at each end of a private rugby pitch. A short distance away, another set of rugby pitch poles could be spotted, showing that there was more than one pitch for these young boys to train upon. Nick smiled at the thought of this being the Twickenham of the Wild West.

The school was situated not too far away from the village, built on a hill, above the houses and cottages lining the river Avon in the valley below. Nick could only imagine that much of the village was constructed after the huge central building, became a school. Whatever the huge building was at the end of the drive before it was a school, it now stood as the central picture view to a giant complex of outer buildings that made up this private facility. The views out across the countryside green vale beyond were stunning. With the sun fully up in the cold February sky, it was even more obvious why so many rich parents sent their children here to learn.

Many would pay huge prices to look out on this vista alone.

This was the same view the estate agent had framed in a picture behind his desk when Celia and Nick had come to look at the house ten years ago.

Driving down a narrow lane, twisting along a steep hill descending into the small village, Nick remembered this road as it reached the river along the shallow valley. It was deeper than he first remembered, not as pretty with no flowers or leaves on the trees, but it had been late August when he first set eyes on this place, not a bleak Tuesday morning in February.

The same picturesque stone houses bordered the riverbanks, with three newer properties still in various phases of construction. The Church in the centre of the village still looked to be the largest building around, which sat centrally inside a loose stone wall within the grassy village square surrounding it. Around the church grounds, old gravestones rested at every angle, each with the names of people who had once called this village home.

As Nick drove by the old stone houses that huddled tightly around a narrow high street, his Sat Nav called out he was about to reach his destination.

At the end of the high street, the houses thinned, emerging out to the church green. Slowing his car to a crawl, he could see his destination without checking the texted address, simply by the number of police cars now gathered and press vans setting up outside of a house, next to the church.

Stopping his Audi TT in an already crowded layby, he sat and took a double take at the house in concern, which was alive with police activity.

Two constables were already busy constructing a taped police line. Several locals were watching the action, but it was not crowded. Two dogs on leads were barking disapproval, one out of frustration that he could not run free across the grass as it was usually allowed to do and the second out of fear of the strangers gathered there.

One press photographer was standing as close to the house as he dared, talking to the policeman pulling tape, snapping occasionally at different people as they came out of the house.

An ambulance was flashing its blues, with its rear doors wide open and the ramp lowered to the ground.

Behind the ambulance, men dressed in white overalls wheeled a fully covered body into the back of the emergency response vehicle, carefully angling it to keep as much hidden from sight as possible. Behind the wheeled bed, a woman with long red hair was being held back, wailing as a man did his best to comfort her. Still dressed in her pyjamas and slippers, the dressing gown looked far too thin to give any kind of warmth outside on this cold February morning.

Even though Nick's professional eye had observed all these things, he was unusually oblivious to any of them.

All he could do was look at the house the police were swarming inside, in disbelief. The swollen river behind the house looked to be flooded with the lower half of the back garden submerged.

The wooden sign hanging on a little garden gate leading to

the front door of the cottage was still as crooked as the day Celia and Nick had first witnessed it when they had come here to view this same house ten years ago.

*The Old Rectory.*

# Chapter 3

## Murder One – Phillip Stevens (16)

### Timeline—16 March 2018

PC Sally Gunel delivered a full tray of six coffees and a plate of digestive biscuits over to the morning meeting. It was not because she was the only female in the room, it was purely out of respect that she was the youngest and least experienced officer in the room.

Working at the Bath station had been great, for every one of the men she worked with, each took shifts in making the brews each day. There were no expectations that the junior was the tea girl, for everyone, right up to DS Murray knew and would often turn the kettle on.

Sally liked to make the first cup for the day team, as often she would find herself far too busy manning the phones as the day went by. Today, was Friday, and like most Friday's, DS Nick liked to have a proper update from his team at this regular time.

Handing out each of the cups to the officers in the room in turn, most thanked her quickly as they listened to the boss talking at the front of the room. Only Sergeant Parsons, a young full of himself promotion seeking police officer had stopped and whispered to PC Gunel, "Racing to get the job done as usual. Officer Sally Gunel delivers excellent service to the team. She deserved that gold medal." Taking the hot mug away from Sally, he purposely touched her hands for far longer than he needed.

Smiling, PC Gunel ignored the stupid comment and carried on handing out the drinks.

Sergeant Parsons was still carrying a flame for her, Sally knew this. A year ago, Sally had accepted a date night out with him, only a week after she had first arrived at the station. It had not been a great evening as all Mike Parsons wanted to talk about was how he would one day reach the position of DI. According to Sergeant Parsons, he would promise Sally that if she stayed loyal to him and if anything bloomed from their date, he would not leave her behind when *his* promotion came calling.

Sally had not been rude, and when he asked her out again on a second date, she had told him gently that she wanted to first focus on her career before committing herself into any serious relationship. The divorced sergeant had been good with this, thinking that given time Sally would be interested and come to him again.

Over the last year, Mike had tried to become a close friend to Sally, but like many men who flirted in female friendships, some of his little comments were over the top and often just too far. Making up pet names, sharing and whispering tales out of school, if the Sergeant had not outranked her, Sally would have told the man to clear off by now. His latest tease was a wisecrack about her deserving a gold medal, which was purely from her name being the same as the famous Olympian gold medallist.

Sally had told him twice that the Olympian who had won the gold medal for four hundred-metre hurdles in 1992, was spelt with two n's and two l's, so was different to her name, but the sergeant thought it still to be hilarious. As he cracked the gag to others in the team, most would smile once, barely cracking a chuckle. Mike Parsons was using it every day, which Sally found infuriating.

However annoying Sergeant Parson's was, Sally loved the job.

DS Nick as she could call him, was a very good, kind, and professional policeman, who was from the same part of the world as she was from. Born in the Queen Elizabeth hospital in Lewisham, Sally was the daughter of a London nurse. Sally did not know her father, but there were rumours she was the result of a rape attack. With Catholic grandparents, much of Sally's childhood had been spent wondering why her dad was never mentioned in conversation.

It was partly the reason why she had joined the police force, as she thought that one day, she could discover the truth to whatever secrets her family were hiding.

Sally served that last of the teas and turned to go back to the front reception desk, where she spent most of her day. The morning briefing with DS Nick was well underway, and much of what they were talking about was way above her current paygrade.

Walking away from the room, DS Nick called out to her, "PC Gunel, would you mind giving us a minute, please. You were on duty the night our young victim was poisoned. Can you tell us when you first came to know that something was happening in Stockton-on-Avon please?" Nick said.

Each of the officers in the room stopped sipping from their mugs and turned to face the young, twenty-five-year-old woman, known to most in the room as Sal.

Sally could feel the weight of their eyes on her, as she was asked to answer the boss.

For a moment she stopped to gather her memories of the night, two weeks ago when the call came in. Making sure she got things in the correct order, she carefully began to talk to the room, her voice a little nervous but clear.

"A call came in just after ten p.m., Boss, it was a call from the ambulance driver… Eric McCulley. He said that they had arrived on site to attend a call from a panicking mother, who said she could not wake her son up. When our team of officers arrived onsite thirty minutes later to assist, the boy was already pronounced dead. Eric McCulley thought the boy had been dead for a couple of hours from his first medical opinion."

"The ambulance team said they needed immediate police assistance as there was little they could do for the boy.

I kept the driver on hold whilst I despatched Sergeant Parsons and officer Plumber… that was around ten-fifteen p.m. The ambulance driver gave me the address in Stockton-on-Avon." Sally said trying to recall the very quick conversation with as much detail as she could, "Excellent recall PC Gunel. Do you remember anything else?" Nick said.

Sally nodded, "Yes, about an hour later, DS Johnson called into the station to state that he had called forensics and a full investigation team to attend the scene. DS Johnson wanted me to find out the name of the school on the hill in the village.

King Alfred's school for boys, yes, that's right. The DS told us that the boys' parents were both teachers at the school. I called the DS back about two minutes after I found the schools name on the internet.

DS Johnson was grateful for the info and hung up on me as Molly Symonds from the forensic team was just arriving on site.

The next time I heard anything about this case was at 05.20 a.m., when DS Johnson asked me to call you to the scene DS Nick." Sally said honestly.

DS Nick moved over to his fully loaded old fashioned

whiteboard, "Thanks, Sal, I appreciate that information. It is important that whoever is on the front desk remembers calls and the times as well as our young PC here. Good work Sal, you can go back on the front line now." DS Nick smiled.

Sally nodded and moved back towards the phone desk. Sergeant Parsons gently grabbed her arm as she walked past,

"Good work Sal. Another gold medal for you." he chuckled taking another biscuit from Sally's plate.

Sally smiled, but it did ruin her moment.

DS Nick moved across to his whiteboard. There were several photos displayed, including the face of the dead young teenager. The boy's lips were the colour of ripened plums, but apart from this, he looked to be normal.

Next to the dead teenager, two photos of the boy's parents were shown. The red-haired mother, listed as Felicity Stevens was shown as a geography teacher, next to the bald father shown as Mark Stevens, a History teacher who was also head of the year.

Below the photos, several links were shown to invisible faces that were yet to be questioned.

From early investigations, the young teenager, named Philip Stevens, was said to be a bright, well-liked boy, popular with his friends and family. The boy was a part of the rugby team in his year but was not a shining future star. The teenager received average to good grades and had never really been in any trouble. As a student of teachers working in the school, he was one of only a few who did not live on-site, but this did not mean he had not fitted in.

Another line of investigation had shown the parents to have only moved into the Old Rectory three years ago, moving their careers together across from another prestigious school in Dorset.

The investigation had already uncovered the back-story of

the teenager's family. The schoolteacher parents were from middle-class backgrounds, who had both been educated in Keel University, Stafford, where they had formed a relationship. They only got married ten years ago, on their twentieth anniversary. Phillip Stevens was by all accounts an accident after a holiday in Rome, but they had loved the child, giving him a good home with everything he could ever need.

DS Nick had looked to focus on the cause of death. Whatever had caused the swift, and what forensics were saying was a painless death, needed discovering quickly. Whoever wanted this teenager dead had known that it was a one-way ticket, which meant it was a murder investigation as this was not meant as a warning. Phillip Stevens was targeted by someone who did not want to fail at the task. But, at the same time, whoever had decided to end the young life was not a brutal killer, as there was no evidence to show that Phillip has suffered in any way. The teenager had just fallen asleep and never woken up again. If it were not for the autopsy report of his stomach content and the brilliance of the onsite forensics team, there would be no other clue that there had been possible foul play.

Suicide was not yet completely ruled out, but again, Phillip Stevens had not revealed any clues or reasons to want to kill himself. He was looking forward to a trip to Russia next month, followed by another summer expedition to a Norwegian glacier, which the teenager's mother had told Nick had been a dream of his since he was young. Phillip Stevens was also said to be a passionate eco-friendly child, who attended many of the local societies and clubs in the school. His bedroom was covered in posters of Greenpeace, Greta Thunberg, and various scenes of climate change. One wall was completely covered in a map of the rising seas levels across the world. This was a popular topic for the younger generation, and Phillip Stevens had felt a need to be amongst their numbers. Having a mother who was just as keen to *change the planet for good*, had fuelled Phillip Stevens into furthering his knowledge together with his mum.

A year ago, Philip and his mother has spent two memorable nights camped out in a street of London, when Extinction Rebellion had been actively rampant across the country. His mother explained that she had been arrested for chaining herself to a statue, which Phillip had told her was his proudest moment.

But Nick could not see any obvious links that these activities would lead to someone wanting to actively murder the young teenager. Wanting to save the planet was no real motive for someone to want a 16-year-old boy dead. Phillip Stevens was a million miles away from the activist Greta was proving to be. No U.S. President knew Phillips Stevens by name.

DS Peter Johnson entered the briefing room. Sally had already provided the DS with a cup of lukewarm tea, but his other hand was filled with a half-eaten sausage roll that he had purchased at the local petrol station. Chewing as he walked up to the front of the room, several officers had to move to let him through.

DS Johnson was the most senior policeman in the station. None knew why the man had not moved onto a DI position as he had served this Bath branch for well over twenty years. Sadly, over the last ten years, the huge ex-front prop of a local Rugby team had bulked out further by a lack of any exercise. Most put the DS at around twenty-two plus stone as he lumbered rather than walked anywhere these days. DS Johnson was the sort of man to drive hundred yards to a local shop rather than walk.

DS Johnson's Nissan Juke would physically wobble each time he sat in the driving seat. With thinning black hair swept across, and a 1970's bush moustache to match, he was not the most well presented. Most weeks, he cycled between two pairs of very faded brown cord trousers and a black or blue jacket that had not visited a dry cleaner in years. Yet, DS Johnson was a very popular person in the station. Rarely was the DS grumpy or in a bad mood, his personality was upbeat and known for his appalling crude jokes. Married with two sons, the DS now prided himself on a son who was looking to be a promising talent to a few Rugby coaches in the area.

"Sorry I'm late Nick, the petrol station was packed." DS Johnson chuckled, taking a quick and welcome seat. Taking out a blue inhaler, the DS took the second puff he had needed since walking in from the car park.

DS Nick allowed his partner to sit. Smiling, he knew all too well that the forecourt of the petrol station was probably free of traffic. But the tempting call of queuing for a sausage roll and Greg's morning coffee had probably been more the cause to be late. Watching the large DS take a second puff of the blue inhaler, he could not help but smile as three huge pastry flakes fell from his moustache to the front of his blue jacket, already covered in enough to prove that this was probably his second pastry.

"That's fine Pete. We have covered nothing you have not already seen. We need to get a proper handle on how the boy died. It seems that whoever decided Phillip Stevens should be dead if we are all agreed this is a murder investigation, they wanted it done fast and painless." DS Nick updated.

DS Johnson put his inhaler into the slightly ripped pocket of his jacket. Scrunching the paper bag that had earlier held the three jumbo sausage rolls, he looked across the team in front of them, "Thanks, Nick. Yes, I agree with you. When we found the lad that night, it was clear his mother had tried all the usual things to bring him back. The time of death is looking to be six-thirty p.m., that's about thirty-five minutes after he arrived home from the private school. His mother got home at around 7.20 p.m. and did not go up into the boy's room until around 9.10 p.m. By the time she dialled for an ambulance and started CPR, the boy was already gone."

"Have we ruled the mother and father out yet? Has anything come back from tech on the boy's laptop? Did the boy drink or eat something that day, he would later come to regret?"

"We hope for the family sake it was a terrible mistake or a complete accident, but forensics say that from what they found in his stomach, we cannot rule out foul play. I think water is important here. Phillip Stevens was known to drink at least three to five pints a day. Reports tell me that he was never known to be too far away from a water bottle. He always carried his water in a purple metal flask, as apparently, he hated plastic bottles. Something to do with the oceans and all that." DS Johnson picked up his now cold tea and drank deeply, guzzling the cold contents down in three huge gulps.

DS Nick moved back to his board. Pointing to a photo of a tall purple steel bottle with the name Phillip written in italics, these types of containers were now very popular with young people as they carried both hot and cold contents. Turning back to face the room, he addressed the officers again, "DS Johnson is right. This water flask we think holds a clue and it is why we are looking for a possible murderer. Forensics are telling us that they are picking up traces of a substance on the lip and inside the flask that is yet unknown, but it is the same as what was found inside the boys' stomach. If someone tampered with his water, it must have been at the school as we have checked the taps in the boy's house and there is nothing to suspect any contamination in the plumbing here. With no other students or teachers ill, we must rule out that there was anything wrong with the school water supplies either. They have an onsite plumber who only recently cleaned the tanks through. His report came back clear of legionnaires or any contaminants.

"Sergeant Parsons went to the school yesterday and spoke to some of his teachers and friends. Do you want to update everyone here on what you told me last night Mike?" DS Nick looked across to the sergeant who quickly snapped back to attention from looking at a pretty blond woman talking to Sal at the front desk.

"Yes boss, of course. I went to the school yesterday to talk with a few of Philip Stevens closest friends. They are obviously all still shocked as Phillip Stevens was well-liked. He was involved in several clubs and activities throughout the school. He played an important rugby match on the day of the murder. Scored the winning try."

"Quite a talented artist by all accounts made most of the posters about climate change across many of the buildings. Some are very good, drawings of dead seals and rising sea levels…you know the kind of thing. According to the head of the year, he was usually, a quiet lad, not much to say for himself. Quite bright, not a straight 'A' student, but good enough not to struggle in his subjects. The only time anyone had ever seen him angered was the debating club for climate change. Like his mother, he is passionate about this subject. I think this is a line worth investigating boss."

"The boy did not have a huge circle of close friends, as he was a day student. Many of the groups of kids tend to be boarders. Phillip was one of only twenty kids in the school that do not stay on-site, but I do not think there was any ill-feeling or isolation because of this. Could be another thing to follow up?"

"The only thing that did come back to me from everyone we spoke to, was Phillips eating habits. He was a staunch vegan, like his mother. You know, only put food and drink inside him that was not from animals or test tubes etc. I do not get it myself, you cannot tell a Lion not to eat an antelope, so why should humans not eat meat? Anyway, Phillip Stevens was a long-time vegan. Only ever drank water from his purple flask. Each day he would fill his flask several times from one of three fountains and drink them dry completely. He liked the idea of pure clean water inside. Said it kept his body clean."

"We have taken these fountains offline to check them, but so far, they look to be clean. No one else is ill. I will ask Sal to chase up the forensic report today. We can go through them together later today boss and come back to you." Sergeant Parsons summarised.

DS Nick nodded and walked back to his board again.

"Thanks, Sergeant Parsons. Those results are very important to this case. Ask Sal to send me and DS Johnson an update as soon as you know anything. Today, we are going to focus our attention on anyone who came in and out of the school that day. You know, caterers, contractors or anyone who was just visiting the school. There were quite a few extra people at the school that day, as you have said, they had a big rugby match. Lots of parents and friends, so anyone could have had access to that bottle."

"DS Johnson is going to interview the parents again and I want to go up to the school and speak to a few more of those teachers you spoke with Mike and try to get a list of the supporters for that Rugby match. A bit of a tall order, but no harm in trying. There is no clear motive yet, we have the very strong possibility that this schoolboy was poisoned. I want to understand if this could have been a prank gone wrong. Was there anyone who may have wanted to show Phillip Stevens that even living a pure lifestyle can lead to severe illness? Who had access to that water flask that day? Did someone have the chance to put something inside it on purpose or was it something Phillip Stevens was given to put inside the flask?"

"Busy day ahead team. Remember Pete and myself are happy to speak to you if you come up with anything important to the case. Let's get out there." DS Nick said.

The sound of floor scaping chairs moving on tiled floors echoed out across the room, as some of the officers went back to their day jobs. DS Johnson was thumbing through screens on his mobile phone.

"Sorry, Nick, you might have to fly solo this afternoon. I have a doctor's appointment at 2.25 p.m. You know, blood pressure and all that. I also said I would watch Keenan play rugby tonight at six p.m. Might be a bit off the circuit, today mate." DS Johnson told his colleague, reading another concerning text from his doctor, that he was not expecting to see.

*Mr Johnson,*

*Please can we change your appointment time from next Wednesday to this afternoon at 2.25 p.m.? Doctor Sanjay has seen your results and would like to speak to you asap.*

*Many Thanks*

*Burbank Surgery.*

Nick nodded and smiled, "Probably just routine mate. You know how doctors are Pete. Tell you to keep off the sausage rolls and start eating more apples…" Nick chuckled, as he added another line onto the whiteboard.

DS Johnson laughed out loud and threw the paper bag into

the bin. Struggling to get out of his chair first time, he felt a sudden sense of guilt and hidden worry that today was just another bag of his usual five a day!

As DS Johnson left the room, Nick watched as the large man stopped at the reception desk. Leaning on the long wooden countertop to gather his breath, another quick gasp of his inhaler was needed.

PC Sally Gunel was talking to a blond girl who had come in from the street, but it looked like Sergeant Parsons, was now asking the girl to follow him into a side room.

Nick turned back to the board, genuinely worried about his friend and partner of eight years. In the force, he had made many good friends, but most had been just working colleagues. Pete Johnson was more than this. Over the last five years, Nick and Celia had been over to Pete's house in Netheravon many times for meals and drinks evenings. Celia loved Pete's wife Mary and their two teenage boys were something both the parents should be proud of. Last year, Pete had needed to take three months off to recover from what was reported to be a minor heart attack, but Nick knew something was underlying that Pete was not allowing anyone to know.

Nick was so pleased when the huge man was given the green light by his doctors to work again as a friend, but selfishly the man was also a very good copper to have around the place.

Nick was convinced that Pete had declined promotion more than once, probably due to health reasons. Since returning to work five months ago, Nick had seen a real decline in Peter's health again.

Lately, he had started missing small details where once this man would have been straight on the mark.

Nick was the only one in the station, apart from the weekly

visit from DI Jenkins, who was able to ask Pete if he was still fit enough to work. It would soon be time that Nick would need to approach his friend again, both out of the personal concern and a genuine worry that he was fit enough to still be in the demanding job. The unsociable hours alone, made this a difficult position to run, let alone the stress of it all. Nick hoped that the doctor's appointment today would decide before he needed to say anything.

There was something unusual today, as this was the first time Pete requested time off to watch his son play Rugby. Mary would often joke at the dinner table that Pete had watched the boys grow up by either photo, phone videos or newspaper clippings of their successes.

If Pete wanted to be there today to watch his son, Nick would not be the one to stop him. With the heart attack last year and the lung illness before that, which Peter did not know Nick knew of, it was important he spent as much time with them as he could.

Drawing another single line out from the photo of Phillip Stevens, he took the pen line to a small picture of the purple water flask that was found empty inside the boy's backpack. It had been Pete who had first looked at the flask that evening and thought it worth checking into further. Carefully opening the lid of the screw top flask with blue plastic gloves, Pete noticed dry, white crystallised granules of residue around the lip of the flask that seemed to be out of place for just water.

In true Pete style, the flask was bagged and tagged immediately, ready for the forensic team to examine. As it turned out, it would become the key evidence to the entire case ahead.

The following morning, DS Nick received a phone call from Sal, just after he had finished clearing his windscreen from another severe frost. Jumping into the warm blowers of the Audi

TT, he clicked the Bluetooth button to switch his mobile phone over to the in-car speaker system.

"Hi Sal, sorry, just needed to get back in the warm, fed up with this weather," Nick told his constable.

Sal chuckled, which was always a good sign as it meant the message, she was about to tell him was not frantically urgent.

"That's why I cycle to work. No scraping required Boss," she said, as everyone knew Sal was a keen cyclist.

Nick chuckled and spoke again, "What is it, Sal. Do you have something for me?" Nick asked, knowing that whatever she wanted to say was important enough to call him.

For a moment Nick could hear Sal tapping on a keyboard before she replied, "A couple of things Boss. DS Johnson's wife has just called in. He is not going to make it in today. He has said sorry for the late notice, but something came up last night that has caused him to need to call in sick."

"Secondly, DS Johnson asked me to check his emails as he left his phone here on Saturday night. DS Pete said to check if anything has come in on the Stevens case. There was a couple of emails about the profiles of the boy's parents, nothing out of the ordinary. Seemingly normal schoolteachers. The mother was a bit of a 'burn-your-bra' girl in her youth, the father looks to be a purely academic, but nothing out of the ordinary." Sal explained, reading the email back from Sergeant Parsons line by line.

Nick turned down the heater of his car, as it was now turning into a sauna. Putting the seat belt around his frame, he clicked it into place, "Thanks, Sal, that's useful. I will be at the station in thirty minutes. Can you send the report to my email please?" Nick asked, knowing Sal had probably already done this.

Sal replied instantly, "Of course, Boss, already done. DS-Johnson also wanted me to forward you the report back from forensics yesterday. The email is password locked so I have sent this over to you by text. It should be with you now. DS-Johnson told me that this was important, something you were both waiting for. I have texted the password so both things are not together." Sal told DS-Nick.

Instantly Nick turned the car key to the off position. Lifting his phone, the text message was flashing with a password that would break a seasoned hacker.

"Thanks, Sal, I will read this when I come in. Did Pete sound all right to you?" Nick asked, his concerns of the doctors meeting now worrying.

At the end of the phone, he could hear Sal talking to another person who had come up to the service desk. It was clear this was not going to be a quick conversation, "Sorry Boss got to go. We have just had a report of a missing car come in.

"It was Mary, Pete's wife who called in for DS-Johnson. We can talk when you get here. Bye Boss," Sal said, hanging up the phone, obviously with a busy desk in front of her.

Nick thought this could only be bad news. To ask Mary to call in and for Pete to instruct the constable from afar was very unusual. Something concerning was up that did not need any police work to find out.

Nick planned to call their house line when he got to the station.

Opening the email that beeped its way to his smartphone, the password screen appeared. After four attempts of getting the hyper crypto password wrong, finally, the screen opened the forensic report.

In typical forensic style, the document was headed up in standard-compliant media.

**Everlan Police Forensics**

*Original Narrative: No Follow up: YES*
*Case Number: DD14-1566*
*Report Date: 01/03/2018*
*Related Case: Bath Spa # DD15*
**The subject of Forensics Examination:**
*Examination of chemical analysis of purple steel water container. Possession of Phillip Stevens (Deceased)*
*ITEM #1*
*Steel Purple Water Container. Small dent on the lower rim. White Painted "Phillip" on the container.*
*Results of Chemical Testing: Residue of absorbed chemical both on the outer lip and substantial residue inside. Chemical biological report to follow. Conclusion 98.76%*
*Water soluble Pentobarbital.*
*Officer Signature: P Lensy Date: 03/03/2018*
*Approved Forensic Lead by M Symonds*

The document went on to a second page, full of ticked analysis and chemical numbers that meant very little to Nick Murray. He was not trained to be a chemist, but he was more than aware of what Pentobarbital was and worryingly what this possibly meant to the case. This was presenting itself as either a suicide or a murder. The only other person Nick could remember dying from a huge overdose of Pentobarbital was Marilyn Monroe. But, from how they found the boy, this did not seem to be a suicide. In nearly all suicide cases Nick had been involved with, suicide was tidy.

It was common for anyone choosing to kill themselves alone in their room would either leave a note to explain why or have half-filled water cups with more pills nearby. In teenage suicides, stories of either isolations or bullying were always quick to discover as an underlying condition. With Phillip Stevens, a popular, well-liked, and happy teenager, with no previous history of any illness or depression, he was found face down, fully clothed as if he had just chosen to take a nap when he got home from school.

With the water bottle, DS-Johnson discovered inside the boys' school rucksack, there was no sign of any other pills or any trace of the white grainy substance anywhere else in the bag. The bottle had been "used" and put away, sometime, up to a few hours before Phillip arrived home, throwing his bag into the corner of his bedroom, like every other teenager keen to be rid of school for another day.

From the forensic report, it was clear to Nick that the water flask was probably tampered with at the school. If Phillip had wanted to be discovered at school, he would have taken the overdose far earlier. This was feeling like murder, which would not be an easy conversation to the parents, who were no longer looking to be suspects.

From Nick's first thoughts, someone else in the school had purposely chosen Phillip Stevens as their victim. Using a drug that was fully soluble and without any lasting taste, how much of the drug and been added to make this drug fatal.

The murderer had known that too much of this drug would be fatal.

Nick changed from the view on this phone and started surfing the internet for more information. Soon he was looking at the page showing that anything over two hundred and fifty milli litre of this soluble drug could be fatal, taking anything up to two to three hours to be effective. This same drug was often used in euthanasia, giving people wanting a painless option to end their lives, without a side effect apart from falling asleep. In small doses, Pentobarbital was prescribed by many doctors as a cure to short term insomnia. Nick was sure the boy had not suffered at the end.

This put pressure on Nick knowing and investigating who was on the school premises that day, and who could have had access to the boy's flask to give him the fatal dose.

Nick needed to press Sergeant Parsons, for he was at the school yesterday, interviewing the staff and many of the boy's so-called friends. One of them was now looking to be a murderer. Nick had not yet heard anything that would lead to any of them having motive or reason to kill the boy.

Thirty minutes later, DS-Nick Murray walked into Bath Spa, Little Street police station. Walking up to the main desk, Sal was looking concerned.

"Hi Sal, sorry, I wanted to check out the forensic report before I came in. What's up constable?" Nick asked, knowing that Sal only frowned when she was under severe pressure.

Moving to the back room, Nick followed his officer through the frosted glass doors.

"Sorry Boss, I have been trying to call you. DI- Ian Kleverly has just phone us from Salisbury station, wanting to speak with you urgently. This is his number. Told me to say that it is to do with the Stevens case." Sal said, knowing more than she was letting on.

Nick took the number and walked over to his office. Picking up the desk phone, he dialled the number. Across the other side of the desk, DS-Johnson's seat sat empty.

Nick waited for the dial tone to turn into a full ring.

After just two pulses the phone on the other end was answered, "DI Kleverly!" the deep, growly voice answered.

Nick sat down and lifted a pen to his notebook, "Good

morning, this is DS Nick Murray from the Bath station. I was asked to call you." Nick said, writing the date and DI Brian Kleverly onto the small leather-bound pad. Across the desk, DS Johnson's identical blue pad was neatly filed next to the desktop keyboard. Both notepads had been secret Santa gifts last year. How he and Pete had laughed when they opened each other's presents to one another, and it was the same thing. They both believed their wives had colluded on the joke.

The man on the end of the phone could be heard closing a door. Nick deduced he was making sure the call was private.

"Thank you for calling me DS. Murray. I wanted to speak to you about a new case we are investigating here in Salisbury. Information came me to me last night that I think we will both find interesting. I tried to speak with your colleague DI Johnson last night about something he was investigating. I believe he is not in today, but I hope you do not mind me dealing with you directly. It is important, I promise you." DI Kleverly said, his voice low not to be heard.

Nick stood and moved around to Pete's notebook. Opening the page, he could see the same on Pete's contact list.

*DI Brain Kleverly, Salisbury Station. "Bulldog"*
*Must call him Monday about their new case. Links!*

Nick continued the phone, "Not at all DI. How may I help you?" Nick asked intrigued.

DI Kleverly continued, "A day ago, my team was sent to a flat in Salisbury to investigate a suspected suicide. Young woman, twenty-seven, with no boyfriend or husband. We have been looking into the circumstances leading to her death, but we yet have not discovered anything to lead us to think this was anything but a sad case of suicide.

I wanted to speak with Pete, sorry DS Johnson, about the

case as we go back years. I used to play Rugby with the big man, he was a good player in his day. Pete was a monster on the field, they caused to call him sausage rol… anyway, sorry to digress, he was telling last week about another case your team is looking into. I saw the case on the TV. The Bath schoolboy… Stevens." the DI explained.

Nick moved back to his chair, "Yes, we have been trying to keep it low-key, but the press got hold of it and you know what it's like. Teenage suicide makes good documentaries. Papers love a story like this." Nick answered, now remembering Pete mention this policeman before. Looking at Nick's desk, amongst the myriad of photos of Mary and his two boys, there was a photo of Pete and the winning rugby team holding up a cup many years ago. Nick imagined that one of these men in the photo was the man he was now chatting to.

DI Kleverly spoke again, "Yes, the press are parasites for a story like this. Anyway, what has recently come to light is that the young woman we discovered on Sunday night, died by what we believe was a huge overdose of a soluble Pentobarbital. Our investigations our concluding that over four hundred milli litre of a powdered pill was mixed into a bottle of water she was carrying in her bag. Sound familiar?" DI-Kleverly asked the silent Nick.

Three days later both cases were improbably linked. Two murders within fifty miles in just over two weeks with the same method used in both. As with Phillip Stevens, the new murder in Salisbury was again not showing any clear motive.

Two complete stranger's dead, using the same drug that killed Marilyn Monroe.

# Chapter 4

## Joshua Wright – A Good Man

### Timeline—13 January 2018

After nearly a year of devout personal study, training the mind and constantly listening for signs from God, Joshua Wright had finally succeeded in hearing what most never would.

Twelve extremely thick hardbacked books, ten audiobooks, countless links into various websites and hundreds of YouTube videos, had given him everything he required to find his personal salvation. Literature and the true followers of the Lord God had shown him the path to Eden. Hard work, and utter devotion to the cause had done the rest.

Unlike any other Sunday, the congregation sat inside the small village church around him, none of them yet knew the real glory of the revealed Lord God. As they sang out with a faithful gusto to the hymn 'All Things Bright and Beautiful' following their invisible obedience to the old vicar, the forty-six-year-old plumber, felt both 'Wise and Wonderful. Knowing that being amongst God's chosen few had helped a lost, broken man become blessed and anointed to perform *His* work.

It was this revealed truth that made his heart sing louder than a thousand congregations could ever call out.

Learning *How to Hear the Voice of God* had changed his life forever.

Once he was lost, on the edge of total despair, but God had found him through His divine grace. Joshua had been alone, but God taken pity and given him, companions to love and cherish. Once he hated the thought of the next morning, now he relished every single day.

God had filled his heart. God was with him, always.

Five years before, Joshua Wright had been through a terrible year of despair and personal suffering.

Losing his beloved mother and father in a fatal road accident, followed by the company he had worked for since leaving school collapsing due to the recession leaving him unemployed, Joshua was left alone with no hope or prospects of a better tomorrow.

Joshua contemplated suicide so many times, for there seemed no way out from the darkness he found himself in.

Many times, he had prepared a note for nobody to read. Many times, he had stirred countless pills into filled whiskey glasses. But Joshua was just not brave enough to follow through with his wish to die, he was a coward.

Twice, Joshua had placed his mouth over the end of his Dad's old twelve bore rifle.

Luckily, he could not reach the trigger.

Luckily, he had knocked over the whiskey glass.

Luckily, the words for the suicide note never came to him.

With no love left in his life, living in a small one-roomed bedsit in the city of Wells in Somerset with just a bag of rusting plumber's tools, each day was long and lonely, apart from pointless occasional trips to the jobcentre, where he was made to feel like a complete waster.

Joshua Wright had never been religious. Born into a family that only went to church for weddings and funerals, there was never really much time to talk or think about God. As the only son of a bus driver, and a mother who had never worked as far as he knew, childhood had been one of few opportunities, little prospects and fish fingers, chips & beans after school.

After a largely uneventful school life, Joshua left the Bristol comprehensive at 16 with minimal qualifications and without any real ambition to succeed. It was his father that managed to talk to a good friend that got him a place as an apprentice plumber. Working as the plumber's mate for two years had been good money for a teenage boy. When it became a full-on apprenticeship, complete with a day release to Bristol college, Joshua was fortunate enough to learn a properly skilled trade.

By the age of twenty-two, Joshua Wright was a fully qualified plumber in his own right. Taking up a position in a local property service company, he found the work and the salary very stable, which allowed him to earn good money, eventually allowing him to move away from his parents' house, into a rented room in Wells.

For a while, there was even a brief relationship with a young admin clerk who worked in the firm, but it had not lasted more than six months. Joshua had soon discovered the young girl was extremely open with her favours and loyalties, with three men claiming to be "going out" with her at the same time.

Joshua had needed to call it off with the girl, but sadly this had been the last time he had found any degree of romance.

For the next few years, Joshua continued to work hard, earning enough money to put a good deposit down on his own house.

Joshua spent a very long time trying to find the right property. Twice, he almost made offers on properties, but nothing ever felt as homely as his mother and fathers house in a village just outside Bristol.

Over the space of three years, Joshua viewed over thirty properties. It was on his way home from viewing a small three-bedroom house, which was strangely next door to his long dead Grandmother's home in Bristol, Joshua had finally decided to put in a formal offer.

This house seemed to give him a strange feeling of home, which was not surprising, considering the amount of time Joshua and his mother had spent in his grandmother's house, when his father served in the army during his younger years.

Just moments before he had picked up the phone to speak with the Brymore estate agents to put down a firm offer, another phone call came in from the local police which had changed his life completely in an instant.

For the next year and a half, Joshua was taken through the terrible drama and trauma of losing both parents at the same time. As an only child, Joshua inherited the whole of his parent's estate, including their house in a small village outside Bristol. Instead of buying the house near his Grandmother's in Bristol city centre, Joshua decided to move back into his parents' house, finding it easier than having to go through the whole mess of organising a rapid house clearance and selling up.

It would also give him the time he needed to grieve.

Only three days after the coroner's verdict of accidental death, ironically detailing how his father was driven off the road by the very same school bus he drove weekly, a phone call came in from the boss of his company.

In a usual sorry, management style approach, Joshua was told that due to huge cutbacks and a lack of confirmed future orders, there was no way they could continue to have two full-time plumbers on their firm. Joshua and another young plumber were put up for redundancy. They were each told that only one of them would be retained.

Joshua knew there was no chance he would keep his job, as the other plumber was the owner's recently qualified son.

With just £3800 in redundancy and a letter of how sorry they were to lose him, together with words of *if anything changed, they would call him,* Joshua became unemployed.

Joshua had never heard another thing from anyone in the company since.

For the first few months, Joshua tried without much luck to apply for several local plumbing jobs, but work was proving hard to find, especially with the number of Polish workers asking for sometimes less than half of his wage. Each time, he was given the same answer, "You are well qualified, but we have nothing for you at this time. This recession is awful for everyone."

After eight months of nothing but false promises of call-backs and outright rejections, he sat alone inside his parent's old tatty kitchen, with a sense of complete hopelessness. There was nothing left for him in this world.

Joshua flicked open his dated slow laptop and began to search for painless ways to commit suicide.

To his surprise, there were hundreds of links into sites that could help him on his next journey. For days, he found himself looking at euthaniser sites, for painless drug methods used to help people peacefully move into the next life. There were countless articles about common overdose drugs, most of them also used for either date rape or other sinister crimes. GHB, Rohypnol, and Ketamine made easy reference to ways of numbing the senses enough to find an easy way to end it all.

The various methods to die for a coward were plentiful.

Even alcohol could be used to induce comas, but this was an unreliable concept as most people just reached a state of drunkenness that could easily be recovered if the medics got them in time. Joshua was in no mind for anyone to find him and recover, this was to be no cry for help in the dark, he wanted a painless finality to it all.

Researching each page in some detail on easy methods of committing painless suicide, Joshua was shocked to see there were just as many hyperlinks and adverts leading off to self-help sites. There was always a number to ring, or a person Joshua could speak to if he so wanted, each site claiming they could confidentially and discreetly help him find a way back from despair, mostly through God.

Joshua had even tried to phone the Samaritans once, speaking to a wonderful person who listened and offered very good, comforting advice. But when the reassuring voice was gone after the call, Joshua's parents' house fell silent again, and his brief moment of hope was again just an empty void to nothing.

For days after the call to the Samaritans, Joshua had planned and written down ways that would best suit his painless suicide. Joshua decided to leave no suicide note, nor was he going to tidy the house before taking his chosen method of painless drugs.

Suicide was going to be final, for he wanted no way back.

Choosing a Monday, as he always hated Mondays, tonight would be his last.

Sitting alone with a clear glass of cold water and an empty box of Pentasol, which he had easily ordered from a site on the internet with no questions or medical records needed, Joshua was surprised how clear the swirling water was after 400ml of white powder had all but disappeared. Just a light dusting line of white crystal residue lapped the glass edges at the top of the water level.

Picking up the glass slowly, Joshua went to take his first sip.

That was the precise moment God found him.

That was the moment God saved him.

A knock at the door made him spill some of the water over his hand. It was a sound that he rarely heard since moving back into his parents' home.

Only the odd delivery driver knocked on Joshua's door, and most of them were during the daytime. It was nearly eight fifteen p.m., he was hoping to be dead by eleven p.m.

Walking over to the front of the house, he opened the old wooden door, which squeaked through a lack of oiling. On the doorstep, three people stood smiling at him, two men and a large woman, whose beautiful white teeth shone like the pearls around her neck.

"God loves you, sir. God hears you and He loves you." The large black woman said, holding out her hand to shake.

Joshua Wright felt compelled to take the woman's hand. It was fat, very cold and the most welcoming contact he had felt in years.

Immediately as if drawn to a mother's embrace, Joshua felt the woman's other hand on top of his.

Without any knowledge of knowing why, what, or how, Joshua fell to his knees and sobbed like a baby. The woman moved in to embraced him fully, gathering Joshua instantly into her flock.

Ten minutes later, he was inside his parents' home again, with the large black woman sat next to him, still holding his hand. One of the men who had arrived with her was searching the kitchen, making them all a strong cup of tea, whilst the other older man sat in his father's old chair speaking in a soft, almost preachingly healing manner, "Sometimes, we believe we are sent to help those who cannot hear. You are not the first man to feel this way when we have knocked on their doors, Joshua. The Lord works through us, we hear his voice and sometimes we are guided to those we feel need our help."

"Your pain is shared with us, sir. Do not feel you are alone. My friends and I all belong to a local group called Eden's Echo. We are a small but loving congregation, as each of us has received and heard our calling through His grace. Once anyone learns to pass back through the gates of Eden, God can be heard. Only those, like Adam and Eve, who were cast out of Eden are forced to walk a lifetime of sin, are silent to the Lord's voice. We believe that God is calling us all back into Eden, where he waits to speak to us as his children. Eden is the heaven all men seek."

"Tonight, brother Joshua, we are looking to invite any who hear our voice, to join our numbers. Our knock on your door I think was divinely led. There is always room for another who looks to seek the entrance and hear Eden's Echo. One as lost as you need to know we offer salvation and more importantly, true guidance on a new pathway."

"Chaplin Mary Grace is truly one we have learned to love and follow. Mary hears the Lord, for she has already found the pathway back into Eden. She has written many books to help those who have lost their way. These are the guides back to Eden, where God will again be heard to those who seek His salvation. We can show you there is another way, Joshua, for a rich life, in the knowledge that God and his son Jesus await us in Eden. Mary has saved me from my sins. Mary will help you too." the older man, who had introduced himself as Fredrick Bannister to Joshua, made the sign of the cross over this chest.

Taking out a thick paperback book, from what looked like a backpack full of the same book, he gently placed it on the table in front of Joshua.

"Mary has written this book which we want you to read. It is not for all and cannot be found in any shop or website. It is only to help souls lost like your own, where only despair remains. For the small price of just a few pounds, God's voice can be heard to you. God hears your prayers Joshua, you just need to learn how to listen to his voice." the man explained, using his softest but a well-trained sales pitch.

The second man introduced at the door as Bradbury Barnes appeared with four cups of hot tea. Joshua guessed this man was of west Indian origins, given his complexion and easy voice. Placing the tray down on the table next to the glass still filled with water, he handed a cup to Joshua, "Drink my boy. Tea is always a good healer. Tea is from heaven alone. This fine china is perfect for such a brew. Think of this tea as the first taste on your road to recovery. Soon, like me, you will know love again. Through Mary here, your heart can be full again. God is listening, He knows you, my brother." the man said, taking a seat next to Fredrick.

Joshua took the tea. It was good, filled with what he could only think were twenty sugars. Far too sweet, but it was good. This tea must have been in the cupboard for years, as Joshua could not recall either of his parents drinking tea or ever producing fine china cups and a proper teapot. Wherever Barnaby found them, it was a good find.

Mary smiled fully and spoke, leaning towards Joshua, "Come to our church tomorrow Joshua. I think you will find a sense of peace here. Eden's Echo is filled with hope. You will be with friends and you will know of God. I feel it in you. You have a strong spirit, Sir, that God will know, he hears your pain. Take my book, read some pages tonight, and if you do not want it, bring it back to us. I will accept no payment from you today, for

I know tomorrow you will start on your path to salvation and come to us, happy with your £10." squeezing Joshua's hand, Mary Grace released him, to pick up and sip on her hot tea.

Joshua smiled and reached for the thick paperback book. On the cover, there were pictures of fluffy white clouds floating in a crystal blue sky. At the centre of the cover, almost floating between the clouds, words written in black italics were lined with embossed gold.

### *HOW TO HEAR GOD*

For a while they all chatted, talking about the book and the small faith group they belonged to. Joshua had heard of religious groups like these before but always thought them to be crackpots or filled with desperate losers. Frederick and Barnaby were explained to be both ex-prisoners, Mary was their prison Chaplain, who had saved them both.

Today, they had all saved his life and in truth, he was a desperate loser, who could have easily ended up in prison.

The least he could do was offer them an ear.

When they eventually left his home in the early hours of Tuesday morning, Joshua found himself thanking them, and agreeing to attend the church group at seven p.m. sharp. As a token of thanks Joshua had paid for the book anyway, which now sat next to the drugged water glass.

Walking back to the couch, he sat for a while and looked at the book and the water glass.

Which one should he pick up?

At ten a.m. the following morning, Joshua Wright woke up on the couch. The water glass had been accidentally kicked over during his sleep. The new book was open on the arm of the couch at chapter twelve, one hundred and fifty pages in.

Eden was calling out to him.

Seven p.m. that same night, Joshua entered the small doors to the Eden's Echo building, to the surprising sound of rapturous applause from Mary Grace, Fredrick, and Bradbury, who sat on the front bench seat of a small chapel hall, "Welcome brother Joshua, we knew you would come. God told us all you were a good man. You have taken your first steps alone, but every other step you will take on this journey will with friends. The path to Eden's Echo is hard, but with our guidance, you will not fall." Mary said, standing to deliver today's sermon, as more people came into the hall.

Sitting on the front bench next to Frederick, twenty other people came through the doors of the hall, each receiving the same applause. Every man, woman and child were all from different walks, colours, and creeds of life. All of them were smiling as if lifted from the burdens they carried outside of the walls of this small meeting hall. Taking up seats on the ten lines of benches, all facing the table at the front of the room where further copies of Mary's book were stood and stacked high, the huge woman opened her hands and welcomed them all. Pointing to a picture of God reaching out to Adam, giving him the spark of life, Mary began to preach to her flock.

Those had been the days that saved Joshua Wright from committing suicide. Soon after becoming a member of the Eden's Echo group, he found the courage to start his own small business as a plumber. Mary, Fredrick, and Bradbury seemed to have many friends with plumbing issues, all needing his trade skills for help. Work was never hard to find, most contracts coming from the church group directly. Within six months he had found the strength to redecorate his parents' house and start to build it back into a home once more.

With the help of Mary Grace, the book she wrote seemed to make sense to him, almost providing a map of life to follow. Joshua found a true sense of purpose that through Eden's Echo, God was hearing him and helping him rebuild his life. The book promised that God was close, choosing only to speak to those who truly wanted to find their way back into Eden.

With his new friends in Eden's Echo, Joshua found time to help in many of their good community causes. Twice a week, on Tuesdays and Thursday nights, Joshua would join Frederick, as he walked the streets of Bath, helping to feed the homeless. Hearing some of the sad stories that had led to these poor people living out on cold streets, exposed to the elements every day, made Joshua realise that his life was not so lost. Even in the darkest days that had led to him almost taking his own life, he had always had a roof above him, keeping him warm and protected.

That was much more than any of these poor homeless friends ever had. Joshua loved to help these people.

For a while, Joshua had even taken two young men into his house, giving them free shelter and a chance to find another way back to a proper life. This had proven to be beneficial to all of them, as Joshua enjoyed having others in the house living with him.

In just eight short months, Eden's Echo had given him a way back to what many would call normal.

Life was good. Life was pure.

Joshua Wright was a good man.

Eden's Echo had given him the chance to live again, or as Fredrick told him, Joshua was "Born Again."

Living just a little too far away from the Bristol chapel

building where the people of Eden's Echo gathered daily, Joshua also became a member of his local village church congregation.

But, on Monday's, which he now loved, every week he would travel back into Bristol just to listen to Mary Grace preach from her special holy book. There was always something new to learn from the wonderful lady, as she slowly revealed the secrets for how to hear the voice of God.

Mary's book had been the key and given him a new purpose, Mary's words were the gateway into Eden.

Over the year, Joshua read many books on the same subject of 'How to Hear God', which all showed the reader how with trained focused obedience, God was listening to those who spoke to him, and one day He would choose to answer their calls.

With a new fast laptop surfing online, Joshua found further fuel to follow his passion, as it seemed Mary was only one of the thousands who had learned this skill to hear God's voice. Many would claim that God had spoken to them personally, something that profoundly changed them into knowing that God was the truth and the only way back to salvation. Audiobooks were another release, which also provides a friend via headphones through the quieter nights.

Everything was a wonderful brightness, that shone a light in Joshua's renewed heart.

But that light was suddenly ended on the day he not only learned how to Hear God, but suddenly, out of nowhere, driving home on a Monday night after learning the final chapters of Eden's Echo, God decided to answer him as he sat waiting for a traffic light to turn green.

It had taken a huge 18 wheeled truck behind him to lean on the horn, to make Joshua move his car forward after the lights had long turned green.

Mary had shown him the way.

God had shown him the light.

Joshua discovered Eden was real.

But, in order to reach it, Joshua was given a Holy mission that he needed to obediently follow without question.

# Chapter 5

## Murder Two – Jemma Evans (27)

### Timeline—19 March 2018

DI Iain Kleverly sat in his office alone.

Outside, his inner facing window revealed the whole of the main open office of the Salisbury special investigations room was nearly empty. In the corridor beyond, a cleaner worked with a vacuum cleaner, her ears plugged into white headphones with music so loud it almost forced her to dance as the hoover moved back and forth.

It was already 9.34 p.m. Most of his team would be either at home or sitting in a nearby pub.

Outside his external window, Iain could see beads of water moving slowly down the pain of glass as rain fell. It was cold enough for snow, he could only hope that the night would not lead to this, as snow always hampered investigations with the inability to travel easily.

The pages of case notes in front of him were scattered across his desk. They were all very detailed, written by some of his best officers, yet none of them made any sense as to why he was looking at a murder charge.

In nearly every investigation of murder or suspicious death he had ever been involved with, eighty per cent of prosecutions came from the victim knowing their killer. It was a sad statistic, but alarmingly true. But, on the other hand, it always made police work that much easier, as looking for anyone the victim was either close to or friendly with often was a good place to start.

But, in the case he had been working on for the past few days, every line of inquiry from known associates or family members had drawn a complete blank. DI Kleverly had even asked his team to look at any of the girl's previous relationships, going right back to when she was just thirteen, but so far, this had presented nothing but a silly fight when a boyfriend had once eaten meat in front of her.

The only real connection that made Jemma Evans, who was a qualified estate agent originally from Bath, anything close to not being quite normal was that she was said to have been a bit of an activist and vegetarian. There was no record of her going completely vegan, but from three witness statements, the girl did not eat meat and liked everyone to know this fact.

This fact alone was not a crime, but had it caused anyone to kill her for it. DI Kleverly had known cases where people had killed for less, but this did not seem even remotely seem to be a reason why this single, seemingly happy woman had been found poisoned in her flat.

Jemma Evans was a fitness fanatic. Attending a local gym in Salisbury every morning, she was a keen runner. The DI had at first concentrated on anyone at the Gym who had taken an interest in the woman, but apart from the owner, and one personal trainer, most of the people in the Gym did not even know who he was talking about. Jemma was a regular, that was about as much as anyone knew. She would turn up, most weekdays at seven a.m., run on a treadmill for twenty to thirty minutes and leave by 07.45 a.m. Sometimes she would come to the Gym in the early evenings after work, but this was said to be on rare occasions.

CCTV for three previous weeks before she was found dead, confirmed these timings to be true. There was nobody who came in with her, none that followed her out, or anything to arouse even this smallest amount of suspicion to follow up.

Yet, the pathology report had been clear that Jemma Evans was subjected to a huge overdose of Pentobarbital, carefully stirred into a bottle of mountain spring water, which was something she always purchased from a newsagent on the way into the gym each morning.

The owner of the newsagents had told the police that he liked the girl but did not know her name. She always purchased just a single bottle of water and often a high protein bar, mostly in the mornings, but sometimes in the evenings.

DI Kleverly had not suspected the newsagent to be involved in any way.

As the case developed with no real leads to follow up, this left only two possibilities, both of which he felt were wrong for a seasoned DI. Either the murderer was someone she did not know, or the girl had added the drug into the water herself, making it a suicide. Both were not going to be easy to prove, both would not provide the answers that the girl's father, who lived in Cirencester, needed to hear.

Murder had not yet presented any solid evidence to give DI Kleverly grounds to think this was the truth of it. But that had all changed when a chance remark by one of the pathologists who DI Kleverly knew personally happened to mention that they had just helped on a case near Bath where a sixteen-year-old boy was found dead in his bed.

Molly Symonds was a forensic specialist who served right across the South of England. Known for her dry, non-emotional manner, there was no denying in her abilities. The case about the young teenager was known across the press, as it was coming to light that the schoolboy was killed by foul-play and it was not another teenage suicide as first reported.

Molly Symonds and her team had found something to counter these claims, leading the investigating team to now be working on a murder hunt.

DI Kleverly had not linked the two deaths until Molly Symonds second, a lady the DI had known from his days serving in the Swindon police station, had been working on another case to do with a chemical leak in a factory nearby.

Iain had taken his friend out for lunch to discuss the old days and to catch up, as they had not seen each other for over five years. Over lunch, Wendy Van-Wendrix, who incidentally had recently married one of the best Pathologist in the country, was talking about recent cases she had been working on:

"There is always someone drinking something they should not. It keeps us all very busy. I never thought that my life would end up sifting through the contents and testing what someone's last meal was? But sickeningly, this is what attracted me to Maximillian. He's very good at it." Wendy chuckled, as she pulled apart a chicken leg on her plate.

Iain laughed and replied, "This is husband number three Wendy. Do you think it will last this time?" Ian was eating a risotto, which was cold and not that pleasant.

Wendy shook her head, whilst taking a bite, "MMM… maybe this time. It feels right. Max likes rummaging through dead stomachs as I do. I think it is a match made in heaven. Molly says we are the same. That is something coming from her. She usually just shrugs when I talk about men to her. Not the conversational type. You know Molly." Wendy, said, speaking with her mouth far too full.

Iain nodded. For all of Molly Symonds known forensic skills, she was difficult to engage in any conversation. Yet, she had proven to be the most important person to solve countless cases in police stations all over the country over the years.

"Molly still likes to keep full control. I know she likes to micromanage her department. I do not know how she can keep up these days. It's a big area to cover." Ian said, giving up on his risotto as a lost cause.

Wendy took another bite, "Yes, but my god what a memory she has. Only yesterday we were working on your poisoning case. Molly remembered that the schoolboy in Bath a week or so before was probably poisoned using the same drug. She was not even working on your case, but she had read up all the notes your team submitted. It's incredible what Molly can retain." Wendy had told Ian.

For the rest of the lunch, Iain and Wendy caught up on the last five years, which had seen them both go through a painful and bitter divorce. Iain thought it was good to know Wendy still held their friendship as important, but throughout the dinner, Iain felt guilty as he was only really thinking about one thing.

Molly Symonds believed the poison used to kill Jemma Evans was the same used to kill the schoolboy in Bath…Phillip Stevens. This needed to be followed up.

Driving back to the police station, it was already late in the day. Using the police computer, it had not taken him very long to find out who was leading the case for the Phillip Stevens murder. A local newspaper on his desk also revealed the same name of the chief investigator, so it only seemed sensible to at least speak to the DS in charge to see if he had any firm leads on the Stevens case.

The following morning, picking up the phone, DI Iain

dialled the number from the screen on the police computer. After just three rings, a woman's professional voice answered, "Good morning, Bath Police station. PC Sally Gunel speaking, how may I help you." The voice was clear and pleasant,

DI Kleverly thought that his service desk could take a lot of tips from this pleasant PC's manner.

"Good morning PC Gunnel. My name is DI Ian Kleverly from the Salisbury station. Could you put me through to DS Peter Johnson or DS Nick Murray, please? I must speak with them urgently." Iain asked, hearing a busy office behind the WPC.

For a moment there was a short silence.

"Sorry Sir, I have just checked, and both are out of the station at the moment. DS Johnson is unfortunately away on sick leave, but DS Murray is due back into the office in about fifteen minutes. Can I take a number and I will ask him to call you as soon as he arrives?" PC Gunel told DI Kleverly.

Iain thanked PC Gunel and hung up the phone.

Twenty-three minutes later, DS Nick Murray called him.

Just five minutes after the call was concluded, both men knew they were looking for the same killer, for it was too much a coincidence for these cases to be so closely linked and so similar. As far as DS Kleverly was aware, nothing had yet been released to the press about the type of drug used to kill these two young people. Iain and Nick believed they needed to find a link between the two victims. Perhaps they both knew the same person or belonged to a group. This at least was a new line of investigation.

For the rest of the day, DI-Kleverly had got his team to look for anything that could link the boy and his family to Jemma Evans. So far, nothing had come even close. These two people seemed to be strangers to each other apart from the way they died.

DI Kleverly starred down at the notes of both cases and wondered why anyone would choose to kill two random strangers. Something was still missing. Both cases looked to have used the same murder weapon, of spiking, or heavily drugging water. Whoever this killer was, they only knew one method of how to finish their victims. This had to mean something, for neither Jemma nor Phillip had suffered.

Tomorrow, DS Nick Murray had offered to drive up to Salisbury and go through the notes together. Perhaps, if Iain partnered up with DS Murray from Bath, they could uncover something that was currently eluding them both.

The next morning, after a frosty drive across North Somerset into Dorset and then across Wilshire, DS Nick Murray was already in the station drinking tea when Iain arrived. Iain walked into his office, surprised to see the DS, as it was still only 7.20 a.m.

The DS must have been on the road by five-thirty a.m. to get here so quickly. For this, DI Kleverly was grateful.

With a brief handshake and some quick introductions, the two detectives took no time into getting down to business.

After a short conversation about DS Peter Johnson and the time both of them spent together in Swindon Station, plus the mention of their love of Rugby - playing on the same team for five years - DI Kleverly was sad to hear his good friend and former colleague was so ill.

Only a day after the new Salisbury case, DI Kleverly had missed a call from DS Pete.

He had meant to call him back, as at the time he thought it to be a friendly call as Pete would often ring out of the blue, but DI Kleverly was now beginning to wonder if DS Pete had already started to see a link between the cases.

DS Peter Johnson was a far better copper than his rank displayed.

The notes were still scattered across his desk as Iain had not been in any mood to tidy up before he left the station at eleven p.m. last night.

DS Iain had also been called to assist at a fight at a local nightclub last night, which had led to several arrests after a non-fatal stabbing.

DS Nick Murray picked up the first page, reading how the girl in her mid to late twenties was found. Yesterday, after speaking to the DI, he had tried to soak up as much as he could about this four-day-old case, but he'd not had access to the paper copies seen here.

DI Kleverly gave him twenty minutes to read them through, whilst he prepared a cup of hot morning coffee for them.

DS Nick read the last known movements of Jemma Evans, *Thursday 15 March.*

*Jemma Evans had a very set daily routine, and today she decided to go to the Gym after leaving her job at Brymore Estate agents at five-fifteen p.m. Colleagues reported that this was intended, as she had spoken about her evening plans with her father to three work colleagues earlier that day in the office.*

*The walk across town would be no more than thirty minutes.*

*Myranda Singh of Papers & Stuff Newsagents reported Jemma entering his establishment at approx. 17.40 p.m., purchasing a bottle of Spring Mountain water and a banana.*

*Jemma arrived at Fitness by Design, at 17.50 p.m.*

*CCTV captured her as she entered and when she left, at 18.38 p.m.*

*There are no cameras inside the Gym, but records state that only three people were also using the facilities at that time.*

Two other females, and a gentleman who is very much a regular after five p.m., plus the onsite trainer. These people are all currently in the process of being interviewed.

Jemma walked back to her car after leaving the Gym. The walk back to the car park is only thirty minutes from the Gym. We have good footage of Jemma walking down the high street and heading towards her car, before driving back to her flat in the village of Netherhampton. At no point did she speak or walk with anyone on the journey home.

The time of death we believe was between 21.05 p.m. and 22.50 p.m.

Jemma was found lying in her bathroom, as she was feeling unwell. The toilet has signs that she was sick sometime before she died.

At 20.59 p.m., Jemma Evans attempted to make a phone call to her father but never made the connection. When Jemma's father did call back at 21.20 p.m., Jemma did not pick up the phone. After four more calls, Jemma father finally gave up.

It was Jemma's father, Mr Larry Evans. who discovered her daughters' body the following morning?

The poison used pathology believes was administered into her mineral water bottle. It would take approx. four to five hours for this poison to take any real effect. This again puts us back into the time Jemma attended the Gym, but it may well have been earlier. Forensics think there may be another substance that delayed the poison acting, but this has yet to be analysed.

We believe somebody tampered with her water bottle.

There were several workmen on site that day in the Gym, all of which had worked book for some time before. Two electricians were working on emergency lighting and a plumber was called out to repair a leaking pipe.

*These men are all under investigation, but so far, each of these individuals is not known to the victim had had no previous reasons to consider foul play.*

*DI – Kleverly.*

DS Nick flicked over the page, but DI Kleverly interjected, "The rest of it is just the history of Jemma Evans. Not much of a story - grew up and went to school in Cirencester, an apprentice estate agent in a company called Brymore. Posted to Salisbury about ten months ago." DI Kleverly said, pointing to the wall where the cases notes were made into a timeline of yellow post-it notes.

DS Nick stood and walked over the cluttered cork pinboard, "This is old-school Sir. We are not allowed to use post-its anymore. Not environmentally clean, you know the thing." Nick chuckled.

DI Kleverly leaned back in his leather chair, which creaked under his seventeen stone.

"Neither are we. But I like it this way. You can see where the gaps are like this. Look at what we do not know. There is a small gap between her arriving at the Gym from work to when the CCTV caught her going in. Where did she go for those minutes? Also, the gym has confessed that they do not insist that everyone signs in each day, it is just a membership card that is flashed to the onsite trainer. So, who else was on sight that evening that we do not even know about? CCTV has shown at least four individuals going in and out at that time. None of which the trainer told us about." DI Kleverly said, shaking his closely shaven head.

Nick pointed to the first few post-its, "This is interesting. This says Jemma Evans served as an apprentice in a village outside of Bath for her first years. Worked in the Stockton-on-Avon branch for three years between 2009-2012. That's the same village where Phillip Stevens lived and the house where his body was discovered." DS Nick said, looking at the girl's short career path in yellow.

DI Iain Kleverly nodded.

"Yes, I did see the connection when I was talking to you yesterday. I think it may be worth at least asking some questions at the estate agents. Does your boy or his parents have anything to do with the branch?" DI Iain asked, reaching for this desk phone.

Nick replied, trying to recall the small branch he had been inside with Celia over ten years ago:

"Not that I have found. Funnily enough, I have been inside that little branch of Brymore before. My wife and I nearly moved into the village when we came down here from Kent. The only thing I can remember about the branch is there was a huge out of place painted picture of the private school and countryside beyond, behind the main desk. It was quite old from what I remember, did not suit the small estate agents at all. It was painted before the place was a school. Just the big old house and the views of fields down to the church." Nick told the listening DI.

DS Kleverly seemed intrigued, "That's a little odd. When was this, Nick?"

Nick thought and counted back the dates on his fingers which made the DI smirk, "2008…2009 that's it. Come to think of it, the estate agent did have a young girl working with her then. Pretty little thing, with long red hair." DS Nick recalled, remembering the young girl with them at the pub and viewing that day.

DS Kleverly rummaged through the piles of paper on his desk. Finding a photo, he turned it to face Nick.

"Was this the girl you remember? Might be a bit old now, and her hair is short, but is this the girl you saw?" DI Kleverly asked, pointing to the picture of the victim.

Nick walked over and took the photo. Looking closely, he was racking his brain to remember the young girl with the estate agent that day. She had not been that important as most of the time she had been silent as her boss handled the viewing and the pub meal after. Staring down at the face of the girl looking at him smiling, it was a picture of her holding a balloon with the number twenty-five on it. Yet even though the girl was older than what he could remember, Nick was sure it was the same person.

"I am pretty sure that's her sir. Hair and face look a bit more weathered than I remember, but I would be sure that was the estate agent's assistant." Nick said, surprised where this conversation had taken them.

DS Kleverly took the photo back and looked to place it on the wall.

"Well, this does put another angle on the case, DS Murray.

I have been looking for something solid to link these two murders together. Apart from the method of death, I have been at a loss. But, thanks to you we now have three new lines of investigation to follow up. The first is the estate agent in the village of Stockton-on-Avon. The second and far most important part of this is the method of death is looking to be the same drug. My suspicions are that both victims had their water bottle spiked with poison. I think DS Johnson may had realised this after reading the forensic report, as he did try to call me a couple of days ago.

Good copper DS Johnson often sees things that others miss. Something he has always been able to do. I was made DI when Pete turned it down. Never understood why?

"Anyway, our third line of investigation is a little more worryingly. Perhaps I should be questioning YOU Nick. A strange coincidence that our only real link to both these cases is the copper investigating one of the murders." DI Kleverly laughed as he pinned the photo next to the post-it that said deceased.

DI Nick did chuckle back, but inside he was now feeling a little confused. For a moment he thought of telling DI Kleverly that the boy was found in the very same house he and Celia were viewing that day. They had been inside the house with Jemma Evans for over an hour when she could have been no more than seventeen years old.

This was a part of the investigation he needed to keep for himself for now.

The last thing he wanted was to be the missing link between both murders, but so far DI Kleverly's little joke was worryingly true. Apart from the same poison used, DS Nick was the only other known person in the world who brought the two victims together.

# Chapter 6

## Eden's Echo

### Timeline—24 March 2018

Chaplain Mary Grace had never been a great cook.

It was a skill her mother had tried to teach her so many times when she was a girl, but none of the African techniques had ever properly transferred. But her lack of culinary skills never stopped her from a want of trying to cook good and tasty food.

As the daughter of immigrants which came over from South Africa with nothing but a small suitcase and a tiny baby in their arms in 1952, Mary had been fortunate, as they had both found employment within a private country school.

Mary's father was once a trained man of god, working with various missionaries right across Africa. After new brutal warlords started to take over Uganda and parts of the Congo, together with growing apartheid in her home of country of South Africa becoming the norm, politically, socially, and economically in every province, Mary's parents took the first boat they could afford passage to escape.

Mary had arrived in Bristol as an infant on a boat filled with bananas, with her families urgent need to escape racist oppression.

The private school was already known for its diversely selected students. It did not go unnoticed that many of the first black students were all sons of warlords who relished their children learning from everything they fought to keep away from their country's dictatorships.

Mary's father had been eagerly snapped up by the school, as having a black teacher of religious studies, helped them to secure far more African students than most of the white-only establishments.

Even as far back as the 1950's King Alfred's school had seized the opportunity to educate ethnic minorities, which it had taken other schools over thirty years to slowly catch up.

Mary's mother had worked within the school kitchens. Over twenty years, she made her way up to head cook and had been a very respected member of staff when she finally retired at the age of seventy-one.

For the price of this loyalty, good service and unbroken employment, Mary's parents had been given access to a private tutor, who had educated Mary alone inside the school. Girls were strictly not permitted, which until this day, this law had not gone the way apartheid had happily followed.

Mary's teacher was old, right from the very first day she started teaching her privately. For fifteen years the old woman, who lived in one of the oldest houses in the village of Stockton-on-Avon below, would spend much of her time talking about the school when she was a small girl.

Mary walked over to one of her bulging bookcases in her flat. Living in a new property near to the renovated Bristol docks area, the view out across the narrow water was best at night when the city lights reflected the growing construction of waterside living. Carefully, Mary pulled out a very old book which was so thick with written pages, the cover had been stitched manually onto the leather hide spine.

Walking outside onto a tiny balcony, it was cold, but fresh just as Mary liked.

Mary pulled open the huge book at a set marked page, like the water below her, the Chaplain reflected on lights from the past.

Mary was just fourteen when she had first been shown this book. Her old teacher, Miss Emerald Down-Lacey, had been keen to share this huge tome with her only student. Mary was quite used to the old woman talking for hours on end about the school before it was a school, but on this day, she wanted to explain how the book had come to be written.

It was the sort of book almost impossible to start at page one. The young Mary had preferred to randomly flick through the old pages, stopping at several of the bookmarks her teacher had already placed.

It was like flicking through a Bible, Miss Emerald had told Mary, *only God will know what he wants you to read next*. It had been a strange saying, but as Mary came to understand the truth of what the book was and how it had come to be, it made more sense each time she held it.

Sitting on her balcony, Mary opened the book at a random page, it fell back three hundred- and seventy-six-pages in. This study, as almost every page was properly titled, spoke on relaxation of the mind, and techniques to clear one's thoughts. Mary had read all this before, much of which had provided the research to write her own books, which over the last ten years had sold extremely well both in print and online.

Bradbury Barnes was a true friend, one who now understood the pathway to Eden. The bonus of him being extremely good with computers and creating her an author's website to sell across the whole world was and had been a huge success.

This was not a night she needed to read. Tonight, like many other nights, she just felt comfortable having this book in her hands. This was more than a cherished gift from her old teacher Emerald. It had provided her with the very knowledge of why she was able to speak directly with the almighty.

As she scanned the old handwritten pages with her eyes, her fat fingers casually traced the embossed letters across the stitched cover.

Each letter was painstakingly embroidered in an *Olde-Worlde* font, long before microcomputers offered such a service with ease to this.

*Eden's Echo – A Study of God*

Mary sat back and looked out across the calm water. It had been the same spiritually calming water when she had first heard the old woman speak of Eden's Echo. That was what the school was called before it was closed in 1935 and sold off to the state.

*Miss Emerald had been at the school for longer than when it became King Alfred's school for boys in 1935. The building was far older than what it had been extended to become.*

*Miss Emerald had told Mary of the days in the early 1920s when the owners would hold huge country balls, inviting dignitaries from all over the world, to listen and hopefully convert those who were looking to broaden their knowledge of the modern times ahead.*

*There were even larger balls before the Great War took so many good men away to fight in muddy fields, including Miss Emeralds late finance, a man she always referred to as Sweet Reg.*

*As a young teacher of French and world Religious studies, Miss Emerald had been asked by the estate to privately teach the owners two nephews. The owner was a man who was known to have once been a great explorer, finding and recording artefacts and knowledge from all over the world. The English Empire had provided the family great wealth and with it enough to not only build the Eden's Echo but bring in other great scholars to help the owner with his special studies.*

*The owner, Charles Wyndham II was a learned man, one who was not one to follow the traditional crowd. It was said that his mother was linked in some way to Queen Victoria, but this was never proven when Miss Emerald knew them.*

*Charles Wyndham had been away for many years on his travels around the world, but when he finally returned, it was a different man who settled again in England.*

*After years of studying and learning from an ancient religious cult in Turkey, which had first formed sometime after the Byzantium Empire was all but ruins, Charles Wyndham had come into the possession of a set of texts that claimed some had come out of first-century Jerusalem with the ability to directly commune with God. It was suggested this was what was being termed as the Holy spirit, something the disciples of Christ had all been given after he passed back to God's side.*

*Whatever the owner discovered in Turkey, it had changed him completely from an outspoken eccentric heretic to a man of divine humble faith.*

*Charles Wyndham made it his Holy mission to teach others about what he had found in Turkey. It was as if he had been told by the divine himself that there was a way that God could talk to anyone who knew how to properly listen for Him.*

*Emerald could remember the hundreds of people who would come to listen to Charles. Some would just dismiss him as a lunatic whilst others looked to follow his teachings.*

*One summer, there was said to be over three thousand people that attended a grand preaching in the house grounds. It was during this time that many of the school's outbuildings were constructed, mainly to provided accommodation to any that travelled to the Bath country estate.*

*The original name of the property was built as The Wyndham Estate, but only two years after it was built and Charles came home, he had it changed to Eden's Echo. In what the press was terming a "Wellness Retreat" the estate was opened for anyone to come and cleanse themselves both spiritually and mentally.*

*Emerald was there on the day Charles Wyndham gave his great sermon on the hill, looking out over the little village. Shouting his new truth, he told the masses that they were all sinners, but it was not their fault. Charles promised that any who chose to follow him, he would show them the way back into Eden, where God was there waiting with open arms.*

*Only inside Eden's Echo could God again be heard by man.*

*It had been a speech that had made all the national newspapers. It had been the speech that had led to the Catholic Church demanding he was silenced and condemned as a heretic cultist. Emerald explained that the Catholic Church was a force for good in the world, but when anything contradicted their teachings, they were also a powerful enemy.*

*The onset of war in 1917 had saved Eden's Echo from closure, for the country needed to focus on other problems caused by the Kaiser. When the war was done, and the dust finally settled over the poppy fields, the 1920's saw interest in Charles Wyndham return and Eden's Echo once more spiked.*

*Charles Wyndham died in 1928, after spending the war years and most of the 1920's writing and stitching together everything he had spent his early lifetime researching.*

*Many of the studies for learning to hear Eden's Echo and*

*speaking to God were copied from the original manuscripts Charles Wyndham had stolen from Turkey. There were several other books Charles had added from different learned techniques, including hypnotism, spiritualism, and previous life regression studies.*

*Agatha Wyndham, the sister of Charles and her two sons, Franklin and Michael, inherited Eden's Echo from Charles will, with a condition that it would be used as a centre of religious discovery. Charles believed all who trained under his teachings could one day learn to speak with God, as he had claimed to have achieved many times.*

*At the turn of the decade, on the advent of the 1930s and added interest from Agatha Wyndham's new husband, who was a prominent member of the new Nazi party in Germany, Eden's Echo once more sparked the unwelcomed interest of the Catholic Church.*

*On a dark December morning in 1935, the police arrived at Eden's Echo with two Bishops, three priests and about 50 enforcement officers. Agatha and her two sons were arrested and imprisoned under the charges of the establishment being a religious cult. They were accused on several lawful reasons that Eden's Echo was preaching and brainwashing people into promising a metaphysical-philosophical ideology. Generally, this belief system was outside of mainstream religions where people were openly shown to become radicalised from what was known and accepted doctrine.*

*Agatha's Nazi husband had avoided arrest because he had already gone back to Germany, never to return. The last anyone heard of him, was that he was working in the office of Joseph Goebbels, a prominent German Nazi occult specialist for ancient artefacts.*

Agatha and her sons were released the following year, immediately leaving for Germany, joining the Nazi cause.

Miss Emerald told Mary that Stockton-on-Avon was on the cover of every fleet street paper that week. There was even a photo of Miss Emerald in the Times when one journalist had asked her all about when she worked at Eden's Echo.

Emerald had lived in the village all her life. As the daughter of the vicar, she had never travelled too far. After the war, when the letter of Sweet Reg's death arrived, she moved out from her fathers' home, choosing to live in a smaller house within the village.

Only a week before the Police arrived at Eden's Echo to arrest her, Agatha Wyndham had come down into the village, with several items that she wanted to be hidden with her most trusted employees. Miss Emerald was sure that Agatha knew they were about to be closed down by the church. Across the village, she gave out items of great wealth, saying that,

"When this is all over, I will come back for them." and

"It's probably a lot of fuss about nothing... but just to be sure I would like you to keep these a while."

Agatha gave Emerald a huge book, the same book she was giving Mary on her fourteenth birthday. The other item was far too big for her little home, yet it was also far too beautiful to turn down.

It was a painting, Agatha said was painted around 1908, just after the house was renamed Eden's Echo. Charles had it commissioned by a friend of his, who had taken nearly two months to complete the piece. Emerald had seen it before, telling Agatha how beautiful it was, sitting above the huge marble fireplace of the ballroom.

Now it hung on a cold stone wall, too brittle to move again.

*The picture was of the house, sweeping out to show the village and the church spire. It was especially of interest to Emerald because you could just see the roof of her long-dead fathers' home, the old Rectory.*

Miss Emerald Down-Lacey died in the spring of 1978, asleep in her bedroom. Agatha Wyndham had never returned to collect either the book or the huge picture.

In 1985, Emerald's little house was firstly turned into a village shop and then sold to a small branch of a local estate agent. The picture was still hanging on the wall the last time Mary had gone into the village, nobody had ever been stupid enough to try to move it.

In the final years of her life, Mary visited Miss Emerald many times. They would talk of Eden's Echo and the huge book. Miss Emerald would constantly state that soon she was going to see Sweet Reg again, and they could be together in God's grace. Of this fact, she was convinced.

Mary had smiled at the time, as she had not yet learned everything she needed to reach Eden.

After a lifetime of studying the great book, painstakingly handwritten by Charles Wyndham II, Mary was overjoyed to know that Miss Emerald had finally been reunited with Sweet Reg.

The final written works of the turn of the century explorer had provided a lifetime companion to Mary, alongside the Bible, that was so important, she thought it to be too precious to release into the public domain.

After the reading of Emerald's will, Mary was the sole beneficiary to her entire estate. The little house, Charles Wyndham's book and over £800,000 were left to Mary Grace alone. Two years later, Mary had sold the house to an estate agent and purchased the small hall in Bristol where Eden's Echo chapter house sat below her spacious waterside flat.

Charles Wyndham II had tried so hard to preach what he had learned. Only from a lifetime of compiling stories from the Holy land, learning ancient Hebrew texts from Africa and the spoken words of handed down testimony from secret religious sect in Turkey, had Charles learned the truth of how to hear God's voice.

About a week after Emerald's passing, Mary Grace had been sitting beneath the branches of a weeping willow tree. The sun in the sky was mottled as its beams tried to push through each fallen arched branch. The wind gently moved each branch, echoing a thousand whispers as Mary sat with her eyes closed and her back against the tree trunk. Holding the thick leather-bound book close to her heart, that Emerald had bequeathed for only Mary to keep and protect, she was at a sense of complete peace, tuned perfectly into the frequency of nature.

That was the first time she had truly heard the voice of God.


Joshua Wright had been a fast learner. Mary did not know if this was because he was a desperate man in need of finding salvation, or if it was to fill his emptiness with the food of God. Whatever the man's reasons were for listening to her, his desire, need, and ability was as fast as any other she had ever taught before. Joshua Wright was a good man.

In Mary's vast experience from teaching the book, after forty years of study, most who came to her were already lost or trying to hide from the errors of their sinful past. Mary had taught every walk of life, from dangerous prisoners to deeply holy men. God was *always* the answer, God was *always* the way, she would tell them, seeing hope return to their eyes.

Often, Mary would use biblical scripture to add substance to her words. How many times had she started a conversation or sermon using what she knew to be one of the strongest statements the Bible commanded?

*Hebrews 11:6*

*"Without faith, it is impossible to please Him."*

Mary's initial teaching was to show that God's voice was rarely heard in an audible voice or an act of the supernatural. The book Charles Wyndham II had written revealed that God's words were mostly heard through one's heart, which takes faith, and for those without a strong faith, it was impossible to hear over the general noise of life.

Mary could remember Joshua Wright listening as if it were the first time, he had ever heard anything in his life. That first night, inside the small Eden's Echo chapter house, as Joshua sat alongside Barnaby and Frederick, Mary had touched a man's heart, filling it with God's grace, allowing it to beat again, to the rhythm of a new song.

For the next two months, Joshua had been the first to arrive at the small hall each night. Sparking up friendships with both Barnaby and Frederick, Joshua wanted to help and become a part of their growing community.

Twice a week, he would go with Frederick and Mary to a homeless shelter, where Joshua helped in giving out food, warm blankets, and most of all an ear for those less fortunate to listen to. For Joshua, this was a medicine, for here he had learned a lesson that there were always people less fortunate than himself.

Mary had marvelled at the transformation. In all her time showing others that there was another way than the despair of suicide, Joshua was by far the only one who had changed his life the most.

After only six months, knowing this man was now far off

from the road to suicide and working again as a plumber too many to the congregation Eden's Echo had formed, Joshua was ready to move on again, taking the next step into hearing God's voice.

Mary had looked deep into the man's eyes, and using her skills, listened to his heart to know if this man was right to know more. God had answered her strong and clear.

There was no voice inside her head telling her this was true, just the arrival of a white dove one morning that had suddenly appeared on the balcony of her flat.

This small bird was the sign she had asked for, this was her guidance that God wanted Joshua Wright to hear His voice and know of His grace.

Mary's lessons from the huge book were not given to all of her flock. The book was very specific in that some of the gifts were not meant for all men. Emerald had once explained to Mary that,

"Some men are followed, whilst most are just followers."

This was clear in the book, for each chapter began with guidance on how God wished to be heard, and to be accepted again into a world that was becoming more secular each year. But this footnote was always preceded by words of caution, stating that there would be many who would falsely claim to hear God's voice, and drive followers to do what they said in His name. Kings and great leaders often tried to change the tides of men, when they claimed their cause was with God. Charles had written in great depth of the sorry history of man in the time of the crusades. Both sides, Muslim and Christian fought bloody battles to claim a false victory for the same God. It was all ultimately folly, none had ever heard God's voice, for each one of the men, women and children that died under their religious banners were all part of the same sheep in His flock.

Teaching how to hear God was only given to the true believers who could use this message to further His grace to the followers and the faithful. Joshua had understood this from the minute Mary explained it to him.

In Charles Wyndham's book, after the scriptures of ancient faiths and different ways to experience God's mercy, the chapters at the end of the book were almost separated as a completely new tome. There was a very thick red leather cover, that looked like a bookmark when viewed from the side. This was the book Mary had spent nearly ten years of her life learning, under Emerald's expert tuition.

Many of the first chapters highlighted Biblical stories and spoke of truth and other holy books, including many gospels that had been left out of the Bible. But the second book, was different, for it seemed that Charles had wanted the reader to only use the first section of the book as a reference to what he wanted to reveal.

The internal red leather cover was hand-embroidered with a subtitle, like the main title of the book.

"Entering Eden. How to Hear His voice."

Mary had watched Joshua as he sat transfixed to the first page. It was handwritten, not typed, for this was a book never intended to be mass-produced. The first page of the second internal book was a contents page, written in Charles Wyndham's hand, of what he had discovered from countless journeys all over the world.

Mary, as she always did, had read out the chapters that she would be covering, partly to be sure that Joshua understood he was going to be shown something that only a few had ever seen before. But it was also out of a sense of drama, for it built up a tension that this was a gift of unique rareness.

Reading the words slowly, Mary left a short gap between reading each chapter's name,

**To Hear His Echo is to Know the Righteous Path.**

***Common Ways God Talks to Us.***

**His Word**

**Other People**

**Our Circumstances**

**The Still Small Voice**

**The Actual Voice**

Turning over the first page, Mary started to read and explain the words that Joshua absorbed like a dry sponge to a bowl of shallow water.

Each time Mary had prepared for the first day of training, she cherished this moment the most. ***His word*** was always the first step to show the followers that God was not only listening, but He was also prepared to answer His flock.

Mary had sipped at a glass of pure red wine as she sat back to relish in Joshua's total concentration. It was as if he were about to witness a miracle. In a way he was, but this was a journey of self-discovery, where God would only reveal Himself if the subject were worthy. Mary tried to explain that all men were loved and known by God, but only those He needed to spread His Word, were able to hear Him.

Mary read on, "To hear from God, we have to know some things about God Himself. We must develop a deep understanding of who God is and the way He does things. Fortunately, there is a guidebook to how God is. We call it the Bible. This is a book written over thousands of years to give us detail about how we can expect God to react, what kind of expectations He has for us, and most specifically, how He expects us to treat others. The Bible is pretty good at this, given its age and the changes that were seen across history. We must learn to read His word. We must learn to know His word. The Bible is the written word and should become a reference to everything you need to find him." Mary flicked back to the first part of the huge book.

Joshua now understood why so many pages were filled with biblical references and gospels.

Mary nodded.

"This Joshua is not just a book to help you find Him. It contains everything that God ever wanted us to learn. There are a few old scriptures in here, many not seen in today's Bible or holy texts. Yet, they should not be thought of as less important than those that made the final print."

"Remember Joshua, the Bible was put together by men who thought they knew God. The first council of Nicosia was one of the most important events in known history, for they made the Bible suit their agendas, settling age-old debates about the divine nature of God. The stories and psalms that made it into the Bible are indeed beautiful, inspirational, and full of wonders, but these alone are not the complete account."

"The Bible is *His written* word. This is the place we need to start and will be very much the place where we finish our journey. In the Bible, we will know His word, and Praise Be, know Him. Words are so powerful when written down Joshua, but they are greater still when they are heard and gloried. No book on earth has ever been written where every word ever spoken in a man's life was carefully noted for others to know. We came close with Jesus. But much of what Jesus said was remembered and written down much later, by those who walked with him or just later heard and passed on the stories, but there is still much that we do not know of what he said to others."

"When you learn to listen, Joshua, you must hear and feel every word, for you will never be able to write down all of what God has to say to you. When you hear His words, it will be like spirit water, as it pours through your soul, filling you with His divine love. If God chooses to speak with you, His words will be with you always, and you will come to understand the love in Him.

*"His Word* Joshua is the only voice you will ever want to hear, but before that glorious day arrives, there is a path you must walk, and it is the path of good. Rejoice in the fact that you are saved Joshua, you are safe in His hands. When you hear the echoes of His call, you must be ready to do *whatever* He asks of you Joshua.

"Eden is our heaven where God can be found. The Echo is the sound of his voice as it travels out across the world, for some to hear and know, for others to use as a way home."

Mary stopped and took a breath. Looking up from the book at the man before her, she could see tears drenching the man's unshaven cheeks, she knew that this was a man whose journey was just about to begin.

Mary looked out across the calm waters of Bristol docks.

It was cold, but she loved to sit, think, and remember on nights like this.

Walking back into her flat to pick up a thick knitted shawl, she flicked on the radio, which was usually filled with quiet Christian music.

The hour was just turning over to eleven p.m.

Even as a young woman, Mary was never one to take to her bed before one a.m. She was very much the night owl Emerald had once described to her as.

The local news played its usual ditty before a strong voice, suited for newscasting filled her ears. Sitting back down in her seat on the balcony, Mary listened to the voice in her head, coming as if from the very wind.

It was the same when she had first heard God speak to her. At first, she had looked around the house, trying to see if a TV or radio had been left on. When she discovered nothing untoward, Mary had sat wondering if someone was playing a trick on her. It had taken her another full week before she came to accept the frequency of God's spirit call.

The radio newscaster read out the headline. In usual news order, the headlines went from the range of plain awful, then horrible, through to politics, and finally followed by a lighter story and the weather to end. This was how modern society accepted their daily intake of current affairs to what was happening in the world around them.

As the first story spoke of a huge fire in a local factory where ten poor souls were said to be dead and many others injured, Mary whispered a silent prayer to the lost souls and the grieving families they left behind.

The second story was just as hard, for it was becoming a common theme to other horrible stories she had been listening to over the last few weeks. Whispering another prayer, the voice on the wind spoke to her very soul,

*"In a further disturbing development, to the School Boy murder case in Stockton-on-Avon, another young victim has been recently discovered, in which police are not denying, died by the same method of poisoning as the other two victims. Police have not yet released the name of the third person to be killed in such a horrible way but have said that investigations are ongoing into*

*what is looking to be a possible serial killer. Our sources state that none of the victims are known to each other, and all of them seem to be chosen at random, which is extremely rare for such a case. Police have asked the public to remain calm, as they are following up several leads that they hope will soon result in the arrest and discovery of this murderer. Tomorrow, police will be releasing a photofit of a man they would like to question. The public has been asked to make sure they do not approach this man if they recognise him."*

The newscaster then moved onto a local council election result.

Mary shook her head. What kind of man or woman would ever choose to kill another in cold blood? It was beyond her to know. God had been very clear in the words he gave to Moses. **Thou shalt not murder.**

Lifting her book, she walked back inside the flat, where it was warmer and out of the breeze.

She hoped with all her heart that whoever the police revealed in the photo tomorrow, the person could be saved.

God was always the way, anyone, even a murderer could find their way back to Eden if they choose to. Whoever this sick individual who was responsible for these crimes turned out to be, they were still just a lost sheep in the Lord's flock.

God would forgive them, but only if they asked for and wanted His divine forgiveness.

This poor soul had just lost their way.

They had not heard the echo.

They were a long way from finding Eden.

Whoever this person was they could not hear His voice, no matter how loud God was calling out to them.

Mary closed her huge book and placed it on the large

wooden table she used to often host dinner parties. On the cover, a picture she had become very familiar with, starred up at her.

This was the same picture she had first seen on a huge plaque hanging on the side of the school her father had taught within when she was young. It had been taken down only a few years after the building became a school, as Emerald explained, where it was once the emblem of the house it was built for.

What had happened to the plaque? Mary did not know, but the picture represented everything the house had once been.

On the cover of the book, the picture was embossed in gold stitching. It was a simple design, but its symbology was important enough to have once formed a large religious following.

Tracing the raised stitches with her finger, it symbolised the very centre of Eden, where a perfect apple tree grew, with a snake wrapped around the trunk.

# Chapter 7

## Murder Three - Ridley Goodman (21)

### Timeline—22 March 2018

DS Nick Murray stood on the sheet-covered ground floor of a multi-storey car park outside of a local Tesco superstore. It was not the place he wanted to be at 02.37 a.m. on a Thursday, but on the discovery of a third victim that was reported to have white crystal residue on the edges of his mouth and tongue, Molly Symonds had insisted the DS was called out to the murder scene.

PC Sally Gunel had felt awful getting DS Nick out of his warm bed, but it had been Nick who had insisted that any news relating to the schoolboy case, he was informed straight away, no matter how small or immaterial it was.

The discovery of another body was already looking to show that something was going on which was worryingly linked. But this new body, described by Molly Symonds as a male in his early twenties, was another seemingly random murder.

It was on her first inspection of the corpse that Molly found the sure signs of the same poison used in both the schoolboy and the Salisbury case. This time, however, it was not water that had disguised whatever dissolved invisibly into the liquid, it was a bottle of cheap white wine.

DS Nick arrived at the twenty-four-hour Tesco, which was already awash with pulsing blue lights. Fortunately, the superstore was on the opposite side of the car park, so it was still able to remain open, as officers carefully taped off a section nearby.

Two policemen were holding steaming cups of coffee that looked to be store-bought, which Nick thought to be a small relief for anyone called out to such a grim scene on a very cold night. Allowing the store to stay open would also not incur the heaps of paperwork that would no doubt have come from Tesco trading office, as often ordering the closure of a store the size of this, would never be deemed important enough to allow the police to properly investigate a murder scene.

By the time DS Nick turned off the warm engine of his purring Audi TT, mercifully, all the administration had already been sorted. The police were asked to re-divert traffic to another car park exit, whilst other officers taped off the entire area where a quickly erected white tent was covering a body.

Everyone was able to continue to work. Tesco was happily allowing people in to trade through the night, and the police were self-contained and able to investigate the scene.

Nick got out of his car and walked over to the tape. PC McKinley from the Yeovil station was on duty, and nodded as the DS approached, "They always find bodies like this on cold nights sir. Never seems to be on sunny days in July?" the policeman stated, lifting the tape to allow the DS to enter.

Nick agreed, "I think you are right PC McKinley. I don't think murderers appreciate the cold night's policemen have to endure when they choose their victims. Perhaps we should have considered this when we joined the force." Nick smirked.

Walking past a parked ambulance, Nick came out in front of the small white tent, where several people in full white overall suits carefully examining a body and the ground around it.

Another white suited person was examining items which had been pushed into several Tesco plastic carrier bags.

Looking at the dead body, Nick could see a heavily bearded man, unkempt and still wrapped in a tattered blue sleeping bag, that was ripped in several places. White patches through the tears of inner lining were visible across the entire sleeping bag.

Sleeping behind a main car park stanchion, the man looked to be just one of the many homeless this area was known for.

DS-Nick looked over at the carrier bags, which were all this man had in the world. Inside, he could see a few items of clothing pushed into balls, with half-open packets of crisps and a nearly empty box of cigarettes.

Outside of the bags, near to the victim's dark hair, a brown paper bag was stood upright, wrapping what looked to be an open bottle of white wine.

One of the people in white walked over to Nick. Instantly, through her visor, Nick recognised the woman in her late 50's. Sadly, over the years Nick has served the Bath station, he had seen this woman too many times. But it was good to know she was on this case because it was also well known she was the best person to investigate this type of case.

Molly Symonds lifted her face mask, "DS-Murray, good to see you at this fine hour." Molly Symonds said, without an ounce of humour.

Nick decided to keep it strictly professional, "Hello, Molly. I see you have been busy. What have you found?" he asked, pointing towards the corpse.

Molly moved over to the top of the sleeping bag, where the man's head and arms were outside of the bag. The team had yet to close the man's eyes, as he coldly stared towards the wine bottle.

Molly spoke, "Our best guess is that he died around eight p.m. last night. There are no visible signs of injury, nor was he known to be ill. His friend over there says he had not been on the streets very long but was well-liked. Slept here most evenings but spent most of his day begging in the main high street.

"Nothing strange to a homeless person dying of the cold, but when my colleague looked at the bottle, it was clear that we needed to call you. This is the third time I have seen this in three weeks. This cannot be a coincidence, for even in my long career, I have never seen this substance used like this before. It is not the sort of thing anyone would chance for substance abuse. This would be a suicidal decision. This man was in a bad way, but he was not suicidal from what that girl says." Molly explained, pointing to another homeless person, sat drinking from a steaming coffee cup in the back of a police car.

DS Nick asked a question, "Thanks, Molly, that's my job done. Can you be sure it is sodium Pentobarbital?" Nick asked, already knowing Molly would not be wrong.

Molly Symonds bent down and took a swab stick from her pocket. Carefully she opened the man's mouth and pointed a torch inside. On the tongue, tiny sparkles reflected from the torch beam. There were a few sparkles on his bottom lip.

"I have been looking at this drug in detail for the last couple of weeks. It is the same, I am sure of it DS Murray." Molly Symonds told the detective.

For the next few minutes, Molly explained that they were almost done and ready for the body to be taken. Molly wanted an autopsy as it would confirm her suspicions and she could write up her case after examining and confirming the contents of his stomach. Molly never placed a cause of death on her pathology notes until she was certain of it. Today, she was almost certain of what she was seeing, but almost in the world of Molly Symonds was never good enough.

DS-Nick thanked the forensics team and walked over to the car, where a young, pretty girl under unwashed hair, who looked to have seen a good while living on the streets, stared up at him. Speaking to the female officer who was sat next to her, the PC told Nick her name was Karen Spicer aged twenty-six.

DS Nick walked around to the car door allowing the young lady to make the most of what he thought was probably her warmest night in a while, "Good morning Miss Spicer. My name is DS-Nick Murray. I hope we have kept you comfortable in what must be a very distressing time." DS Nick said, bending on his knees to look into the back seat of the car.

For a moment, the girl just looked forward through the front seats of the police car, watching the ambulance team arrange to lift the body. Slowly she turned to face Nick.

"Ridley was thinking about going home. Such a shame. I liked him. Did not know him very long, but Ridley was clever, not the usual sort you see in the streets." The girl said, looking back to the body now lifted onto an ambulance bed.

Nick took out his notebook, "Can you give me this man's full name please Miss Spicer? What was your relationship with him?" DS Nick asked, trying to keep her attention.

The girl kept looking forward, as the body was wheeled into the ambulance, "We were just friends on the street. You know, people who sometimes shared a place to sleep. I used to sit with him in the shelter. He likes the food they gave him. Sat with him only last night. They served beef stew and dumplings. Ridley was happy with that. Said it reminded him of his mum." Karen said, taking a huge gulp of the cooling coffee.

DS-Nick wanted to understand who this man was,

"Did Mr Ridley have a surname? We need to let his mother know what has happened here tonight?" Nick asked.

The girl was thoughtful for a moment, "He did tell me that... Good... something. I cannot remember, it is not that important on the streets. We were just friends, given a bad hand in life. Ridley was lucky... He only came to be out here after he bucked off university. I think his parents threw him out after that. I thought he was clever, he helped me fill out all sorts of forms just before Christmas. I liked him." Karen said, turning to look up at the DS again.

DS-Nick closed his notebook as the ambulance slowly pulled out of the car park and out onto the main road beyond.

"Tell me, Miss Spicer, do you know how he got hold of the wine bottle. Did anyone else share this with him as far as you know?" Nick asked as he seemed to have the girl's attention.

Shaking her mousey, braided hair, the girl under her homeless disguise was attractive, her story was also important for none to hear.

"He did offer some to me, but I hate wine. Always have. My mum was an alcoholic, used to beat me black and blue after drinking wine. I guess I learned to hate it then. I also hate the taste. I prefer beer, or cider if it's available.

"But to answer your question, I do know where he got this bottle from. I thought it was generous at the time, Ridley did too. We are not given much on the streets, that's why we beg." Karen said, holding out her empty coffee cup as if she wanted him to put some money in.

DS-Nick took the cup, "I will get it refilled for you. Would you like us to buy you something to eat?" DS Nick asked, handing the cup to another officer. Instantly the girl shook her head,

"No thank you. Some fags would be nice." Karen answered.

Taking a tenner out of his suit pocket, he gave it to the officer who walked off towards the Tesco entrance. DS Nick pushed the girl again, "So, who gave Mr Ridley his wine Karen?" he asked, allowing the girl to turn back into the warm car.

"Goodman... that is his surname. Ridley Goodman. I think he was originally from Bath or that way at least. Came to Yeovil with me and a friend from Reading."

"Sorry, you asked who gave him the wine. It was a funny thing. As we queued to get our stew last night at the homeless kitchen, one of the serving men, you know the do-gooders as we call them, asked if Ridley would like something to drink with our meal.

"Ridley said that a fine white wine would be a great accompaniment, which had made us all laugh. Ridley could talk all posh like when he wanted."

"Anyways, ten minutes later the server came over with a bottle in a brown bag. Told us to keep it to ourselves. Ridley was overjoyed when he saw the wine. I did not have any, but I know Ridley drank nearly the whole bottle. He was out of it when we got back here. I went to get my stuff, as I had left it in a doorway. When I got back about two hours later, I found him like he was, all wide-eyed and lifeless. It was then I went into the shop and got them to call you a lot." Karen said, pointing to the Tesco store.

DS Nick finally had a lead, "This man, who served you the meal. Do you have a description?" DS-Nick asked, taking his notebook out again.

Karen nodded, "He wore a large, brimmed hat. Like an old man's hat. Looked stupid if you ask me. But I think that was to hide a bald head, my dad used to do the same thing when his hair thinned. Not much else to say. Bit of a beard, average height, nothing out of the ordinary. Oh... he did wear a big gold ring. It looked like a ten pence piece when I first looked at it. But it was not a coin, it was a symbol."

"I spoke to Ridley about it after he gave us the wine. I said it looked like a tree, a funny thing to have on a ring. Ridley agreed, but as I told you, Ridley was clever. He said it was an apple tree, with a snake around the trunk, I don't know how he knew that as we only saw it for a second or two?" Karen said, happily receiving the new hot coffee and twenty fags Nick had purchased for her.

DS Nick asked if Karen could draw the ring for him in his notebook. Handing the pencil over, it was clear this was the first time she had held a pencil in some time. It was a surprisingly good drawing; the girl had a talent for art. It was also something positive to follow up.

"That's what it sort of looked like. The tree was sticking out a bit. Ridley said it was probably religious or maybe military." Karen said, handing back the notebook.

After finishing the statement, Nick thanked Karen and the officer with her, as she continued to talk with the girl. Nick walked over to the crime scene, where the body had been removed. The evidence items were all being carefully bagged, with the wine bottle already packed up and gone.

Molly was talking to her forensics teams, making sure each item was properly photographed in situ before being lifted and taken away.

However, DS Nick now understood that this was not the crime scene. This was just the place where Ridley Goodman and come back to, only to die painlessly later.

The murder scene was still a place he needed to investigate, where the crime was committed. He needed to have the names of every person who was serving at the homeless soup kitchen last night, as one of them was now his lead suspect in a triple murder investigation.

Taking out his phone, he took a quick snap of the picture Karen Spicer had drawn of the strange ring. Sending it on a text to PC Gunel and Sergeant Parsons, the words on the text were simple to follow. *See what you can find out about this picture. Possibly a ring or religious symbol. Also, I want you and Sergeant Parsons over to the Yeovil homeless soup kitchen first thing tomorrow. I want to know the names of everyone who was helping serve last night. I will be in at nine a.m."*

DS Nick knew that Sally would not be that keen to work with Sergeant Parsons, as he knew the man was still very interested in her. But he also needed his officers to all work together, and as both were on the night shift, the next few hours were vital to the case. Nick intended to drive the thirty-five miles home and grab at least a couple of hours sleep before he was ready to start again in the morning.

Sergeant Michael Parsons had been through enough relationships that he always convinced himself there would be no more. In the last twelve years, since leaving his short-term marriage of only two years, Mike wanted to remain single, for that was a place he understood the rules of the game. Women were a complicated species, that was for sure, no matter how he tried to impress them, there was always something he lacked.

Mike could not ever remember loving any of them, not even his wife, who had doted on his every smile. But even this had been broken when he was caught cheating with her sister. It had needed a swift exit, costing him a flat in Bath and a lot of cash.

But there was one problem with his determination to remain a single man. It was difficult to admit but the rules of the game were not his to control.

Mike Parsons loved women. They were all fair game.

PC Sally Gunel sat alongside her senior officer as he pulled up into a small pub car park. It was only 7.25 a.m., so apart from a lorry unloading two barrels of ale, the place was mostly quiet.

Looking at the police car clock, she knew that her shift was not due to finish until nine-thirty a.m. It was rare for her to ever clock off on time, but as they were over twenty-five miles away from her house in Shepton Mallet, she could only think that today, she would be adding overtime to the weekly timesheet.

The uncomfortable trip to Yeovil this morning with Sergeant Parsons had been a mixture of cheap chat up lines, disguised in talk of the case. Mike Parsons never missed a single moment when an innuendo or suggestive comment could be added with a chuckle and intentional but hopeful look. PC Sally was pleased that she was wearing trousers today, as the perve next to her in the driving seat would be thinking of the stockings and suspenders she often wore as uniform in the station.

As far as Sally Gunel was concerned, there was no future for the Sergeant to keep suggesting they could try. If he kept on, she would play the only card she had left in the game and tell him she was seeing someone else, and it was serious. Even if this were not true, Mike would not know and men like Mike Parsons probably would not care. It would add to his game plan, as the challenge to win her over again would be back on.

Stepping out of the car, Sergeant Parsons walked around to open the door for Sally. She was already out and ready to follow by the time he got to her.

"Chivalry is never dead. Always polite to open doors for

ladies." Mike said, openly disappointed that she had beaten him to it.

"My fiancé says the same Serg. I love that in him." PC Gunel announced, thinking on her feet.

Mike Parsons just nodded. The comment had certainly struck a chord he was not aware of. Instantly Sergeant Parsons turned towards the building behind the white-walled pub and pointed, his voice again professional and police like.

"That's the place, Sal. It will probably be closed at this time of day. This is the only homeless soup kitchen in Yeovil, it must be the place the DS was talking about." Sergeant Parsons said, adjusting his helmet and walking away.

Sally agreed, looking at her phone. The searches she had spent nearly an hour looking into, had all come back with the same answer.

*The Lord's Pantry, soup kitchen and communal food bank. Operated by the local churches, The Salvation Army, and volunteers from across the region.*

Sally could see that it was not due to open before nine a.m., but she was sure that there would be people already around, warming a tea urn and preparing for the day.

As the two police-officers crossed the busy road leading towards the tall brick building, there were already a few homeless people waiting nearby.

When it became clear that the police-officers were heading to the door of the shelter, two of the homeless men shuffled off in the other direction, wanting nothing to do with any police questioning.

Sergeant Mike Parsons knocked on the large white door. The echo behind was a hollow sound.

On the door a sign was pinned up, offering anyone who

wanted to give anything chartable to be here between nine a.m. and nine p.m.

The was a symbol of the Salvation Army and a telephone number to call if anyone desperately needed help. For many, this was the only place any of them could find hot food, or a means to feed their hungry children.

Many of these places were often manned by religious organisations or groups of individuals who needed to feel that anyone who had fallen on hard times had at least somewhere to come. Across many of the bigger cities and towns of the area, there were many institutions and buildings set up to offer places of hope and warm meals, but in Yeovil, this was said to be the only centre.

PC Sally took a note of the name on the door. Father Stephen Ovett, Priest of St James Catholic Church. As quick as a flash, Sergeant Parsons had already made the connection,

"My God Sal. Another Olympian. Steve Ovett was a long-distance runner in the 1980s. You are in good company here, another Gold meddler if I recall right." the Sergeant said,

PC Gunel just smiled, without rising to the joke. Happily, the door opened before she needed to comment back.

In the doorway, a little old woman smiled. She was tiny, not more than 4'10" in height. Both officers had needed to look down as the woman smiled back up at them.

"Good Lord are we in trouble?" the lady said, opening the door fully to the policemen.

Sergeant Mike shook his head, "Good morning, my name is Sergeant Mike Parsons, and this is PC Sally Gunel. If possible, could we come in and ask a few questions about the service you gave last night. We are investigating an incident." the Sergeant told the old woman.

For a moment, the old woman continued to smile, looking both officers up and down, then slowly moved to the side to allow them in, "This is a place where no invite is needed. All are welcome to come into the Lord's Pantry. We were just about to open anyway. Please come in. Can I get you a cup of tea?" the old woman said, moving away from the door. PC Gunel closed it behind her.

The room inside was bigger than it looked from outside. A huge what looked to be old school hall was completely laid out with old tables and plastic chairs. On the walls, posters were showing many organisations. Numbers were shown for help with drug abuse, mental health and of course the Salvation Army.

But it was the sign hanging over the serving bar at the end of the room that had the biggest impact.

"JESUS LOVES YOU AND KNOWS YOU."

It was so big that it was almost intimidating. PC Sally thought it was probably to show that most charity places like this were all set up by the church. These were souls that all needed saving, these were the flock that had fallen on hard times.

Moving across the room, the old woman had not even waited for the policemen to answer. Shuffling with two white cups that looked almost bleached, she filled each with milk and tea from a piping hot urn. Carrying them back to Mike and Sally who sat at one of the head tables, she turned to walk away.

Mike Parson called out, "Excuse me, can you tell us who we need to speak to. Thanks for the tea," he said as she shuffled back behind the serving counter, which was already filled with a selection of toast, cereal and fresh fruit.

"John is in charge today. He will be here soon. I was not here last night. My days of serving late into the night are well behind me. I am in bed by seven p.m., ready to say my prayers at seven thirty p.m. my dears. John can answer your questions officers." the old lady said, busily taking bread out to make more toast.

For the next ten minutes, Mike and Sally just sat drinking the far too milky tea. They looked about the room, which was not somewhere anyone would consider being comfortable. It was a place built for short term solace. A meal, a drink, and the prospect of another cold night in a doorway.

Sally wondered if it would be of more use to convert this huge room into a safe place for everyone to sleep.

At nine p.m., the place was closed, and empty until it was unlocked again in the early hours. For all the solace this room gave, it could be so much more.

At precisely nine a.m., people started walking into the room. Most gave the two officers a very wide berth, as they made their orderly way to the front serving bar. The little old lady was joined by a younger girl, who happily helped to serve tea, coffee, and toast as breakfast. Many were just here to take the edge of the bitter night, pleased to be inside, even if it was only for a while.

As Sally finished her tea, a man came into the room, dressed in a three-piece black suit. Walking up to the police-officers, he introduced himself as John Mole. From his look, this was a man who was far past retirement age but still liked to dress smartly. Seeing the police-officers, the man did not seem very taken by their presence.

"Good morning officers. My name is John Mole, I guess you are here about the terrible goings-on in Tesco's last night. I thought we would receive a visit today, but you work faster than even I imagined." the man said in an Irish accent. Taking a seat opposite, he smiled and put his hands on the table like he was prepared and ready.

Sergeant Mike introduced both him and Sally and was quick

to start questioning, "It seems news travels fast in Yeovil. You are right Mr Mole. The incident last night is serious. A body was found, we have been led to believe he spent his last meal inside this room before going back to his... place of residence." the Sergeant explained.

Sally did not like the way Mike had termed the homeless man's home. Quickly she intervened before the man had thought on the Sergeant's ill-chosen words, "We are keen to know if you have a list of who was serving last night. We are keen to talk to the man who served that was wearing a hat over a bald head." Sally added quickly.

John Mole was not a man who liked policemen at all. All through his life, he had seen run-ins with the law. Eight times he had been arrested and charged for crimes, mostly just for petty theft and once he was involved with an armed robbery at a nearby post office.

John Mole had done the time.

John Mole had served for the crime.

But that was all long before he found God in prison. John Mole was a born again Christian, and proud of it. Managing the Lord's Pantry had been his salvation, for here he had repaid his debt to his wrong life choices many times over.

"I liked young Ridley. He was a clever lad. Once he even helped me fill out a passport application form. I could never understand how a brainy kid like that ever ended up on the streets. But, in this room, we do not ask. We are here to provide a place for them, it is not a place to ask questions. God bless them all." the man explained to the policeman, not directly answering the question.

Sergeant Mike politely asked again, "The name of the victim has not yet been announced. However, we are keen to see the records you keep of the servers. There is one man, like PC Gunel has said, who served a girl and a man a bottle of wine. Would you have his name anywhere? He is important to our enquires?" Mike asked, taking out his notebook to look official.

John Mole looked down at his huge hands and just shook his head, "We are not in this game for checking people's credentials officers. This place allows many volunteers to come in and help. We have many here, like old Ethel, who comes in every day in her own time to serve and feel they are doing something for the community. We have several church groups that often come in to help us out. But many just arrive and want to help those who are less fortunate. This is a place where all are welcome. We do not keep records or books, hell most evenings I don't even know the names of the people who are here either serving or receiving." John Mole answered honestly.

A couple of the homeless people called out to John, "Morning John, no trouble, I hope. He didn't do it officers." was mentioned as a few others chuckled.

PC Sally smiled, trying to win the man's attention back, "I think what you do here is wonderful. A real lifeline to the community. I have served in places like this before, there is a real sense of well-being."

"But we were told that one of the people who served last night was balding, and wore a huge ring, with a tree shape carved into it. Very distinctive, do you recognise who I am speaking about. Have you seen the ring before?" PC Gunel asked.

Little Ethel was over again with a cup of tea for John. The room was now quite full of people talking quietly and drinking warm tea.

John thanked Ethel as she tottered away. John Mole knew all too well the name of the man these police-officers wanted.

"I don't recall any ring. Could have been any one of the six we had in last night. Three were Salvation Army, I know that. There were a couple of bald men, I did not ask their names, they were just getting on with the job. It is not as if they are paid, so we do not watch them or tell them to work harder. We are just grateful for the help." John added, lifting the hot tea to drink. John had no intention of being the man who would squawk to the police. Many who came here, are looking for the same sense of duty he had felt until God had shown him another road. John had found God, but he still had no time for the law or policemen.

Ethel turned and smiled, walking away she spoke out, "That's a ring that stands out. I saw it a week ago. This man came in to help us in the afternoon service with the same ring. He was so lovely, so kind and caring. He told me the ring was the apple tree from the Garden of Eden. An apple tree. How beautiful. I think his name is Joshua. Such a beautiful Christian name." she said, walking back behind the counter.

John Mole nearly spat his tea out across the table.

# Chapter 8

## The Path Back to Eden.

### Timeline—15 October 2016

Joshua Wright was a good student. More importantly, Mary Grace was a very good teacher.

For the first five months, Joshua attended every church meeting, prayer session and private tuition that Mary was more than happy to give. Joshua was never late, always keen, and ready to involve himself in whatever activity the church was holding.

Fredrick Bannister had also taken a special shine to the newcomer. Every week, they would speak for hours after each church meeting, sometimes going off into other activities. Fredrick made sure that Joshua was always included and made to feel welcome.

Fredrick was a well-known face amongst many of the homeless shelters and soup kitchens across the entire south-west, so it had been easy for Joshua to not only help but become a part of this special community. It was Frederick who introduced Joshua to the various clergy and religious leaders. After learning of Joshua's trade as a plumber, well paid and honest work soon had Joshua filling his days, in making sure all the hundreds of religious buildings were maintained and repaired. It did not take long before Joshua's weekly schedules were full and needed careful booking.

In just eight months, Joshua went from someone who was a loner, desperate and on the verge of suicide, to a person much loved by the faith community.

Joshua Wright was a good man.

Chaplain Mary Grace was not only impressed with how fast Joshua was learning from her teaching, but she had felt a raw passionate hunger in the man to know God.

It was the same when she had first seen the old texts.

When Emerald had first begun to read her the passages from the huge book of Charles Wyndham, Mary was already a God-fearing teenager. As her father was a vicar and Mary's mother, the wife of a vicar, along with their deep African missionary roots, most of the psalms, stories and passages were biblical accounts of what she had known and been taught from birth.

But there were other passages, older hidden texts unknown to her that had perked her young interest. Testimony was written around the time of Matthew, Mark, Luke, and John which had been lost, or hidden and found again.

Emerald explained that these were all a part of the life work of Charles Wyndham who had searched the world to rediscover these lost religious writings, giving a broader, much fuller account of the times of Jesus. Charles Wyndham also discovered many accounts that were taken away from the old testament, all of which he tried to expose to the world.

These were fascinating, although some of this Mary had later discovered came from a single source, where a shepherd had stumbled across some ancient pots buried in the desert. Inside the pots, hundreds of fragile, tattered scrolls were revealed to hold unknown accounts of Christ.

For the young Mary, this archaeological discovery was wonderful, but it was Charles Wyndham's much earlier expeditions that had truly changed her life.

For Emerald, Mary needed to understand the importance of Eden's Echo truth. To know the power this book contained, Emerald explained to Mary that it was vital to know how they had come to be in her hands.

Emerald was another good teacher. Mary was a good student.

Mary was told that as a young man in his mid-twenties, Charles Wyndham had been one of the eager new breeds of explorers that excitedly left Victorian England in the search of adventure. Like most of the other keen rich gentry explorers of the time, he eventually found himself in Egypt, working alongside other great explorers, including a young, confident Howard Carter, who later went on the discover the tomb of Tutankhamen in 1922. Howard Carters later fame, fortune and fate were known to all.

Charles's discovery was a few years earlier in 1916 but somehow lost within the world's passion of Egyptian treasure seekers. England had a thrill and a desire to see the gold of the Pharaohs and a thirst for the gruesome mystery of ancient curses.

When Charles moved away from Egypt to explore the Holy lands, he spent his next ten years scouring the mountains of Jordon, near to the ancient valleys and city of Petra. His discovery of a cave tomb containing hundreds of age-old scrolls had been nothing but a few uninspiring lines on page twenty of the Times newspaper.

Yet, what Charles had found was far greater than anything dug up in Egypt. Emerald could still recall how angry Charles used to get when he told his story to those around him.

After the translation of the ancient Hebrew texts was finally completed in 1921, it revealed hundreds of old testament stories where a man had learned to speak with God. In the Bible, there were only a few accounts that had ever been written to show where a man had conversed with the almighty, but Charles discovered not only was this untrue, but the scrolls contained the secret on how this was achieved.

Just like the new testament, Charles came to understand that the old testament was the same, only revealing stories that were chosen to be included. The scrolls quickly revealed there was much of the old testament that was missing, which for Charles gave him a completely new outlook on life. Charles had tried so hard to prove he had found something of deep religious value, but the Catholic, Protestant and Greek Orthodox churches all wanted nothing to do with his discovery. Instead, Charles was ridiculed and called a heretic by many, with some even saying he had made it all up. There was another piece written in the Times, commissioned by the Catholic church which sadly Charles Wyndham became better known for. Printed as *The Enemy of God's words* this news story, which ironically made page 2, was enough to make Charles the laughing stock of the great explorers' world. It was this public damning that had forced him to set up his cult following, determined to prove the truth in his discovery.

After learning of the newspaper article, soon after his return to England, Charles founded Eden's Echo, where from his home in Stockton-on-Avon, he invited people to personally come to understand what was missing from the Bible, and more importantly how to speak with God.

"Why call it Eden's Echo?" Mary could remember her young self-asking Charles. It was a question she had been asked at least one hundred times herself.

Emerald had smiled when Mary first asked this question. Pouring a perfect cup of boiling tea into a china cup, from a china teapot, Mary knew that Emerald was pure old school, a woman of her age.

Sitting down in her favourite chair that faced the huge painting of Eden's Echo and the village beyond, she stirred the tea and adjusted her 1950's pointed spectacles.

Mary recalled sitting on a very hard chair, as Emerald opened the huge book on page one. It was a handwritten forward, penned by the quilled hand of Charles Wyndham. Emerald explained this forward was a later addition, it was written just before he died in 1928. It was just a few lines, but it had formed the entire focus for both Emerald and Mary Grace to follow their life paths.

Reading out loud to the eagerly waiting Mary, Emerald spoke clear.

**Eden's Echo**

**Why Eden's Echo? it is a strange name that I choose.**

**But it is the very heart and secret of finding God.**

**When God first created Adam inside Eden, they would talk as a family, such as their relationship and union of father and son.**

**Eden was paradise, where God and Man were together in peace and harmony.**

**Yet, we are all taught from birth that we were born as sinners.**

**The original sin of man was when Adam ate the Apple given to him by Eve, A simple single rule is broken that had dammed mankind for eternity.**

**When God cast Adam & Eve out of Eden, God's voice instantly became silent to them and everyone who came after.**

**We could no longer hear Him,**

Leaving Eden was a terrible loss for both Adam and God, for He had never wanted man to be alone in the world. God's voice cried out from Eden, sending his Echo across the world for man to come home.

But God never stopped loving Adam for he was the first. To this day God still calls out from Eden, hoping that those who hear Him will return to His divine guidance.

Eden's Echo is the faint whispers we hear on the wind as God continues to call out to us, ready to guide us home once more back into His divine protection.

As the sons and daughters of Adam, God continues to call out to us, for we are all His children and all deserve salvation,

God still tells us what is right and what is wrong, each echo is a ripple back to Him inside the paradise of Eden. God speaks to all of us, hoping we can hear and one day walk back into Eden, where His Echo first formed.

God can truly be heard by all. After my years of research, I have learned that with a strong faith and certain learned skills, we can hear His voice.

For seven thousand years, these skills have been known to man, but we have chosen to block out God's voice because of the sinners we are meant to be.

I have discovered and will teach you dear reader that Gods voice can be heard again if you choose to hear Him.

These pages are just the beginning of your journey home, back to the grace of Eden. I will show you that you can again know God as Adam once did, as a friend and father to us all.

God will guide you. Obey his call, for His word is the truth. Only through His voice can you find the way home where salvation awaits. Hear His voice and glory from it, for once you have heard Him and know of His true love for you,

**Eden can truly be found again.**
**Charles Wyndham Esq.**

Emerald closed the book as Mary sat in wonder. Mary had used the same technique when she had read these words out to Joshua Wright.

Eden's Echo was a path back to the almighty, where ancient scrolls had not only revealed that many men had spoken with God over the ages, but they had also written down *how* they were able to hear Eden's Echo.

Emerald had asked another question the day she had first introduced Mary to the book. It had seemed odd at the time, but as Mary came to know more, she could see her point.

With the book now firmly closed, Emerald took a sip of her still hot tea. Placing it back to the china saucer with a satisfying china clink, she asked her question.

"From what you know of the Bible, how many people can you name from the stories within that spoke to God?" she asked smiling and taking a home-baked biscuit from a plate.

Mary had sat back and thought deeply. Mary thought her Bible knowledge was quite good, especially with a vicar as a father. The Bible was one of many texts that gave man knowledge of God. As a whole book, it contained everything one needed to find the Lord again. But as she thought about the question in detail, Mary was suddenly aware that only a few names came to her. Mary knew there would be more than she could remember, but the number was not millions, it was less than ten?

Mary Grace could remember politely smiling and replied sheepishly.

"Adam, Moses, Abraham, Noah, Samson, David, Jesus, Mohammed?" Mary said, remembering that it was not only

Christianity that followed the same monotheistic God. After this small list, she was stumped.

Emerald was pleased, "Well done, Mary, that is three more than most say. But as you can see, there is not a huge amount of people that claim to have spoken personally to the divine. Why do you think that is?" Emerald had asked her, taking off her spectacles which indicated to Mary that today's lesson was ending.

Mary sat back and tried to think of a good answer. Nothing came to her.

"I am not sure Miss Emerald. I know that there must be more people who have spoken to God, but they are often treated as madmen." Mary had said.

Emerald nodded, "That is the correct answer. Not only have we all forgotten how to hear God's voice, but we are also in fear of confessing that we have heard or tried speaking with him. Strangely, we accept prayer as our way of whispering to the divine, and we all hope that our prayers will be answered. But there are very few who will openly admit that God spoke with them after He heard their call."

"Only a few men were ever listed as speaking openly with God. But that is not the truth of it. We will learn together Mary, that God is always there, and His voice is waiting for you to hear Him." Emerald told the young Mary Grace.

Mary's knowledge of the old book from both Emerald's teachings and the long life of her own research was complete. Mary could not possibly give a number to the times she had not only heard God's voice but spoken with him openly, as he guided her on the path to Eden.

For the acolyte, several techniques needed to be understood

and learned, but for Mary, her path back to Eden was definite. Mary had heard the Echo and knew the way home. All she wanted these days was to show others the same glory of God.

Teaching Frederick Bannister had been another student she had completely enjoyed. Like Joshua, this was a man who had not only found hard times, but he had also served time in her majesties prison for the terrible crime of taking life.

Redemption for Frederick had come from Mary first hearing his name whispered to her from the Lord. This, Mary thought was her gift, for in her abilities to hear His voice, God would simply reveal the names of people He wanted her to save.

It was not always in the sound of His voice. Sometimes she would hear it on the breeze. Other times she would find her eyes drawn to names inside newspapers or local magazines. Often, the mention of a name by another would stay with her, keeping Mary awake at night until she could find and help the person.

Frederick Bannister's name was shown to her in a newspaper, soon after the man was convicted by a jury to serve five years in prison. Back then, Frederick was a twenty-five stone single man, who had worked for ten years driving buses across the region.

One dark stormy, rainy night in late November 2011, Frederick was asked to drive a bus route home he had never driven before. With the wind howling and pushing the bus all over the narrow Somerset road, just outside of the village of Stockton-on-Avon, it was taking a huge effort for the windscreen wipers to keep the screen free of rain to just keep the way forward visible.

In what Fredrick, who had changed his name after leaving prison, believed to be the worst moment of his life, a small car appeared out of nowhere, hitting the front of his bus and careering off the road into a tree. Fredrick had stopped the empty bus and ran across to assist, but the car had burst into flames, trapping, and killing the two passengers instantly.

Frederick Pearson, the long-haired, fat, fully bearded bus driver had been given five years for manslaughter, which although harsh, he thought to be just.

In prison, Chaplain Mary had found him, helped him, as she loved to come to prisons and read the Bible to those who wanted to hear. It was inside prison she had begun Frederick's journey back to the Grace of God. When he left prison, it was Mary who picked up the clean-shaven, short-haired man, who was eight stone lighter than when he first went in.

Leaving prison, Mary had helped Frederick rebuild his life. Frederick wanted to repent for his crime, and as he came to learn of God's voice and Eden's Echo, Frederick wanted a completely fresh start, changing his surname to Bannister.

Frederick had now devoted his life to Eden's Echo and helping others find God. Mary had thought him to be her best student, alongside Barnaby Barnes. But compared with Joshua Wright, Frederick was a very slow learner.

Mary knew that Frederick had found his pathway back to redemption, but it was a dangerous road he had chosen to walk. Unlike most of the people God chose for Mary to save, through Frederick wishes and pleas for her to help him, Mary had come to know of Joshua Wright.

There was no inner voice saying his name to her, there was no newspaper showing Mary that Joshua Wright needed her help.

This time, the truth of knowing that Joshua Wright needed to be saved by Eden's Echo came from the very man who had served five years for killing both of Joshua's parents.

# Chapter 9

## The Apple Tree

### Timeline—8 April 2018

PC Sally Gunel had finally negotiated her way out of working on the night shift.

A new constable had recently joined the team, after requesting a transfer down from the Gloucester station. The new constable, PC Roland Briggs, was very keen on working the night shift for reasons neither PC Gunel nor DS Murray cared to want to hear. Sally completed her last graveyard shift a week ago.

Sally was just happy knowing that she now started work at seven a.m. and was usually off shift by seven p.m., depending on current situations or case developments.

It also meant she no longer had to deal with the late-night drunks who often were abusive as they were made to spend a comfortable night in a station cell.

It had taken a couple of weeks for her body clock to fully re-adjust. To fool her body into knowing that sleep was again a night-time activity, she had taken to running into the Bath station, nine miles from the village of Radstock, near to Shepton Mallet. PC Sally had always been a very keen runner. In her youth, she had run in marathons and could have gone professional if the call to the police service had not been so strong. It was probably for the best that she chose the police, as a second Olympian called

Sally Gunel would have been a strange coincidence for the UK history books.

Sergeant Parsons had twice said that he would like to run with her, but Sally had been pleased when both times he had found an excuse to pull out, always making a joke that he would struggle to keep up with an ex-Olympian.

The police stations single shower was OK, nothing special, but allowed her to clean up and put her uniform on for the day. The only physical problem with the shower was that it backed onto one of the main investigation rooms, which meant that everyone could hear her singing as the water poured down.

Twice she had been teased for terrible renditions of Adele and Katy Perry, which had been a constant form of amusement for Sergeant Parsons. Sally had shuddered when the Sergeant had threatened her that if she did it again, he would have to personally come in and arrest her for breaking the peace.

DS Nick was already inside his office when Sally arrived at 6.55 a.m. The new evidence of the man called Joshua, with the apple tree ring, seemed to be keeping the DS busy looking for possible leads, as the schoolboy killing was still not giving any clues to why this child was murdered.

The murder case in Salisbury of the young girl Jemma Evans was not moving any faster than theirs, but everyone was now sure that the killer must be the same person. As nothing had yet been officially released about the poison used, the police and Molly Symonds all suspected heavily that these cases were all somehow linked.

The press was all over this story, with headlines of "Who is Next on The Murderers List?" which did not help the public unease. The story had now become national, which hindered progress as everyday DS Nick was expected to deliver a press conference to reassure everyone that the case was nearing an end.

DS Nick wished with all his heart that his friend DS Peter Johnson was fit enough to work again, for he was sure Pete would have found something by now. Peter was an excellent copper, with the ability to know a lot of people, which gave him the edge when investigating local crime. Peter was also very good with dealing with the media, something he would have happily taken off DS Nick's shoulders.

The murders now had a name that all newspapers liked to badge. It did not help the police, but it was a way to bind together these seemingly random killings of young people.

"The Spiker" was not only awful, but it had become a real public worry. A person who was randomly spiking drinks with enough drugs to kill someone. It was grim but sadly proving to be completely factual.

DS Nick was delighted after hearing Sergeant Parsons report from the Yeovil soup kitchen. When Nick heard the name of "Joshua" and that this man wore a ring matching the same description of what Karen Spicer had explained to him on the night Ridley Goodman was killed, it was finally a positive lead to follow up.

It was now an investigation of finding out if the ring meant anything to anyone, and did the man known as Joshua belong to this group.

There were no records kept from the soup kitchen about who served, but since the murder, the man in question had not been seen working there again. The man in the wide brimmed hat was Nick's main person of interest, this was the only real lead any of the two branches investigating this case had to follow up.

DI Kleverly in Salisbury was concentrating on those in the local Gym who were caught on CCTV but not signed in. So far, nothing had come up as suspicious. Two out of the five unknown members who attended the gym that evening had been traced, interviewed, and released without charge.

Sally came into his office, with her short, shaven at the back, black hair, still damp from the shower. DS Nick smiled and welcomed her as Sally pushed a fresh cup of steaming black coffee onto his desk, "Morning Sir. Black and hot, the last one looks untouched?" Sally said, reaching to take a rancid plastic cup filled with last night's coffee away.

DS Nick chuckled, "Celia always tells me off for not drinking my drinks when they are hot. I forget I have them, that's my problem. I think the therapy and relief caffeine gives to me comes from me getting off my arse and putting the kettle on. I tend to chuck away far more than I ever drink. Probably for the best on the caffeine intake." the DS said, picking up the new hot mug to drink.

Sally walked out with the old coffee cup and returned with her mug. It was an all-red mug with a white tree on this side. Sally sat down in front of DS-Nick's desk and spoke, "Any luck with the ring boss? I was looking online last night but couldn't find anything like it. I do not think it's military, I ran it past a friend of mine who served in the army for nineteen years. He's a bit of a geek when it comes to army stuff, but he confessed that this was not a symbol he knew of." PC Gunel said, lifting the cup to her mouth.

DS-Nick looked up from his PC screen. Watching Sally drink, he looked at the mug, "That cup has a tree on it. Not the same, but I wonder if the ring is linked to a sports team or club membership." DS-Nick asked, picking up his notes with Karen Spicers sketch openly on display. Tuning the notes to the same way around as Sally's mug, he could see it was not the same tree.

Sally turned the mug to face her and chuckled.

"This is my Nottingham Forest mug. I have had this mug for years. My dad was a supporter and naturally thought his daughters would be too. I never had the heart to tell him I hated football. I like this mug though. It reminds me of him. I think this is an oak tree, not an apple tree like the ring." Sally told the DS.

DS Nick nodded and replied, "It's nearly all rugby in this part of the world. I have never liked football much either. But the ring might be a sporting symbol. Let us get onto it. Can I ask you to keep on this please Sally? I have sent Sergeant Parsons back to Yeovil with Kelvin the photofit artist. He should be back later today after he had a full description of the bald man, Joshua. Mike is going to try to find Karen Spicer again to see if Kelvin's picture matches who she remembers."

Sally agreed and stood to leave, "Does PC Parsons know where to find Karen Spicer? It is a weird fact that often homeless people are the hardest to find!" PC Sally told DS Nick.

DS Nick agreed, "Yes, I have heard that before. I am sure Mike will be fine. Say what you want about him Sally, but he is a good copper beneath his brash nature." DS Nick said, knowing the fractured relationship his young officer had with his sergeant.

Sally just nodded and walked out.

Moving across to a small computer on the main empty reception desk, she began to surf the internet for anything to do with an apple tree. There were plenty of references to the apple tree. It was known to be the symbol of love, peace, truth, beauty, honesty, remembrance, and fertility.

Sally took in a deep breath. Where on earth should she start as all these things could have meaning and several associations linked to them.

Sally took up her notes and looked at the little sketch she had made from DS-Nick's briefing on his faithful whiteboard last week.

DS Nick had added this evidence to the white board, putting the names of Karen Spicer, Ethel Reading, and John Mole in lines leading up to the Lord's Pantry soup kitchen. From Karen Spicer and Ethel Reading, two lines were drawn to the name "Joshua" and a small hand-drawn picture of the apple tree ring.

Sally looked at the drawing. There was something on the apple tree around the trunk, which Karen had seen, but Ethel had not mentioned it. Karen had told DS Nick about the snake coiled around the trunk.

Sally looked back at the screen. A small underlined blue search link caught her attention.

*The apple tree was the symbol of creation and a reasonable sense of creativity.*

PC Sally clicked on the link and watched as the slow internet page change. A few new pages were showing the apple trees origin within different cultures.

In Greek mythology, the golden fruit of an apple tree grew in the garden of Hesperides, where Aphrodite, Hera and Athena lived.

In China, the apple tree blossom was used as a sign of mourning and sorrow.

There was a long paragraph where the apple tree was shown to represent the power of love and devotion to God, where a man could commune with God. This was said to be the spiritual symbol for the search for the divine.

Sally sat back as it was all quite deep. Sipping her coffee, she causally flicked through the pages until a shape on the screen stopped her clicking. It was obvious now she saw it, but this made much more sense to Karen Spicer's description.

Looking at the screen, a picture was shown of a half-naked woman receiving an apple under a tree, given to her by a coiled snake. The page was titled "The Forbidden Fruit" giving the account of an apple as the symbol of sin.

As Sally worked her way down the page past original sin, temptation and Adam and Eve, this seemed to be a closer link to the ring than any other meaning to its representation.

Sally cleared her searches and typed afresh.

"Adam and Eve".

Surprisingly, there were three pages of children's games that first came up in the google search. Scrolling ever downwards, Sally came to a link that she was hoping to find.

It was not the same symbol that was shown on the ring, but it had all the same features. The page was called Eden, showing countless depictions of Adam's fall from grace throughout history. There were paintings right back to 1520, which had both a naked man and woman, standing under an apple tree where a snake tempted Eve into giving Adam, God's forbidden fruit.

The internet page went into huge detail about the fall of man and the concept of original sin. To Sally, none of it made much sense, but from what Karen Spicer had described about Joshua's ring, she was sure the symbol represented The Garden of Eden.

Sally was about to continue with her searching when the phone rang on the desk, making her jump. Picking up the receiver it was DS Peter Johnson's wife, Mary Johnson.

"Hello, Bath Station, PC Gunel speaking, how many I help you," Sally answered, still half concentrating on the screen.

"Hello, Sally. It's Mary Johnston, DS-Johnson's wife." a voice said, clearly shaken.

Sally stopped the search and focused on the call, "Hello, Mrs Johnson. How may I help you today?" Sally asked, guessing this was not going to be good news.

"May I speak to DS-Murray, please. I need to speak to him urgently." Mary Johnson said, clearly holding back tears.

Sally put the call through to DS Nick. Ten minutes later he came out of his office and called his team together.

DS Nick was never one to show much in the way of any emotion. He was not a cold man but found the job an easy way to overcome his innermost feelings. DS Nick was a professional, who had years of training to deliver bad news.

This was different.

With around ten people gathered inside the main police office, DS Nick walked up to the front of the room. Shaking his head slowly, he was still trying to come to terms with the news he had just received.

"Good morning team. This is not the way I wanted to start the day, but I have just had some very bad news. There is no easy way to say this to you all. Our friend DS Peter Johnson was taken into the hospital late last night, after a suspected heart attack.

"I have just got off the phone with Mary his wonderful wife. I am sorry to have to tell you all that Peter did not recover and died in the ambulance."

"I hope you do not mind joining me for a minute's silence as he was a good friend and colleague to us all. I know some of you knew him personally, so if you need time to digest this awful news, I completely understand. His family wanted us to be amongst the first to know as Mary says he loved working with us all." DS Nick bowed his head as his team followed, he needed to wipe a single tear away from his eye.

Sally bit her lip but failed to hold back the tears. Around the room, the officers were looking down at their desks shaking their heads as they were all shocked by the news that this popular, larger than life character, who had been one of them for over ten years had lost his life so suddenly.

Everyone knew he had been ill for some time, but none of them had expected this.

For the remainder of the morning, the team found comfort in quietly talking together. Sally explained that DS Nick had only spoken to Peter a week ago, and he was feeling much better and hoping to return to work by the end of the month. It sounded as if the heart attack was sudden.

DS Nick sat in silence. he had just come off the phone from his wife Celia, who was also broken with the sad news. Throughout the ten years, Nick had relied on DS Pete. It had been Peter who recommended him to the DS role, and as a potential rival to his position for promotion, DS Johnson could not have been more supportive. There was very little Nick could say about the man that he did not like. He was messy, and his car was always a rubbish bin, full of empty sausage roll bags and chocolate wrappers. But that was nothing compared to the lovely man Peter was. Nick was going to miss him both professionally and personally.

Sally came into DS Nick's office at three-fifteen p.m. Her eye makeup was still smudged from the tears she had shed today. Placing another hot coffee to replace the cold one on Nick's desk, she sat and sighed, "How are you, Boss? I know you and DS Johnson were close."

DS Nick sat back, grateful for his PC's concern, "Thanks, Sally, I must confess this has hit me hard. But this is a job where you learn to live with bad news. We will all miss Peter. I will for sure. But Peter would want us to get on with the job, I know that. We will have time for our sorrow at his funeral, but Peter would want us all to just buy a sausage roll and crack on." DS Nick said, forcing a smile.

Sally Gunel found a wry smile.

Everyone knew this was DS Johnson's trademark, so much so that he was on first-name terms to the two ladies who served at the local Greg's store.

Sally nodded and thought it was time to get DS Nick away from his sombre thoughts.

"I have found something that may be of interest boss. The ring worn by 'Joshua' I think represents The Garden of Eden. I know this was mentioned before, the snake around the tree is significant here." Sally said, giving DS Nick a printout of the web pages, she had found.

DS Nick seemed welcome for the distraction, "That makes sense Sally. Perhaps we should focus our attention on religious groups that have links to Eden. I know there is an evangelical group called the "Children of Adam" in Bristol. Can you call them to see if they have anyone called Joshua in their congregation, please?" DS Nick asked, moving to his screen. DS Nick began typing.

PC Sally stood to leave. DS Nick called over to her, "Good work Sally. You are a real asset to this station. I am very happy we have you in the team. I know DS Johnson liked you also. He once said to me that you would beat us both to DI with your professional attitude and sense of duty. I think he will yet prove to be right." DS Nick said, pointing to DS Johnson's desk.

PC Sally kept walking. She was determined that DS Nick was not going to see the state of her tear-drenched eye makeup that now ran across her cheeks.

# Chapter 10

## The Good Book

### Timeline— 1 February 2017

Joshua was never late to a lesson.

Mary Grace had proved to be a good person, a friend and now a mentor to Joshua's new life.

Learning from Eden's Echo had already been a revelation to him, as God's word was slowly revealed.

They were now on the third chapter of Charles Wyndham's teachings, which was moving into Joshua knowing some of the more advanced techniques of knowing God. The first chapter on **His Word** in the book was heavily based on and referenced to the Bible. This included a huge number of links into the newer stories left out of the Bible, which Charles Wyndham had found and added.

The second chapter focused upon the words and actions of **Other People.**

Much of the content Mary had discussed within this chapter and the techniques needed to know God were common practices and one she believed to be blessed with knowing closely.

Mary Grace had been very keen for Joshua to understand her, for this had personal meaning, "Many times, God will use other people to try to get through to us. God can use anyone at any time, but I find more messages coming from people who are practising Christians than non-practising ones."

"Those who are already tuned and accept God's divine grace, have already begun to listen for his calling. They all seek the path to Eden but are yet to know how to open their hearts to feel his love."

Mary had closed the book that day. Looking into Joshua's eyes, he wanted this message to be personal.

"I am simple woman Joshua. That is why I sometimes need God to spell it out to me. Let me try to give you an example.

"Mary moved to her small Bible and opened it to a known page. Reading from the text, Joshua listened in silence.

"Exodus 18:13-17-The message"

*"The next day Moses took his place to judge the people. People were standing before him all day long, from morning to night. When Moses' father-in-law saw all that, he was doing for the people, he said, "What's going on here? Why are you doing all this, and all by yourself, letting everybody line up before you from morning to night?" Moses said to his father-in-law, "Because the people come to me with questions about God. When something comes up, they come to me. I judge between a man and his neighbour and teach them God's laws and instructions."*

Mary closed the Bible and smiled,

"This Joshua always makes me smile. The people knew Moses was a man who heard God's voice. This man was an expert who could talk with God and because the people knew this, everyone would go to him to ask their questions.

But what this meant was that they stopped going to God themselves. People have learned that the only way to God is through Popes, Imam's, Rabi's, and other Holy men, they can only speak to God through others. They are so wrong Joshua."

Joshua nodded. He understood the message. Mary

continued,

"Has it ever crossed your mind, "What's the point?" Have you wondered if it matters if you hear God's voice at all? Well, here is your answer: When you listen to and obey God's voice, you will have the strength to carry out God's will for your life and all the people you impact will flourish also. That's huge!

Let me explain my journey, Joshua, "At first, I was having a hard time hearing God. I thought I needed to be in a deep trance-like state, so I took to drinking heavily and taking strong sleeping pills, so my sleep was sound. I heard nothing."

"Many of my friends would say to me, stop drinking Mary, you will become addicted. Those pills should not be taken each day. All these were messages that I failed to hear. I would pray to understand why God would not speak to me. I reverted to experts for help, religious men who told me that God wanted me to stop, but I thought them just concerned for my physical wellbeing."

"When I finally submitted and listened to their advice, I gave up every vice in my life. Then floodgates opened. I now hear God with such clarity, but if it were not for the experts, I would have never found the way to listen, as they were speaking from the heart out of their concern and love me. But I now know that God was speaking to me through other people. He was asking me, and I finally obeyed to his will through others."

Joshua understood, and was about to speak before Mary stopped him with an upraised single finger, "The last part of this lesson is very important Joshua. The chapter of Other People has one warning that I must stress you listen and understand me, child."

"God places certain people in our busy lives to play certain roles for specific seasons. Look for the ones he has placed near to you and around you. They are there. And when it is time for them or you to move on, obey this call. Remember, God will not ever leave you. And when you need other 'experts,' he will be certain to guide them into your path."

"Do you understand me, Joshua? There will be times when you will again need to walk alone, but with the skills, I am showing you, this time you will have the strength to seek out experts." Mary said, wanting to impart a sense that even if Joshua needed to move away or his new friends moved on, he would no longer have a sense of hopelessness, where she had found him on the brink of suicide.

God had spoken to her, through the redemption needed for Frederick. Through Others, she had come to be his expert. But Mary was only there to be a teacher, to show that all men could hear and know God. How they chose to hear was their own choice. What they did when they chose to follow his words through others, was completely for Joshua to follow.

The third chapter was stronger than the first two. Mary had purposely waited for several weeks before calling him back to her side.

Alone in her flat, this time it was a discussion over dinner.

Mary loved to cook but in truth, she was never that good at it. Cooking was a gift from her mother and her African roots, Mary was very adept in turning something quite ordinary into a feast for a King. Her mother used to say to her that in Africa it was essential that families learned how to make sometimes only one item of food taste good, as it was often the same thing they would eat for several days. Mary's mother was an expert in many things, and even as an old woman, she still missed her every day. Mary had learned to live without her expert help, though inside her heart had died a little the day she left her some thirty-eight years ago.

Finishing a simple stew of beef and vegetables, it was as good a meal as Joshua could remember. Nothing inside the huge single bubbling pot with a wooden ladle resting within was special. Everything was just simple ingredients of carrots, swede, potato, and root vegetables. The meat was not from the finest pastures, matured and feed on the green grasses of Somerset. It was just supermarket cheap cuts, stuck into plastic packets and taken out to boil. The only special ingredient that had turned these simple ingredients into a pot to bubble and boiled for six hours inside an oven, was love. Mary had added love, for she had wanted Joshua to enjoy the meal, and with that and through the skills of her mother's teaching, they had eaten a meal together which sat well with them both.

Mary offered a single glass of wine, as she knew Joshua needed to drive home later. Mary, as a recovered alcoholic, had learned to limit herself to only one glass served with a good meal. Most of the time she only drank cold, fresh water, as it was pure and known to be the very nectar that Adam and Eve shared.

Mary lifted a glass and spoke, "Tonight Joshua, we have fed our stomachs and now I want to feed your mind. Chapter three is short and does not need to be readout. I will speak to you and you will know of it."

**"Our Circumstances"**

"This Joshua is a simple message. Sometimes the only way God can teach us something is to allow circumstances in our lives to lead us to and *through* the very thing we need to discover. I think you are already on such a journey my friend. Despair is a common circumstance that can lead someone to change. For some, it can take them into dark places where only God can call them back. For others, they use the circumstance leading to the event as a catalyst to change. Let me try to explain,"

"It's important not to stretch this method of hearing God and knowing His will too far. God does speak through the circumstances of our lives, but we must be careful how we interpret 'what' God is saying through the circumstances. I believe this method of hearing from God should be used to help you answer yes or no questions and not questions about God's pleasure or displeasure with you. I want you to learn to listen to Joshua and truly know His intentions."

"Sometimes God will ask things of you that are not what you would think to be right or normal. But these are often the most important."

"For Example, if you asked God to reveal if you will ever be rich, and it does not happen, this does not mean he does not love you. God rarely shows His favour through material possessions."

"Therefore, this method of hearing God's voice and knowing His will for your life through overserving the circumstances that happen in your life should only be used to answer yes and no questions and not questions about God's love for you or His will. Sometimes God does not bless us with what we want, we are here to follow His will. Only through obedience to His will can we find our way back to Eden."

Joshua looked uncertain, taking a sip of the weak wine, he listened as Mary tried to explain further, "Knowing the will of God through circumstances is possible but it requires us to properly interpret what God is saying through the details in our lives. Just because something is happening and God is saying something through these events, we are still the ones who are responsible for interpreting things properly. I must confess that how I came to find you Joshua still worries me, but it has proven that my thoughts were wrong. I am glad we have met, and I am glad we are now friends. The circumstance that brought me to you was blessed, although I did not see it."

Joshua raised his glass to toast the large woman.

Mary smiled and laughed in her booming way.

Mary began to recite a well-rehearsed biblical text to drive home her lesson.

"Circumstances ordered of God must be submitted to and accepted, whereas those arranged by Satan must always be resisted. If we are not sure we can pray something like this, Lord, I do not know whether this situation is of thy ordering or from Satan. But I do want thy bidding at any cost. Save me from being deceived and thus missing thy best. If this is from thee, I accept it joyfully. If it is from Satan, I resist him and bind him in thy name."

"You see Joshua, sometimes circumstances will ask you to question His bidding. There will be certain times when you will stop and wonder if what has been asked of you has come from Satan. This will come down to a question of trust Joshua. Do I follow God for only he knows the road to Eden, or do I stop and fall to self-will?

"This is something I cannot teach you, for these will be circumstances only you can learn to live through."

"Whatever you chose Joshua, God will continue to love you. This I can assure you." Mary said, raising her glass back to the bald man.

Although this was to be the shortest of the lessons Mary would teach, it was probably the most important. This one simple meal had changed his life completely, for this was the moment he chose to follow God's will, whatever the personal cost to his or anyone else's life.

# Chapter 11

## Respect and Honour

### Timeline—-18 April 2018

DS Peter Johnson's funeral was only a week and a day after his untimely, far too early death. DS Johnson was only fifty-five when he died.

The week inside the police station was sombre, with many of the officers and senior policemen preparing eulogies.

Mary, Peter's wife had asked politely that anyone invited to the cremation, kept their words short, as the crematorium had another funeral after Peter's on a Wednesday afternoon. There was to be a wake later in a local bowling alley, where many of Peter police friends would come to show their respects. The wake in the bowling club would be done in full police honours, but the cremation was purely for the family and very close friends.

DS Nick sat reading his words, to try to memorise as much as possible. None of it was going in, no matter how many times he read them. Nothing he had put on paper seemed close to what he felt for his friend and partner. Putting ten years into five hundred or fewer words for a man who could talk for an hour without stopping was almost impossible.

Nick had spent days talking to his wife Celia about what he should say, which was more painful than he expected it to be.

Celia had answered in the same way she had done when she

lost her mother to a hit and run., "Just speak from the heart, Nick. That is all Peter would have ever wanted." Celia said, knowing how much pain her husband was secretly feeling.

Sergeant Mike Parsons had not been so sympathetic to the loss. Since hearing the news, he had pretty much gone on as normal. Most knew that the sergeant had never been close friends with Peter, but it was DS Pete who had suggested Mike was promoted to Sergeant.

To be fair, Mike Parsons had never known this, but without DS Pete, he would still be walking the streets as a plain old constable.

DS Nick looked out across the office. He could tell most of his team were in no mood today to do police work. They were all just awaiting the two p.m. chime of the office clock, before filing out to the small minibus that had been laid on for them all. PC Sally Gunel was the usual rock they all needed, organising the bus, the flowers and helping Mary with the bowling club venue. DS Nick was as ever grateful to his young constable, she was on the fast path to promotion.

Taking up his silver Keno pen, which was a fiftieth birthday gift from DS Pete and his family a few years ago, he looked over to his friends' desk, which had yet to be touched in any way.

The picture of Peter's young boys stared back at him, smiling in their dirty rugby kits. Behind them, the tall white rugby posts of the pitch stood framing his sons who were now without a dad.

Clicking the pen to a close, DS Nick decided to write nothing. What he needed to say would come from his heart, not a pre-scripted piece of paper. DS Nick owed Peter that. When he stood up, he would speak openly and know that even if he were a stuttering idiot, Peter would be smiling down, as he loved people making arses of themselves.

DS Nick walked out into the main office. All his officers were looking extremely well-polished wearing their shiny black uniforms. Two of the men were busy dusting off helmets and buffing shoes, whilst others spoke together in hushed tones.

When DS Nick appeared from his office, all of them stopped and turned, expecting the detective sergeant to say something to them all. DS Nick was not there to say anything, but thought he needed to speak as the room was silent, "I know that today will be the hardest, but it will be a time to say goodbye to our friend and colleague. For us, this will be a time to reflect, and then we must remember and move on.

"For Mary and her sons, this is just the beginning. From today, they will have to learn to live without DS... Peter coming home. We all have our memories of the big man. He was a very special copper. Today, through our sorrow, can I ask that we are strong for Mary's sake. It is her time to say goodbye, as he was always a husband and a father before he was a policeman. I want her to feel that today. Sometimes, when I have attended police or army funerals, it is like they were married to the forces they served. DS Peter was a great policeman, we all know that. But Peter Johnson was a better husband and father." DS Nick said to a room who nodded and understood.

Sergeant Parsons felt a rare touch of emotion. He was the first to react and started to clap. In the room, the rest of the team joined in.

Staring at the beautiful wreath that the flower shop had made into the shape of a long sausage roll, the photograph of DS Peter Johnson smiled from the centre. On the card, a simple message was written by DS Nick.

"From your friends in Bath Station Pete. You were the best

of us mate. We hope the sausage rolls are good wherever you are now."

DS Nick turned to walk back into his room, forgetting completely about the coffee cup he had come out to fill.

As he walked past Sergeant Parsons, Mike stood with a small piece of paper in his hands.

"Boss, sorry to talk shop today, but I just wanted to show you this. I have just had this back from Kevin, the photofit artist. This is a likeness of Joshua, from the descriptions of Karen Spicer and Ethel Bryant. Both have him wearing a brimmed flat hat, both think he was bald underneath. Do you want to release this to the press, today Boss? I know they have been asking for something." Sergeant Mike asked.

The DS took the photo and looked at the pencil image of the man staring back. From the image, it was the picture of a man in his early forties, with a wide nose, and large full lips. The eyes looked sorrowful but seemed quite piercing.

Sergeant Mike Parsons spoke again.

"The man here known as Joshua is white, around 6 feet tall and of slim to stocky build. We know about the apple tree ring, but I suggest this is not mentioned when we release the image. We don't want to alert anyone that we know about this, as this man will take it off." Mike said, pointing at the face of Joshua.

Nick was pleased to have his mind away from Peter for a moment.

"Thanks, Mike. This is a good image. We will release this to the press tomorrow morning. I am expecting a report from Salisbury tonight which will update me on the murder case of Jemma Evans. They have something solid that they want to tell me about. It seems the newsagent where Jemma purchased her water every day was not as empty as the owner says it was.

Someone else was in the shop." DS Nick told his sergeant.

Sergeant Mike was very keen to know more, "Did the shop have CCTV?" Mike asked, knowing this was a significant development.

Nick shook his head, "Sadly, only a single web camera, pointing at the till. The owner says that he can remember someone coming in wearing a scarf around his face, which was not unusual as it was bitterly cold outside at that time of the evening. The man did not buy anything. The newsagent says he remembers the man knocking over some of the bottles where Jemma was picking up her water. He left, soon after making no purchase. The owner swears he can remember seeing the man hand Jemma one of the fallen bottles from the fallen pile." DS Nick whispered.

Sergeant Mike was about to ask another question when PC Gunel came into the room, "The minibus has arrived. Can we all make our way out, please? I said we would be at the crematorium before one thirty p.m. We have forty-five minutes." she called out to the room. In a sombre silent exit, everyone made their way towards the minibus and the funeral of DS Peter Johnson.

Mary Johnson sat on a plastic seat at the front of the crematorium in tears, her sons on either side of her, all holding hands. In the centre aisle, before a packed room, a long wooden coffin sat upon a metal stand, draped with flags of the local police force and Bath Rugby Club. A small silver-framed photo of Peter Johnson smiled back into the filled room, with another photo of Mary and the two boys close by.

Inside the crematorium, the sound of swing low sweet chariot played out over the speakers, as this had always been Peter's favourite rugby song. As an ex-rugby player and proud father of two sons who had followed their dad into the game, this was the song that had deep-rooted meaning to them all.

Although Mary's tears were very visible, she remained in complete control, mainly for her two sons.

When the music slowly faded to an end, a vicar stood up and began to speak about the great life of Peter Johnson. It was a simple message of a man who loved his family and the work he had done. It was a warm, embracing recall of a man who loved sport, his dogs, and the taste of Somerset cider.

Several carefully worded rugby stories caused the room to chuckle, along with a heartfelt tale from Peter's brother about a pushbike they both shared as kids.

Paul Johnson was three years younger than his sibling. Paul explained to the room about the day when Peter had sold their shared pushbike for cash to a school mate, telling his parents that his little brother had lost it.

When his father saw the bike for sale in a local magazine, he had secretly bought it back again, leaving it in the garage for Peter to rediscover.

When Peter saw the bike again, he panicked, thinking his brother had stolen it back when he saw it at their school.

Peter's conscience finally got the better of him and he had confessed to his father about selling the bike, because of the trouble he thought his brother could now be in.

For three weeks his father kept him worried, stating that several policemen had been by the house to investigate the theft.

When his father finally revealed that he knew of his deception, Peter had physically sighed with relief.

Peter's brother told the room that it was this act of nearly being on the wrong side of the law that made him become a copper. Peter always loved to play the criminal mastermind, but his good heart and love of friends and family always turned him back to the policeman he was going to become.

After a few other family members had spoken, DS Nick was asked to walk to the front of the room. With no paper in his hands, he stood up from a chair near to the back of the crowded room. Letting go of Celia's hands, Nick made his way down to the front platform. For a short while, he looked down at the coffin, silently thinking of his friend within.

Taking a deep breath, Nick spoke to the room,

"Peter was a good friend. Peter was a great colleague and Peter was one of the best people I have ever met. When I first met Pete, he was sitting on the little wall outside of the Bath police station, eating what I can only describe as a giant family-sized apple pie. We all know how much Pete loved his food.

"When I approached him, he just smiled and continued eating, with bits of pastry all over his moustache.

"Twice I tried to ask him a question, but each time he stopped me by raising his hand and continued to eat the pie, slowly, looking me up and down."

"When Pete finally finished, he sat back and asked me what I wanted. I told him I was looking for DS Johnson. For a while, he just told me about the delicious apple pie, where to buy them in the city and why he always chose a single-family sized pie. He said that the small individual pies were a waste of time as they were never enough and you always ended up with six metal cases, rather than just one single one to chuck away. He then went on to say that bought apple pies were not the same since Mr Kipling got hold of the recipe. Too much sugar and the apples were far too sweet. Not sharp enough."

"I was about to walk away from this obvious street nutcase when he called me back again. 'Where are you going?' he asked me, looking very hurt. I said I had an appointment with a DS inside the station, and they would not be best pleased if I was late. Peter chuckled and pointed to the sun in the cloudless sky above."

"Good day to meet outside, a good day for a picnic. My name is DS Peter Johnson, pleased to meet you, DS Nick Murray. I knew it was you, as that is the good copper in me. You, however, I can see need some work. We are not in London here mate. This is the wild west."

"From that day, I became good friends with Peter. I am honoured to say I am friends with Mary and the boys too. I have learned many things from Peter over the years but the most important lesson he ever taught me was on that first day. Never judge anyone too quickly. Sometimes even those you think are complete nutters can prove you quite wrong. Rest in peace, my friend. The team will miss you terribly." DS Nick walked back to his seat.

Mary smiled as he walked by, whispering the words, "Thank You, Nick."

The remainder of the funeral was just a few of Peter's copper companions, who were close enough to be called friends. The rest of Bath station and many from the Bristol branch were waiting back at the bowls club.

With the coffin slowly lowered below, and the flag of the police force folded neatly by two of his old Rugby league friends, Peter Johnson disappeared for the last time.

The vicar softly invited everyone to convene again on the little terrace that looked out over the pretty gardens beyond.

Nick stood with Celia ready to make their way out, following the family members. Celia was very upset as she had always loved Peter. Holding Nick's hand tightly, she caught the eye of

Mary, who smiled back at her. Mary's heart was truly shattered, she was barely holding it together.

In the little entrance hall of the crematorium, people stood around chatting quietly as they slowly filed out towards the little terrace. It was one of those times where nobody knew what to say to each other, so many strangers stood with the very upset family.

Nick stood back with Celia, next to a tiny table that was covered with dozens of religious pamphlets.

Celia walked over to speak and say a personal sorry to Mary, who seemed to have rallied a little. Mary knew the next few hours would be the hardest for her.

Nick watched as the entrance hall slowly began to clear. In his quiet corner of the room, he waited for his wife to finish speaking before they needed to descend the steps onto the outside terrace. Nick could see that people from the cremation chapel were now gathering with a glass of something, again talking in quiet remembrance.

Looking back to the wall behind him, there were a few pictures of Christ and the disciples. Nick smiled when he saw a leaflet for a local pizza shop. This was a strange leaflet to have in such a place.

DS Pete would have loved this and would have probably placed an order to be delivered!

Thinking of Peter again his head dropped to the many pamphlets littered across the small table. There was everything here from self-help, the Samaritans to specialist religious groups in the area.

DS Nick picked up a leaflet at random, more to look like he was interested than any real need to read it. As his eyes loosely scanned the paper, he caught sight of something in the corner of the front cover that instantly snapped him back to reality.

Perhaps DS Peter was there with him, he was a great detective.

On the pamphlet, it was almost plain red, apart from a tiny symbol of an apple tree and a snake around the trunk in the top corner. The text in the centre of the page was in an old italic style, inviting the reader to call a group to know of God's Grace. DS Nick was about to read on when Celia came back across to him.

"Time to go love. Peter is with God now," she said, taking his hand again.

# Chapter 12

## The final chapters

### Timeline—10 December 2017

Chaplain Mary Grace was never one to gloat. But teaching Joshua Wright had been one of her greatest achievements.

The man had not only become an avid believer, but Joshua was also one of the leading figures in their little group, always available to take part in any activity Mary set up and organised.

Mary thought that this man would possibly know enough to one day go on to take on her mantle, to be able to teach of Eden's Echo. Many of the people Mary had shown were strong believers, but only a couple had shown the ability to teach. Mary was like a spiritual fuel to Joshua, filling and driving him for his passion to find God.

The final chapters of Eden's Echo were sometimes more than even Mary had ever truly understood. Charles Wyndham was very clear that only a few could ever really reach this level of knowledge. Charles wrote that he had only ever got to chapter four personally, but he had known others who were able to truly hear and speak openly to God.

**The Still Small Voice** chapter, Mary had taken days to share with Joshua, reading it with him many times before the man understood. The key to knowing God through His small voice was within reach for everyone, but most who heard this call dismissed it as madness. Mary explained that this was the true Echo of God, where a man could finely tune into the Lord's song, like listening to a radio.

Mary tried to explain this in her own words, "Most of the time, God uses a tiny voice inside us to let us know when we're not on the right path. Some people call it 'the voice of peace.' Whenever we are contemplating something and we do not have peace about it, it is a very good idea to stop and carefully look at the options. There is a reason you do not feel peace about it.

"You must be aware Joshua, for His spoken word is rare. Samuel was told of this in the Bible. Samuel asked, God, is that you? If so, I am listening."

"You will hear other voices that claim to be God, but you will know which is true, for the still small voice of God is calming, overwhelming, and above all else, love."

"Sometimes you may be too busy to notice.

*You will seek me and find me when you seek me with all your heart,* Jeremiah 29:13.

Being ready and willing to respond to God when He speaks requires obedience and total love in him."

Mary continued, her voice low like that of a schoolteacher,

"Be humble Joshua. God does not just speak to special people. He speaks to us all. You must recognise that hearing God speak is normal and part of our lives. But we must not allow pride to sneak into our hearts when we hear Him. Staying in humility positions us to fully receive and respond to the messages God may share with us. It is a wonderous gift, that I know you are ready to receive my friend."

Mary tried to explain to Joshua about when Adam and Eve first heard God when walking in the Garden of Eden. Adam had hidden until he began to know that it was God's voice he could hear.

"Never expect to hear God in a mighty roar or with a clap of thunder, for this is not His way. The still small voice is to know that it is not your imagination playing tricks. There will be a warm feeling, that will whisper and answer you. I have known this many times Joshua, for this is how I came to know that teaching you was what He wanted." Mary said, closing her book.

The final chapter Chaplin Mary Grace had taught to Joshua was in the presence of her two other star students. Fredrick Bannister and Barnaby Barnes, both born again Christians, who, after serving time in prison, had come to know of God through the grace of Eden's Echo.

Both men were looking for a way of paying and repenting for the sins of their early lives. Both men had come to Eden's Echo through the prayers and words of Mary Grace.

After a large diner of off the bone lamb and burnt roasted potatoes, they were all quietly chatting about their daily lives over a glass of fine red wine. All of them were now good friends, happy to be in each other's company.

Before the dinner, Chaplin Mary Grace had spent all afternoon preparing carefully for the evening, as tonight she wanted to be special. Cooking a large meal and buying a fine quality wine, it was all in the readiness to show her friends of Charles Wyndham's final chapter. To mark the occasion, Mary had given the three men a uniquely special gift.

Mary wanted them all to know how special they were to her and what they now had become to the people of the Eden's Echo congregation. These three, the men Mary had chosen and known would be the strength of her community once she was dead and gone. Emerald had handed her baton to Mary. Mary was passing it onto three men she trusted and loved.

After the meal was complete, Mary opened a drawer below a large bookcase and withdrew three very small velvet-covered boxes.

Smiling, she was excited to see their reaction as she placed one box on the table in front of each man.

"Open the boxes at the same time. I have had these made especially for you. You are all very dear to me. You are all important to each other. You are the path into Eden's Echo and others will come to know His voice through you. This is the sign of your brotherhood; Glory is to God." Mary said, clapping her hands together.

Each of the men took up the boxes and opened the tiny hinge outwards. Inside each box, it contained the same large ring. It was a gold band, with a circular, five pence sized coin on top, carved with a little apple tree, its trunk encircled with a coiled snake.

"These are the rings that bind you all together. These show you are a part of Eden's Echo, acolytes of the path back to Him. I have one too, given to me by the lady who showed me the same pathway. I wear mine around my neck on a chain, here, see."

Mary lifted a short gold chain out from her purple blouse. Pulling it clear, away from a small gold cross that also hung around her neck, she revealed a smaller, more delicate ring, showing the same apple tree symbol.

Holding it out, she whispered, "In Eden, we find His voice." Mary closed her eyes in prayer.

Barnaby thanked Mary first, "These are wonderful. I am honoured to wear this and know that my brothers are bound to the same ring. I feel as if we are all family, something that I lost and miss." Barnaby said, placing the ring on his finger.

Mary nodded, "We are all family Barnaby, in God's grace. I should thank *you*, Barnaby. Redemption is a righteous path to back into Eden." Mary said, reaching out to the man.

Barnaby Barnes was a complicated character. In his twenties and thirties, he had been a rich, prosperous shopfitter, with twenty men who worked to the bone to make him lots of money. Married with three wonderful children, Barnaby had thought his empire would soon dwarf the wealth of his father's huge retail business in clothing.

Barnaby had grown up in an area where the sons of Jamaican immigrants were supposed to be the labourers and not the employers of large companies.

Living originally as the only coloured skin family in the North Somerset area, Barnaby had known and seen racism many times first-hand.

But racism had not stopped his father from setting up a single clothes stores, which soon became three. People needed clothes, which had always been a more powerful message to his father than any racist slur against him.

It was true that Barnaby had been given his first major contracts to fit out his father's shops, but this had only kicked him on to build what grew into one of the biggest shopfitters in the west of England.

Barnaby had earned enough to buy a holiday home in Jamaica as well as several smaller properties that were rented out to students. Just when Barnaby thought that his charmed life could not get any better, in just six months his world came crashing down, shattering his life completely.

Barnaby was a loyal, trusting husband who loved his wife. Sadly, she had not been the same. After two affairs, she just walked out of his life, taking the three children and half of

Barnaby's considerable fortune with her.

Once his wife's solicitor had bled him nearly dry, Barnaby was left alone in a house that was far too big for one person. Lonely, and lost he turned to the sin of the bottle.

For months he became a total recluse, and through heavy alcohol and some substance abuse, he lost the facility to see his children. Slowly the business crumbled, as profit turned into debt.

Barnaby had needed to sell all but his large house just to keep paying the money his wife had settled upon.

One night, it had all got too much and something inside Barnaby just snapped. Mary would later say that it was the Devil himself who had found his way to play on Barnaby's anger and whisper evil into Barnaby's soul.

Taking his 12-bore shotgun, he decided to drive over to his wife's new house to commit terrible murder, followed by violently ending his own failed life.

That was the night Barnaby believed God had begun to take an interest in him. Driving through the village of Netherby just outside of Bath, it was late on a Friday evening.

Barnaby could not remember how many glasses of whiskey had led him onto the dark path, but it was enough to blur his vision as he drove at speed in his Porsche.

Although the hour was late, the roads were mostly empty.

All apart from a single little old woman who was walking on the footpath without a care in the world.

When Barnaby mounted the curb and struck the old woman from behind, the woman was dead before she even hit his bonnet.

Barnaby had instantly changed his plans of murder, for he had already caused a death. Without stopping to help the woman who he knew was already dead, he drove away at speed from the scene. It was just two days later when the police arrived at his door with an arrest warrant. The policeman in charge of the case was a DS Nick Murray, who turned out to be the dead old lady's son-in-law. Barnaby later learned that DS Murray had been the first to attend the scene with his wife, which had been an awful discovery to make.

Barnaby Barnes had pleaded guilty to the charge of dangerous driving, causing death, and his sentence had been six years and three months for the crime. Barnaby had served five years and two months for good behaviour.

During his time in prison, Barnaby had found a sense of peace in Mary's preaching at the small chapel. Learning of Eden's Echo and its chance to find salvation and redemption, he discovered that only through God words, could forgiveness ever be found.

Mary had tried to ease Barnaby's pain by saying that she thought it was God who had purposely put the old lady in his way that night. One woman had died, which was truly terrible.

But how many would have died if Barnaby had reached the home of his ex-wife? Would his gun have gone on to murder his children and her new husband who had another five children?

Mercifully, this tragedy was spared to the world.

Mary believed that Barnaby Barnes had been saved from the path the Devil was carving out for him to walk.

God had known Barnaby's heart and loved him.

God had changed the day. Mary explained it in simple words,

*"God had created the Greater Good."*

Since meeting Mary, Barnaby had been on the long pathway to redemption for three years. Although he was yet to hear God's voice, Mary was confident he was close to Eden. It was only a matter of time before God revealed His grace to him, and in knowing the last chapter of Eden Echo, Mary was sure Barnaby had everything he needed to bask in the voice of the Lord.

Barnaby was not looking for forgiveness. To him, the past was lost, another life ago. Barnaby only ever wanted to look forward, wherein knowing and serving God, he would find his salvation through the people around him.

There was always a part of Barnaby that had wanted to say sorry to the wife of DS Nick Murray for killing her mother. For nearly a week, Barnaby had once sat outside their house, waiting for his chance to say sorry. Each time he saw the woman alone, something inside Barnaby had told him to stop and wait. There would be time, but it was not today.

Mary believed this had been the Still Small Voice inside.

Frederick and Barnaby were good friends. Both having pasts they would prefer to forget. They were kindred spirits in both wanting to start again. Mary had seen this, and through her special gift, she had seen the good in them both. They were both more than born again Christians. They were born and living again, in God's forgiveness.

Mary had been certain that God wanted them both back inside his flock. They were important, for Eden's Echo had flourished and grown since they had found His words and welcomed her embrace.

Both were now free of their prison binds, both physically and spiritually.

Joshua had just as quickly become another part of her flock. Both Barnaby and Frederick had taken to the man as a friend, treating him as a third brother. All of them were stronger than any of the other forty-eight members, who had not yet truly learned what Eden's Echo offered.

**His Actual voice,** Mary whispered, opening out the huge book onto her large dining table.

Around her, three men sat in silence wearing their new rings, all of them waiting to hear what Mary would reveal from Charles Wyndham's years of dedicated holy research.

Mary had built up the power and ambience. Four scented candles burned as the main lighting of the room. The smell of incense filled the flat. On the radio, Mary had tuned to a Christian channel that played soft hymns with a hundred choir boys, calling out words to God's embrace.

The door of the flat leading out to the balcony was wide open, allowing a slight breeze from the evening tides to move into the drawn curtains. It was like the scene of a séance, but the reality of this night was completely the reverse.

Tonight, Mary was not looking to speak to those who had died long before. Mary had no interest in try to hear if friends had passed over and we're safe in God's arms.

The last chapter of Charles Wyndham's great book was about the truth of His love. Tonight, she wanted all of them to find salvation.

Tonight, she wanted to teach them how to hear the actual voice of God.

If tonight, was going to be like anything she had experienced when Emerald had been through the same chapter, it would be both terrifying and wonderful at the same time. God had come to Mary like a rush of a wave upon a shingle beach. Mary had known silence as the sea was calm inside her, but, when the waves crashed down upon the stones of her mind, God's voice had filled it, and it had stayed with her, complete, loving and allowing her to knowhow to get back into Eden.

Mary asked them all to join hands. It was more and more like a séance. Asking her friends to just breathe slowly, she wanted them all to be completely at peace, knowing the love in the room.

All of her students obeyed without complaint.

Reading gently from the book, Mary began to read the final chapter,

"*His Actual Voice*. Think of this, my friends. The real, all-knowing, all-loving voice of God. He is waiting for you, I know this. Soon you will know too and with this knowledge, you will rise, awakened in His grace."

"Sometimes we're able to "hear" something in our spirit that sounds to us like an actual audible voice. Or suddenly, you just know you heard something. Pay attention to those occasions because it is very likely God is trying to tell you something."

"There was once a time when you had to work to tune in to a program on the radio or television set. You had to find the right frequency. You never questioned if it was broadcasting—you knew it was—but you had to do your part to find the frequency and tune in."

"Most often, we miss His frequency because we are tuned in to hear some huge revelation; when, in fact, He is giving you just simple instructions. That is what He will do when you first begin to hear from Him—and He will continue to do this for the rest of your life here on earth. Obedience in the simple things is very important to God—it reveals the willingness of your heart."

"Sometimes, the small things He asks of us may seem unimportant or involve giving up things we think we enjoy. But to reach a level of intimacy with God where we hear His voice, we will know new places in our spirit,

***obedience must become a non-negotiable in our lives***."

Mary looked up as if staring into heaven itself. This line was important to emphasise. Even Charles Wyndham had underlined it to make sure this was understood.

Her smile was full as she took three deep breaths. Looking back at the three men around her wooden dining table, she could see each of them were alive with what she was telling them, their souls soaking up what she was saying. Opening her hands out wide, Chaplin Mary Grace whispered, finding the frequency of her listeners.

"You are so close. I can hear Him. Praise be my friends, open your minds and know Him. He is asking for you. Lord, these men I return to your love and grace. They were lost from your flock. I have brought them back to you. I am just one of your shepherds, hear me, Lord." Mary said to the room.

Barnaby was the first to speak, "I cannot hear Him. I do not hear His voice!" he said, looking desperately across to Mary.

Mary reached out to Barnaby, "Just be patient. You will hear, but only when you let go of your heart Barnaby. If not tonight, then soon my friend."

Frederick was the next to speak, keeping his eyes tightly closed, he gripped the other two men on either side of him as if they were falling away.

"I can hear a something, a low whisper. Something is there, it is so quiet, so peaceful, so loving. Is that you God, can you hear my voice?" Frederick said, allowing his sound to flow towards Mary.

Mary smiled and gripped Frederick's arm, "Your Salvation is close Frederick. You have everything you seek in your hands. Redemption is so close for you. Frederick, soon, I can feel Him reaching out to you. Such a love no man ever knows. Eden has a place for you."

Mary felt the desire to hear God in her students. His voice was in the room. His voice was with them. His voice was always with them. They had just forgotten how to listen to Him.

Mary opened her eyes. Frederick and Barnaby followed her lead. Smiling like they were heavily drugged, something had just happened, certainly to Frederick. Barnaby did not have the same experience but was still in a state of joyous wonder.

Mary had built up this scene to a crescendo, telling them all God was in the room, speaking to each of them as a father to a child.

They were all so close to hearing the actual voice of God.

Sitting back, Mary, Barnaby and Frederick turned to the only man who had not yet spoken in the room. With his eyes still closed, he seemed to be talking in silence, his eyes blinking rapidly, without ever opening.

Mary stood and walked around the table. Placing her hands on Joshua's shoulders, she bent and whispered into his ear, "Joshua, can you hear Him. Is He with you now?" Mary asked, squeezing the man gently.

Joshua stopped and suddenly opened his eyes wide. Turning to Mary, he began to weep. Mary leaned in to embrace Joshua.

"Did you hear God my son? I know it can sometimes be overwhelming. The first time is always the hardest and most frightening." Mary told him, holding the man in a full hug.

Joshua turned to Mary and through his tears, he whispered something into her ear.

Mary just continued to hold the man, her heart thumping in total disbelief. Taking Joshua outside onto the balcony to get some fresh air, she asked him again to repeat what he had heard God tell him.

For a while, she sat talking to Joshua alone. Mary always knew there was something special about Joshua and his ability to learn from Eden's Echo so quickly. But from what Joshua was saying, something was very amiss. Had Joshua found another frequency that was not God's voice?

Moving back inside her flat alone, she left Joshua sitting on the balcony, calming himself in the December breeze. Frederick and Barnaby were both eagerly sitting and waiting.

Fredrick sounded very concerned, "Is our friend Joshua all right. We are both worried. You looked like Joshua had contacted the dead?" Frederick said, looking across to Barnaby.

Mary took her seat at the table again. Shaking her head gently, she closed the huge book.

"No more learning from this book tonight Gentlemen. Joshua needs to rest. Joshua heard a voice tonight. Joshua believes he heard God's voice. For each person, the revelation is different. Joshua needs time to reflect and be sure he heard God." Mary stated, making the sign of the cross on her breast.

Frederick smiled, "That is wonderful. Joshua has found his way to Eden." the older man said, placing his right hand on the huge book.

Mary shook her head, "This indeed is a wonderful thing, Frederick. But I have never seen a man receive God in this way, in any I have ever shown before. Joshua was given a message. A mission. A commandment." Mary explained, shaking her head to try to understand what Joshua had told her on the balcony.

Barnaby was the next to speak, "What was he told to do?" Barnaby asked.

Mary looked at the two men before her. She knew the book had always contained a very special power. But until today, Mary had always believed that she was the only person who had learned to master how to hear God's voice, better than any other.

But Joshua had surpassed anything she had ever heard before. Joshua believed he had heard Him, and God had wanted Joshua to hear his commandment. For He had given Joshua a message that Mary was unable to comprehend.

Mary placed her hand onto the small cross that hung around her neck, as she whispered to the men next to her, "Joshua says he has been chosen. He told me that God has asked him to complete a holy task before he can ever reach the gates of Eden. It is up to Joshua now, for only he knows what he must do." Mary said to the stunned men.

Frederick broke the short silence, "If this is true, we must help him Mary. Does the book not tell us, obedience must become non-negotiable? Joshua has been blessed this night and we must rejoice in this. Whatever God has asked of Joshua, I will be there by his side."

Mary nodded but could not bring herself to reveal what task God had asked Joshua to do, as it went against everything she knew her God to be.

# Chapter 13

## Dramas & Photofits

### Timeline—20 April 2018

A mass gathering of press and media people stood under dripping umbrellas as the police briefing was called for the morning. With all the various tv and radio crews crowded into the small Bath station courtyard, which faced three curved concrete steps leading up into the station, they formed a solid media wall of flashes, faces and lenses, all battling for headlines in tomorrow's news.

Inside the station, DS Nick looked through his pages of notes. This was a part of the job he never found easy. Nick was a copper, not a public speaker. Whenever he faced a group of press, he felt anxious, sometimes nauseous. This was where DS Pete Johnson was so good, as calming a sometimes-over-eager press pack came naturally to the big man.

DS Nick stood and walked out to the reception desk. Sally was standing behind the desk, guarding any of the eager reporters against entering to steal the first scoop.

Yesterday, on DS Nick's instruction, she had fed information to one local paper that they would be releasing a photofit of a man they would like to question and that it was linked to the three murders across the west country. Within an hour, every newspaper, tv station and blogger were running with a headline about the face of the Spiker to be revealed.

Sally could feel her boss's resistance, as he fiddled clumsily with the top button of his shirt. Running murder investigations was no longer just a question of policing and organising meetings to try and piece together the evidence. The job also demanded a public image, for the majority who took their news media digitally. There would have been a time where the chief investigator's name was just a footnote to a radio or newspaper story. These days, every click of a camera was saved, stored, and uploaded into digital heaven, for all to see the face under the helmet, the man behind the badge.

PC Gunel followed DS Nick outside. Under the dripping concrete entrance roof, it was at least dry, out of the rain falling steadily beyond. At the bottom of the steps, DS Nick could see the short brick wall where he had first met DS Pete Johnson. How he wished Peter were here today, eating that giant apple pie.

DS Nick had secretly hoped the continuing rain would deter many of the mainstream media and journalists, who could just as easily poach their evening story from other reports later. Not surprisingly, it seemed news of "The Spiker" story was growing fast and starting to attract national interest. With the killer still at large, the public was both uneasy and fascinated in equal doses.

As PC Sally Gunel walked out behind Nick, she could see a couple of foreign microphones erected and pointing toward the steps. One looked French, the other she thought was probably Spanish. In a violent world, Sally was always surprised how stories of murder attracted so much of an audience. Murder was a subject that sold well worldwide. It was a huge revenue stream within every media business.

Across the world, how many nights a week were devoted to the subject. Prime-time TV, was either filled with documentaries about past murders or dramatised into multi-part detective dramas? Sadly, in Britain at least, it was too many to count.

Morse, Frost, Vera, Poirot, Columbo, Sherlock Holmes, Murder She Wrote, Prime Suspect, Ms Marple, Midsomer, Broadchurch, Endeavor, Line of Duty…

PC Gunel thought the list was almost endless. But every one of them was brilliantly engineered around one single subject.

Murder.

Murder sold, Murder entertained, Murder employed.

Sadly, the public seemed to revel in its sinister act, no matter the motives or outcomes of killing. The dark unspoken truth was that the public hated and loved the crime of murder equally.

It was a strange irony that in a modern world which was said to value the words of God's commandment "Thou Shall Not Murder" a huge number of people needed murderers to ignore this divine rule just to make a living. Ending the life of another person, through accident or foul measure was an age-old crime that humanity had never found a way to control. Prevention of this crime would force thousands into immediate unemployment.

Policing prevention of murder was the hope, policing the aftermath of murder was the reality.

Even before DS Nick began to speak into the thirty plus microphones, reporters could not help themselves calling out from the crowded courtyard.

"Do you have a suspect?"

"Are you worried they will strike again soon?"

"Is it true you are looking for a religious person?"

All of these questions were ignored, although the last one did register with both DS Nick and PC Sally that something may have been leaked.

DS Nick remained calm, professional, and determined to

only deliver what he was sadly there to do.

"Good afternoon ladies and gentlemen. First, let me start by just reminding everyone that we are still at a very early stage in this investigation.

"As you are all aware, we have many officers working on this case, day, and night, looking to find the perpetrator of these awful deaths to innocent victims."

"We must remember that when something like this happens in our community, it affects every one of us. All of these crimes are not only a huge tragedy for the families, but they also cause understandable worry across the region. The police are and will be doing everything we can to maintain the safety of the public. I want to assure you all that we will do whatever it takes to pursue and make sure justice is done and will not stop until we have someone behind bars."

DS Nick stopped and turned his page over to the sound of a thousand clicks, "Today, we are releasing a photofit of a person of interest. We are keen to speak to anyone who recognises the face in the picture. We are describing this man as white, aged around forty to forty-five, with an almost completely bald head. The man has dark facial stubble, thick bushy eyebrows with sharp brown eyes. In the photofit, we have shown this man wearing a brimmed hat, very distinctive, but we believe this is something he likes to wear. If anyone matching this description is known or seen, living in the Bath, Bristol, or the Somerset area, please could they contact the Bath police station or contact crime stoppers as soon as possible."

"We strongly advise the public does not to approach this man. We do not consider him a threat to the public in general, but we are keen to speak to him regarding the murders of the three young victims."

"PC Sally Gunel here will be sending the photofit across to all of the media outlets later this morning. You are welcome to take one of the printed pictures from officer Gunel now.

Thank you for your time in this awful weather today." DS Nick nodded and turned to walk back inside.

A question from behind him, stopped Nick to turn back towards the microphones again.

"What about the Apple Ring?" a voice called out.

DS Nick looked into the crowd, "We have investigations ongoing about specific items linked to these cases. We are not in a position to release any further details. Any information released that is not from officers investigating, this case, should be treated as false until we confirm the truth. Please, let my team do the police work. Again, thank you for your time today. Let's all get out of this rain." DS Nick told the crowd.

This time Nick continued to walk into the building, ignoring the barrage of further questions coming at him.

PC Sally Gunel, walked forward, down the steps and into the crowd. With a photocopied pile of paper, each was a single side sheet, which had just one picture of the face both Ethel and Karen Spicer had described to Sergeant Parsons.

Eagerly, the journalists took a copy of the photofit. Within seconds, most were changed into digital copies, as mobile phones and camera captured the picture.

Those who had onsite reporters were already standing before men carrying shoulder-mounted TV cameras, trying to be the first to show the police image of the suspect known as "The Spiker".

Sally knew this was the way modern media worked. Reporters and journalists were like locusts on a wheat field, swooping in, consuming as much as they could, and moving on again to find their next headline. To be first was all.

PC Sally had printed one hundred copies of the photofit. As Sally fed the last of the opened hands, she was quite surprised that no more than ten pages remained. Already, images of "The Spiker" would be broadcast across the world, as the news was now twenty-four hours and three hundred and sixty-five days a year.

PC Gunel was about to turn and walk back inside when a reporter of a local paper walked up to her.

The girl looked young, with blond hair that looked to be very wet. Sally guessed she had probably been stood outside in the rain for some time. This was the price needing to be paid to gain a story.

The girl wanted to speak to Sally, "Good morning PC Gunel." The girl said, looking at Sally's name badge on her uniform.

Sally turned to face the cold looking, very wet woman. Looking at her lanyard around her neck, PC Gunel could see that the girl worked for a local paper. Emma Giles, the reporter from The Western Chronicle.

"Sorry, may I use your loo, please? I am bursting, we have been stood out here since six a.m." the young girl asked.

PC Gunel felt pity. This was another price that needed to be paid to gain a story. Often, basic human facilities were far from the place a story needed to be found.

Sally nodded, "Of course. Please keep it quiet though, we will have all the reporters wanting to come in." PC Gunel walked forward, and the young reporter followed her into the dry, warm reception area of the station.

Pointing down a short corridor off to the side of the room, the sign of the toilets and cells was displayed clearly on the wall.

The young reporter thanked Sally and made her way quickly off towards the toilets.

Sally moved back to her usual place behind the main desk. The phone was already alive with flashing red lights, which she quickly began to answer.

Three calls came in from different media outlets, trying to ask for an exclusive interview with DS Murray. Other calls wanted her to send them emails of the picture. It was going to be a very busy morning.

As Sally picked up her sixth call in three minutes, the young reporter reappeared in the reception room, her hair now brushed and makeup re-applied.

From the girl who had run off at pace into the loo, the woman who returned looked quite different.

Sally was busy, writing down messages. The phone was still alive with lights. Sergeant Parsons was trying to help, taking calls from his desk in the room behind reception.

Emma Giles wanted to be a good a reporter like her mother before. Catherine Giles, founder of The Western Chronicle had once been a well-known foreign correspondent to BBC radio. As the daughter of a multi-award-winning journalist, Emma could only hope to be half as good as her mother had ever been.

As a female young newspaper journalist, it was hard to try to compete with ambitious men and digital outlets, where news was current and able to bring information to readers minute by minute.

Catherine Giles was both a mother and a mentor to Emma. Throughout a long career of broadcasting the news, she had learned many tricks to gain the extra edge.

Emma was using one of them today. Catherine Giles had always tried to position herself in places where other reporters could not reach. Having ears and eyes in the right places could often make the difference in what others were reporting. Catherine Giles had told Emma that real reporting was sometimes like being a spy, often having to balance between what was right and wrong.

Standing purposely at the other end of the reception desk, Emma could see PC Sally Gunel was very busy on the phone. Usually, nobody would ever stand at this end of the desk, as the main door naturally took visitors to the other end. At this end of the front desk, there was only the door that led into the main incident room.

The door behind the reception desk leading into the main police room was wide open. Inside, Emma could see several policemen on the phone and DS Nick Murray, pointing at a huge whiteboard.

Placing her blood-red leather, Mulberry handbag up onto the high desk, Emma opened the clasp and took out her phone. Pretending to text or read an email, she held the phone upright.

Using the triple zoom feature, Emma allowed the iPhone to focus on the whiteboard. Almost instantly the images, names and faces, connection lines and symbols appeared on her screen. Holding the main button, the camera snapped at least four times.

PC Sally came to the end of her call.

Walking over to the woman at the opposite end of the desk, she could see the girl answering a call on her mobile phone, "Hi, Mum. I will be home at five thirty p.m. I can cook if you like. Love you."

Emma Giles placed the phone back into her handbag and closed the golden clasps. It had attracted PC Gunel attention.

"Beautiful handbag. I have a similar one in purple, but I think it's fake. Internet bargain. I love Mulberry bags." PC Gunel said, standing in the way of the doorway.

Emma Giles agreed.

"Yes, this was a present from my Mum last Christmas. I love it, very waterproof and surprisingly spacious. Thank you for letting me use the loo, you're a lifesaver. It can be hard in this line of work when you have to wait so long." Emma told Sally who was still looking at what she could see was a real version of the handbag.

PC Sally snapped back to her professional self. Casually closing the open door to the incident room, PC Gunel spoke.

"If there nothing else we can help you with, have a lovely day." She told Emma Giles.

For a moment Sally thought the young reporter was going to speak. It was pretty obvious she wanted to ask some questions about the case. What a scoop it would be for a young unknown reporter to get the inside police info about "The Spiker." PC Gunel prepared herself to refuse to answer anything concerning the case. There would be nothing leaked through Sally today.

Sally was wrong.

Instead, the young girl just thanked Sally once more and walked back towards the door. In seconds she was gone, back into the rain which was falling much heavier than earlier.

The following morning papers were filled with pictures of the man the police wanted to find to help with their enquires. Headlines and front pages were boldly stating that this was the face of the "The Spiker."

Some mentioned the story of an apple tree, but there was no real substance or relevance to this claim.

Radio news tried their best to describe the bald man with the brimmed hat, stating clearly to everyone that this man should not be approached. Many of the national talk radio programmes did their best to speak with "experts" and ex-policemen about how they imagined the case was progressing. This was providing a topic of conversation that everyone wanted to be a part of, with switchboards alive with theories and possible motives.

But it was one local newspaper based in the West country that seemed to have attracted the most public interest. TV and Radio outlets were all trying hard to get an interview with a young reporter who was known to be the daughter of the famous Catherine Giles.

When everyone else had gone to press with the huge photo of the "The Spiker" on covers and spread across centre pages, the paper "The West Chronicle" had printed far more information than what was said in the police briefing.

Emma Giles had produced a story that linked the man known as "The Spiker" with the real name of Joshua. Emma explained that police were now firmly linking all three murders to the same person.

There was a question in the story that asked the public to come to them if anything was known about an apple tree golden ring. Emma described the ring in full detail, stating it was a solid gold band with a beautifully carved apple tree with a coiled snake set into the top.

Emma went on to explain that this symbol probably represented a link to Eden, the garden mentioned in Genesis at the start of the Bible.

The owner of the paper, Catherine Giles had added a supplement to her daughters' story, offering a reward for any information leading to the arrest of this man.

Catherine explained that as these murders were all in the Somerset, Avon, and Wiltshire area, which was the region her newspaper was written to inform. Catherine announced that it was in her interest to see that everyone was kept as safe as they could be. The swift arrest and conviction of "The Spiker" would allow everyone to sleep easier in their beds.

This additional supplement to Emma's breaking story had boosted the interest of the entire nation.

Catherine had a face that most people could remember reporting from live-fire war scenes and bloody military coups. If Catherine Giles was concerned enough to state this man should be found and locked away, the public thought they should take note.

Emma Giles was immediately being called by fleet street editors. It seemed that having a famous mother and the ability to take opportunist photos was going to pay off.

It was Catherine who came up with the headlines that focused the public's eye, "Who is Next on this murderer's random list?

"Police worry on how to stop "The Spiker" from striking again."

But her best headline had been a real corker, ***"It could be U2 – on the Joshua Tree."***

# Chapter 14

## Phillip Stevens – The Last Hours

### Timeline—27 February 2018

Phillip Stevens hated the feel of crusted dried mud on his hairy legs.

Each time he tried to pull off the caked muddy sections which rapidly dried, it was as much as he could do not to scream out loud. How women did this to themselves every day for reasons of vanity alone was beyond his sixteen-year-old brains comprehension.

Rugby had not been a choice activity Phillip opted for throughout his short private school life. Outdoor sports were never something he relished taking part in, but here in this exclusive high fee-paying boarding school, every student was forced to go out into the weathers of winter and fall about stupidly in Somerset mud. At least it was not summer, as Phillip hated cricket at least three times as much as he hated rugby.

As the son of two schoolteacher parents, Phillip attended King Alfred's school for boys almost free of fees. With many students paying thousands of pounds per term, arriving from all over the world to attend this prestigious education centre, his mother and father believed that the heavily reduced wages they received each month, was worth the ability to have their only child Phillip properly educated.

When his parents had first arrived in the village of Stockton-on-Avon, Phillips's father was the only one of his parents who had a job at the school. It was another two years before his mother also became a full-time educator.

Moving the family down from just outside Cambridge, his father and mother were sweethearts formed as ex-students of the larger Cambridge campus. Knowing his parents love for education, Phillip believed they were both going to be full-time students for the rest of their lives.

Since he was thirteen years old, Phillip knew his place in the world had been a complete accident. One evening, whilst led in his bed living in the Old Rectory, he had listened to his parents downstairs entertaining several other teachers from the school over dinner.

As the wine began to flow, stories of their younger student days were filled with embarrassed laughter.

The revelation of his mother's pregnancy being a huge disappointment to Phillips's grandparents and the fact his father was almost forced into doing the right thing by marrying his mother when they had no intention of settling down, had stayed with Phillip.

That night, Phillip had listened as his mother spoke of her pro-life religious stance. There was never any chance she would ever have thought about abortion as her Catholic bonds were always strong. This was a part of the reason why his grandfather had been so angry when he found out about her sex life outside of wedlock.

Phillip Stevens was born on the 14th of March 2002. For the next ten years, Felicity Stevens life had changed from a well-trained Geography teacher to a homebound mother, supporting her husband, Mark.

To keep her mind active, Felicity had written and worked with a friend to produce a couple of Vegan cookbooks, mainly because of her student educated views on animal consumption. To make ends meet, Felicity also tried without much success to sell her watercolour pictures, many of which she painted from the views outside of the Old Rectory.

Twice she had organised local gallery sales, to sell her artwork, but this had never really given them enough to make a regular second salary.

When a position for a Geography teacher came up in King Alfred's school, Phillips's father had quickly moved in on his wife's behalf. The Dean had been happy to take on Felicity Stevens, for a heavily reduced wage. For this price, Phillip was moved from the local comprehensive school, into the first year of King Alfred's.

Phillip's love of art was definitely from his mother side. This was a natural talent which he spent many of his daylight hours following. Felicity and Mark's views on Veganism, Ban the Bomb, Nuclear Power and Climate Change had also worn off on Phillip. Joining several groups within the school, two of which were run by his mother, Phillip found a place where his opinion was welcomed.

The school was filled with posters and images printed from Phillips's own hand. It was a reputation he was known for in the school, which no matter what the views of the students were, had made him a popular figure.

Even though Phillip Stevens was the result of two bottles of wine and a convenient forgetfulness of his mother's Catholic standards, Felicity and Mark Stevens were proud of their son, and like all parents of gifted students, wanted nothing but the best for him.

Playing rugby had been a true surprise to both Phillip and his family. Phillip was not particularly strong or very well built, but like his father, he was a fast runner. Mark Stevens had competed as a boy at county level sprinting, which everyone assumed had given Phillip something of his father. With each school year that passed, Phillip was always included as a winger even though he hated the sport, but this team membership brought him more popularity with his school friends.

Phillip's ability to get the ball and run like hell was known to the school sports teachers. Phillip was not a fan, nor did he particularly enjoy the Sunday morning training sessions, but as it kept his parents happy and the small fact Phillip felt part of a team, he would never complain and endure the cold, muddy, sometimes painful winter mornings.

As a bribe to keep Phillip interested and keen on the rugby team, his father had offered to pay for Phillip to travel on a school art trip into Russia later this year. This was a trip to draw Red Square and scenes of Moscow. His mother had also made a similar offer to allow Phillip on a trip to see a Norwegian glazier, *"Before it was gone due to Global warming"* so his mother often told him. Getting through winter was going to lead Phillip Stevens into a pretty great summer.

Today was the first proper inter-school rugby match of the season. The Sunday training session yesterday had been full-on, as the coach went through a dozen set plays that he wanted to see his team try.

With a team arriving from another private school just outside of Swansea, the coach, a retired lesser-known ex-England player, was treating today like an England versus Wales clash at Twickenham. Barking out orders and losing what was usually a calm, jovial personality, the coach felt this was his world cup final.

Phillip's team could feel the tension in the dressing room. Usually, the coach would appear just before they all walked out onto the pitch, mainly to wish them all luck and to enjoy the game.

Today, the coach was sat on a plastic chair drilling each of his team on what he expected them to do.

Raymond Blair had only been in King Alfred's school for ten months. In that time, he had gently changed what was a weak rugby team, into something he could finally work with. Today would be his first real test and come through with his promise to the Dean that within a year he would have a competitive rugby team that would bring the School trophies.

Setting up games with schools both locally and further afield, this was going to be Raymond's first full international match. Phillip was asked to create the match posters, which were pinned up all over the school and in the village below. The Dean and a huge proportion of the school, with many parents, would be pitch side today, cheering on the team today. Nothing short of a win would be an acceptable result.

Much of Raymond's reasons for the Dean choosing him to fill the sports teacher role depended on today's game. A lot was riding on it. Raymond needed to push his young boys to realise this.

Phillip listened as Mr Blair told him three times who would be feeding him the ball today. He needed to stay alert and ready to receive the killer pass from the little fly-half. Phillip's job was simple enough. Get the ball and run as fast as he could towards the poles. Sadly, he knew that simplicity in rugby was impossible, as running at speed usually ended with hitting the grass at speed, with someone on top of you.

Nodding to the coach, Phillip knew what he was in the team to do and expected that at some point during the game his job would need to be executed.

To add to the atmosphere, which Raymond Blair said was all part of the occasion, the coach played a CD of both "The World in Union" and the English national anthem, to boost the player's adrenaline. Phillip thought that playing the English national anthem was a little pointless as most of the players in the team were from other countries all over the world. Three Africans, one German and two from Dubai had no idea of the significance of either of the songs.

Phillip tried to think what song would have been more suited for such an international side. Speaking to the four other English players in the team, one of the hookers, and team captain, who was a huge lad with a broad Yorkshire accent, smiled, and spoke, bursting into song for the chorus,

"Tub-Thumping by Chumba Wumba!

*I get knocked down, but I get up again,* that would probably be better for us." to the laughter of everyone except coach Raymond Blair.

As the team were walked out onto the field, led by Raymond Blair, all of the players were surprised to see just how many people were stood at the far side of the field, cheering, and eagerly waving the school flags.

Phillip caught sight of his mother, waving the only flag he knew she owned. It was certainly out of place between the Welsh Dragons and Union Jacks, but the flag of Extinction Rebellion was easy to spot.

Phillip remembered when his mother had first acquired the flag. It was stuck out of the top of a fence post, on the black iron fences surrounding Parliament in London. Phillip had spent three amazing days, sitting on the streets, and living in a tent, whilst the world was told that time was running out.

He could remember his mother placing the flag on the pole of their tent and told him about the symbology. It was a simple black and white design. A black circle which his mother told Phillip represented the planet was surrounding a simple hourglass shape. This symbol clearly stated that time was running out, and unless something was done to address climate change immediately, the world was going to die.

Phillip was a total believer in climate change. He could remember the passion both of his parents had for this just, noble cause. But, in a year when so much was drummed into the world that Climate Change was real and now reaching dangerous limits, November had seen the election of President Trump, who dismissed the facts and signs like they were a made-up children's fairy tale.

Today, the weather was sunny, very cold, but at least the frost was now gone. Two hours before the ground was like concrete, but as the sun worked its magic on the pitch, soon, twenty-three sets of boots would be churning up the mud below.

The first half saw a very balanced game of aggression. The Welsh team were massive, strong, and full of a need to beat the English, just as Mr Blair had said they would be. The score was looking to be going the wrong way for the coach, as the Welsh scored two tries in quick succession on the eighteen- and twenty-minute mark.

But two converted penalty kicks had brought King Alfred's back into the game.

The crowds on the side of the field were a mixed bunch. As the trip down from Swansea was only eighty miles, many of the Welsh parents had taken the day off to watch their young boy's play. Phillip guessed around sixty to seventy people were making a lot of noise. Throughout the whole half, they cheered, as coach Blair paced the line shouting out commands.

It was in the last play of the first half that Phillip found himself alone, with a clear root to the oppositions try line ahead. From a fumbled scrum, the ball quickly moved between the German hooker and the African fly-half. Seconds later the huge captain blocked their fly-half from stopping the pass that fell sweetly into Phillips's hands.

Phillip was already running when the ball fell into his midriff.

Dodging a flying tackle from an equally quick Welsh defender, Phillip was away. By the time anyone got near to him, the ball was firmly on the ground, near to the left-hand post.

Raymond Blair's cheer was the loudest and deafening, easily heard over the cheering parents behind.

Phillip turned back towards his mum and could see her jumping up and down but was instantly lost to his team surrounding and hugging him.

The referee blew the half time whistle, and the teams made their muddy way back into the changing room.

The halftime score was 13-14 to the Swansea team.

Inside the changing room, Phillip refused the orange juice offered by a tall balding man. It was sugared and had enough E numbers to fill the back of the cardboard box. Instead, Phillip walked over to his peg, that Raymond Blair had labelled with his name, again to add the occasion of the day, and picked up a purple metal water bottle, which he had made sure was easily accessible from his bag before the game.

Taking off the lid, Phillip drank deeply. The taste was a little chalkier than he expected, but Phillip put that down to how dry his mouth was from the game. This was water from his home at the Old Rectory. It was pure and much better for him than heavily chemical Orange juice others were busy drinking.

*** 

Joshua Wright was, for the last six months at least, a regular helper at King Alfred's school. Recommended by the local vicar in the village, he was often seen around the premises when work was needed to the old plumbing.

With so many old buildings, there was twice the number of broken pipes, especially in winter when the heating was needed to warm the borders.

The vicar had given Joshua a full reference to the Dean, as he was also a good friend of Frederick Bannister, who had first introduced the vicar to him a year ago. Joshua was keen to know about the building where Eden's Echo had been formed, so working inside the old school would at least give him some idea of the roots of where the good book of Charles Wyndham was first written.

Frederick had not seen any problem with Joshua wanting to learn of Eden's Echo roots, but the real reason why Joshua was here was far more sinister than what his friend was telling him.

Joshua's initial background check had all come back clean. There was nothing in his past life that said this man was not fit to work with children. The onsite premises team had been keen to have Joshua on their list of available people to call in an emergency, as main contractors were expensive, to say the least.

As Joshua's work proved to be cheap and very reliable, his phone was often ringing by the school for urgent help.

Within months, Joshua was given access to get himself into

several restricted areas, helping out around the school, including kitchen maintenance, heating, and toilet remedial. He also had access to the boilers, which were situated next to the school field changing rooms.

Most people did not even look twice at him as he walked around the school with his plastic Adidas sports bag holding his tools. Just one of the largely ignored maintenance men, there to do a job, invisible to the children.

Joshua wondered if any of the school children even noticed him some days, as rarely did anyone attempt to talk to him.

On the day of the rugby game, Joshua had been on site before most had even arrived. With a set of keys and the alarm codes, there were not many places inside the grounds he could not access. Today, he made sure there was plumbing work to do on the boiler near to the changing rooms, where he had placed his orange plastic health and safety signs up, to make sure the kids stayed out of his way.

When the children started to arrive, all of them were far too excited to look at a man in orange overalls and spanners all over the floor.

The coach of the team was sat on a plastic chair talking to the boys. It was a fairly frank discussion with the coach not holding back his concerns and expectations.

Joshua thought this man was being a little harsh on what was just sixteen-year-olds, but from his maintenance cupboard, he continued to loosen old boiler pipes for the heating check. From what he could see, these were the original pipes that must have been installed before the building became a school. They were copper and silver soldered, with many of the original fittings from the early fifties.

When the team lined up and walked outside, Joshua could

hear the cheers of the mothers and fathers beyond. It was good to know that these boys were well supported. Joshua was never a fan of sports but could feel God's love close, for he loved all children in his family.

All but one.

Walking out, into an empty changing room, there were bags and pegs full of hanging clothes. For a few minutes, he waited until the referee's whistle was blown and the cheering increased. For the next forty minutes at least, he would be alone.

It did not take him long to find Phillip Stevens name above the peg.

Joshua had purposely not wanted to know the face of the boy, for this would make him feel much worse than he was already feeling. Over the last few weeks had seen brief glimpses of the lad from afar, but with his Holy mission accepted, Joshua needed to make sure Phillip Stevens did not know of him.

It would be far easier for them both this way.

Joshua knew that preparing for murder, needed careful meticulous planning. Joshua did not want the boy to suffer, he did not want the boy to know any fear. Joshua would do as God had asked him, and that would be all.

For months Joshua had needed to come to terms with what he was told to do, the first time he had heard God's voice. Mary Grace had not been able to give him any clear answers, for God's words went against everything she thought God's love to be. The fundamental rule of *Thou Shall Not Murder* was being tested. Mary told Joshua he was mistaken, but he was sure of what he heard. The voice had been with him ever since and would not be silent until His will was done.

Joshua wondered if something was missing from the commandment that had been added to the other nine rules Mosses had been shown by God.

Mary Grace was certain Joshua was wrong, but her best student's logic was sound.

"Thou Shalt Not Murder Unless I Tell You."

Over many difficult discussions, Mary had told Joshua that he must have misheard the message in some way. She tried to justify the message by using biblical references to Abraham.

Mary tried to explain, "Remember Joshua, Genesis 22:1-18, The Lord God asked Abraham to sacrifice his only child as a burnt offering. But God was testing Abraham to prove his loyalty to him. God, I think is testing you, Joshua. He will stop this before you go through with His command, and you will know love." Mary said to the bald man, hoping in all faith she was right.

But Joshua was sure he heard God clear. Since that first wonderous evening, what Joshua had not told Mary was that voice was still with him. Night and day, he would hear Him speaking continuously. Joshua was tuned into the frequency of God. It was like a louder form of tinnitus, a constant whisper that could only go away once this task was done.

The words from God had been clear, simple, and certain for Joshua to know and understand.

*"Joshua, I have a task for you. You are and will be my shepherd.*

*Do you love me? Prove your love. You must Kill for me. This is your path into Eden. I ask this deed in great pain Joshua.*

*Find Phillip Stevens in King Alfred's School.*

*Even a child can cause great harm to my flock. He is a wolf.*

*You are chosen, Joshua,*

*You must Kill the wolves of my flock, so the sheep can live in peace.*

*Do this Son of Adam and Eden will welcome you home?"*

Finding the boy's name on the rugby team sheet had been a bonus. Joshua already knew a painless nonsuffering way he could do God's will, for it was the same way he was going to end his own life, just a few months before.

Using just three hundred milligram of Pentobarbital pills, ground into a fine powder, Joshua found the boys water bottle in his sports bag, and using his workmen gloves, opened the lid of the purple water bottle.

With tears rolling down his cheeks, Joshua had fallen to his knees, looking upwards, as he hoped God would now tell him that He knew Joshua was loyal and obedient to Him.

The whispers inside his head continued with the same message. *"Kill the wolves, Joshua."*

With a true sense of burden and regret, Joshua added the powder into the water inside the container. Replacing the lid, he shook the bottle to mix it up completely.

Within two minutes, the water would be completely clear and almost tasteless to the inner poison. Anyone who drank down this liquid would be asleep within two hours and dead within four.

Raymond Blair was the first person back into the changing rooms. As each of his heroes walked back into the room, he congratulated them all personally.

The last boy to enter was Phillip Stevens, who had struggled to get out of his mother's cuddles after watching her son place down the winning try, finishing the game 22-20.

Phillip Stevens had been lifted by the boys on the pitch as a hero and the best player of the match. Phillip felt as if he were on top of the world. Maybe rugby was not that bad.

The mud on his legs seemed a trophy, rather than a pain.

Walking into the changing room door, he turned and waved to his mother who was waving and shouting that she would see him at home later.

That was the last time Felicity Stevens saw her son alive.

Phillip drained the rest of his water, before getting changed and cycling the three miles back home.

Even before he got inside the Old Rectory, he felt very tired. Phillip thought the game had taken all his energy out of him.

Filling his water bottle up again from the kitchen sink, Phillip carried everything he brought home from school upstairs into his bedroom. His legs and arms were telling him to have a shower as the mud pulled hard at the tiny hairs.

But Phillip felt too tired to shower. Throwing his bag on the bedroom floor, he dived onto his single bed, where the Greenpeace duvet cover softened his urgent need for eternal sleep.

One hour later, Phillip Stevens died.

# Chapter 15

## Jemma Evans – The Last Hours

### Timeline—15 March 2018

Jemma Evans was in a rush.

The red LED lights on the clock radio alarm next to her bed flashed furiously at 06.22 a.m., as it had been doing each minute for the past twenty-two.

Twice Jemma had leaned over sleepily and hit the snooze button hard since six a.m., which had brought an instant blissful silence to the morning radio songs blaring out her call to the shower. Sadly, the second strike of the button had not been on the snooze for five minutes. Instead, Jemma had pressed the mute button, so the alarm had never gone off again, as the clock radio played on in complete silence.

Jemma swore under her breathe as she startled back to reality. Throwing the duvet off her warm body, she ran across the bedroom towards the bathroom, grabbing whatever clothing would have to do today.

This was at least the third time this had happened to her in so many months. The clock radio had been a present to herself last Christmas, as she was fed up with waking to the sudden sharp blurting of a small alarm clock bleep, but Jemma soon realised that whoever designed the clock radio had never used it themselves. Designing the mute button to be next to the snooze button was and had been a complete disaster.

Jumping into the shower, Jemma was barely wet before she was reaching for the towel. For the next ten minutes, the bathroom was just a mad panic of toothpaste, hair brushing, make-up and remembering to take her birth control pill. As Jemma looked into the mirror before she left, she knew it was not her best look, but today, it would just have to do until later.

Tonight, Jemma decided she would be looking online for a new clock radio, as this was the last time this was going to happen.

In the kitchen of her flat, the cold vegan croissant and orange juice were at least pretty good. Jemma had gone to bed intending to wake up and prepare a good healthy lunch of couscous with butternut squash, but instead, today Jemma would need to waste money she could not afford to spend, on buying healthy food from a shop.

As the clock radio flashed over to 07.07, Jemma was pulling out of Culverwell Street in the village of Netherhampton just outside the city of Salisbury, where she had lived for the past three years. In the distance, the tall spire of Salisbury Cathedral pierced the grey sky, like a rocket on a landing pad. Jemma had often thought she would never be surprised to see the spire blast off into the air, on its religious aim to get to the heavens above.

Jemma likes Salisbury. Although she had grown up in a much bigger city, Salisbury was altogether prettier and much less threatening than Bristol.

Most of her childhood had been spent in Bath, where her mother and father had tried in vain to run a small restaurant. Their private venture had come from her parents successfully running the kitchens in a large school in the village of Stockton-on-Avon. For six years her parents had worked closely together to prepare thousands of meals for hungry boys and staff alike.

When Jemma's mother had suggested they went out on their own, the idea had been exciting, for the whole family. But, within a year of the small Vegetarian restaurant opening in Bath, it was struggling to make a living. Sadly, both her mother and father were far better cooks than businessmen.

On the day after Jemma's sixteenth birthday, the news of her mother having breast cancer had been a terrible blow to both her father and any hope of Jemma getting the GSCE's she needed for a hopeful career in veterinary. Jemma's father closed the restaurant to look after his wife, but within ten short months, Jemma was stood at the side of a new grave, devastated at the loss of a woman she loved dearly.

Jemma's father took the quick decision to sell up and move into Bristol, where he found a steady job in a small pub, running the kitchen. Jemma struggled heavily, needing counselling from her grief and two bouts of anorexia.

If it had not been for the woman who not only mentally counselled her back to life but gave her back a passion for the food her parents used to love to prepare when she was a child, Jemma did not think she would be here today.

A career with animals had never been achievable. Leaving school at just seventeen, Jemma did not have A levels nor the want to move into further education. Instead, Jemma took a job in Bath, working as the apprentice to a local estate agent called Brymore.

The work was surprisingly fun. Taking people around to look at houses they wanted to buy was not as dull as she first thought. It gave Jemma a great thrill to see inside the homes and how people lived, and the money was pretty good for a school leaver.

Within a year, Jemma was asked to be assistant manager to

a tiny branch of the estate agency, taking her back to the village where her parents had worked in the private school.

The Stockton-on-Avon branch was no more than two rooms on the ground floor of an old stone house, decked with a huge painted picture of the school on the hill and village below, but Jemma had loved her time working for the branch manager.

Many of the people who wanted to buy a house in the village and the countryside beyond, were not the sort of people looking for two-bedroom semi-detached houses. Jemma quite often found herself showing wealthy city folk around huge river-hugging properties that supported sometimes over eight bedrooms, stable blocks, and snugs.

The branch manager of Brymore at the time was a woman in her mid-thirties, who had a very similar outlook on life, and like Jemma was passionate about her Veganism and the drive to stop a nuclear power station being built in the Southwest of England. In her years in Stockton-on-Avon, Jemma had not only become a good estate agent but by the time she left, she was a staunch activist, spending her weekends standing with placards outside contested areas on climate change and factory farming.

For three years she served the branch well. At the age of twenty-three, Jemma was offered the position of full-time manager of the little branch when the manager became pregnant, which Jemma took up for eighteen months until a new position of a much larger branch came up in Salisbury. In a year, Jemma found a flat in a village only three miles from the heart of Salisbury, where she now lived in the hope of finding love.

Within just ten minutes of leaving her home, Jemma was pulling into the car park a short distance away from a local Gym. Jemma was completely obsessed with fitness, something that also helped her mind back from the anorexic days.

Parking her hybrid Toyota, she quickly grabbed her sports bag and ran off into the little newsagent that was across the street from the Fitness Now gym.

Inside the shop the newsagent, a little Indian owner was sat on a stool behind his counter, where Jemma believed he slept.

The man never seemed to have any time away from his shop, he was always there, morning, noon, and night.

Grabbing a bottle of mineral water and a Vegan energy bar, Jemma paid the man, who was always smiling and grateful for her business.

At 8.25 a.m., after a good twenty-minute run on the treadmill, Jemma was in the Gym showers, this time making sure she was clean. Alone in the gym, none had seen her train this morning, Jemma was a nobody.

Today, she had four appointments, all outside of Salisbury, each for potential sales of people who were looking to discover the glorious peace of Wiltshire life.

With a face full of free from animal testing face make-up, a white-toothed smile, bobbed, clipped back red hair, Jemma sat in the drive of a huge, six-bedroom house waiting for the first viewing clients to arrive. Considering her alarm clock had put her twenty minutes behind today, she was delighted to think that as she sipped her bottled mineral water, Jemma was five minutes early before the agreed meeting time of nine thirty is clicked over.

Typically, Jemma was still sat in the car at 9.53 a.m. After several attempts to call the viewers had failed, mostly due to the lack of any mobile signal in the area, something she would not mention today during the viewing. A brand-new BMW X something or other pulled into the driveway. Jemma shook her head, mostly out of the fact of how late these people were, but also out of their need to drive such a huge carbon hungry vehicle.

As the monster four-wheeled drive tractor pulled up alongside her tiny fuel-efficient, half electric Toyota Yaris, Jemma could see just two old pensioners inside.

There were no children's seats in the back of the BMW, as both of the people in the front looked far too old to be parents. This vehicle must have been purchased as a choice, rather than any consideration towards the environment. Jemma needed to put on her game face and overlook the utter distaste she was feeling. Jemma was pretty sure that these people were time wasters that liked to look around houses in their retirement. Over the years, Jemma could tell what enquires were genuine, but sadly anyone could call for a viewing.

Smiling, Jemma got out of her little car as the old man in the driver's seat struggled to electrically down his window,

"Sorry, we got very lost. These country lanes are so small. Needed to stop twice for tractors, such a nuisance." a posh voice said, retracting the window to get out.

"I am not very good with maps." the old woman said from the passenger's seat, slowly trying to fold a huge map back into its original shape.

Jemma just beamed back a smile, whilst looking at the huge turned off seven inched screen Sat Nav on the dashboard, which this pair had no idea how to programme or use.

For the next five minutes, it took the two clients an age to get out and sort themselves out ready to follow Jemma inside the house.

Jemma remained ever-professional, passing the time of day, and making pleasant conversation as the couple struggled to work out how to lock the doors of the BMW tractor.

As they walked towards the house with the driver still moaning about tractors on country lanes, Jemma could not help thinking about the fact that this old man was also driving a tractor through country lanes, who was also looking to buy a property that could easily fit a family of twelve people.

Taking a deep breath, Jemma walked towards the huge entrance door with the keys in her hand. Today, she would be looking to try to sell this six-bedroomed home to just two old people who would probably be better in a two bedroomed bungalow. How this pair would ever hope to manage the three and a half-acre gardens behind was beyond Jemma, but this was not of her concern. Anyone could view any property. Those were the rules of this game.

Jemma's 11.20-second appointment was altogether more sensible. A lady in her mid-forties was already waiting when Jemma pulled up outside of the small end of the terrace house.

As they quickly moved into each of the small rooms, it was obvious to Jemma that this woman was looking to move to a new house quickly. Not really listening to anything Jemma was saying about the train lines, bus stops and local amenities, the woman today was just keen that the place had three bedrooms and a kitchen.

Jemma soon discovered that this lady was the victim of a violent marriage and was looking for somewhere to bring her two children after walking out of the marriage. It was funny how many people opened up to her when looking for a house, it was as if they wanted to show they were genuine about the purchase. These were usually the people Jemma knew were not time waisters, as most of them were only keen to know if the price could be negotiated for a quick sale.

Jemma Evans drove back into Salisbury at 2.02 p.m. As fast as she could run, Jemma purchased a Vegan chickpea sandwich and an apple from the M&S near the city branch of Brymore.

Jemma munched away as she wrote up the first two viewings of the morning. Just as Jemma thought, the first had been a waste of time, with the old couple saying that they had hoped the property was larger, which had shocked her at the time. There was no way these people were interested, as Jemma knew one of her colleagues had taken them around another huge house only a few weeks ago.

The second viewing was more promising. Even before Jemma was back in Salisbury, her Bluetooth phone connection in the car was calling her, asking Jemma to make an offer for the divorced woman. Jemma had closed the deal even before reaching the office car park.

After a brief conversation with colleagues in the office, all of which she liked and got on with, Jemma was out again, driving to her third appointment on the outskirts of the city.

Frustratingly, she had forgotten to buy another bottle of water when she purchased her lunch, which meant she would need to go back into the newsagents again today before going to the gym tonight on her way home.

Pulling up on the road outside of the third property in her viewing list of four today, Jemma was surprised to see a man already stood on the doorstep. It was 3.11 p.m. so Jemma was about five minutes late. This house was vacant, so if he had been knocking on the door, there would have been no answer.

Taking her half-empty water bottle, Jemma stepped out of the car and walked through the narrow gateway that was dwarfed by a huge six-foot hedge on either side. The house was mid-terraced, with three steep steps up to the door. As Jemma pushed the stiff wooden gate forward, she greeted the tall, bald man, wearing a wide-brimmed cloth hat at the door, "Good Afternoon, Mr Wright. Sorry, I am a little late. Traffic got the better of me."

Jemma said, shaking the man's huge hands.

Inside the house, the man was very quiet as he looked around the property. Jemma found him hard to judge as he made little in the way of conversation. For a while, he stopped to look out of the bedroom window, which had beautiful views of the cathedral spire in the distance. The man seemed very impressed with the sight and told Jemma he was a regular churchgoer.

Jemma told the man that there were many religious groups and beautiful churches in Salisbury, which seemed to bring his interest in a while. As Jemma usually asked in her routine, she suggested the man have walked around on his own to get a feel for the place.

It was then the man made a request to her that was unusual, but Jemma could not see any harm in what he was asking. As she left the man downstairs looking around the kitchen, she went back upstairs to take a picture of the cathedral from the bedroom window. The man asked if this could be sent to him and as he did not carry a mobile phone, and he hoped Jemma would not mind sending it to him by email later today.

Mr Wright told Jemma that he would decide on the house based on this view alone.

After Jemma took around three decent images, she was sure she could hear the taps running downstairs.

Quickly she went back to check and found the man looking at the pipes beneath the sink.

Jemma was surprised, but Mr Wright explained that he was a plumber and always liked to check the pipework of a property. The man confessed to running the taps, to check the water pressure, which Jemma just zoned out to.

Picking up her water bottle from the kitchen worktop, she was sure it was a little fuller than what she remembered but put it in her handbag without a second thought.

An hour later, Jemma's phone was ringing as she sat waiting outside of her fourth appointment. Answering her phone, it was good to hear her father's voice, "Hi Jemma, it's Dad." the voice said.

Jemma chuckled. Her dad had never understood that the phone told her who it was before she answered, "Hi Dad, are you OK?" Jemma said, sitting back in the warm interior of the Yaris.

"Jemma, I will call you tonight properly. But I just wanted to make sure you are still OK for me to come to you tomorrow. I am about to pack a bag?" Jemma's Dad asked.

It had been a weekend her Dad had been looking forward to for months. Jemma had told him that for his birthday this weekend, she wanted to take him out to three very good Vegan and Vegetarian restaurants, in the area. Jemma's dad was going to stay with her until Sunday, so Friday evening, Saturday evening and Sunday lunchtime were going to be a real pleasure. It had been months since her father had spent any quality time with his daughter.

"Dad, stop worrying. I am looking forward to seeing you. I have a meeting Saturday morning with my Hinckley point group, but apart from that, I am going to be with you. It will be fun." Jemma said, checking her watch.

After convincing her Dad to pack his bag ready, her father said he would check with Jemma again tonight, which made her smile.

Jemma loved her Dad. They had gone through hell together and both seemed to be on the other side of her mother's death. Jemma knew that her Dad had another incentive for coming over this weekend. Jemma knew he wanted to tell her about a new relationship he was in and he wanted Jemma's approval. It was his first relationship since Jemma's mum had died years ago. Jemma had known about it some time ago, when auntie Janice, her father's sister, had accidentally let it out of the bag in a conversation at Christmas.

Jemma knew it was coming and found it sweet her Dad wanted to do it properly. Jemma had no problem with her Dad wanting to find companionship again, he needed to move on, as she had done.

The 4.10 p.m. appointment was almost over before it began. When the family of three turned up to look at the small, detached house in the village of Dinton, the wife had instantly taken a dislike to the interior. Jemma could see that it was the husband who was keen on the garden and outbuildings, but the wife and her young daughter found the house to be uncomfortably small. Twice the wife commented about the fact the house had a "kitchen-diner" rather than two separate good-sized rooms.

What was scheduled to be a thirty-minute appointment, was no more than fifteen. As they were ten minutes late, Jemma was ironically back on time.

Driving back to the office, Jemma wrote up her notes of the day before walking across town towards the Gym again at five fifteen p.m. Jemma liked to walk to Gym in the evenings as it added to her early evening workouts. Leaving the car in the office car park, forced her to walk back again to drive home. This had been very much part of Jemma's routine for the past year. Walking the thirty minutes to the Gym was not so good at night, but the whole root was street lit with plenty of people around. Jemma used this as both her warmup and warm down each evening.

Reaching the Gym, she took out the half-full water bottle. It was not enough to last her tonight. Taking the bottle lid off, she quickly downed the remaining water inside.

Crossing the busy street, Jemma walked into the newsagent expecting to see the little Indian man sat on his stool behind the counter. To her utter amazement, the seat was empty.

Moving inside the shop, Jemma could see the man at the far end of the narrow newsagents, stacking shelves. Another man was in the shop near a tall stack of mineral water bottles she wanted to buy.

The two aisles of the shop were very narrow, as the shopkeeper tried to cram as much as he could sell into a space that was not able to hold it all.

Reaching out to grab a bottle of water, the other man in the shop, bent down at the same time as Jemma, but stumbled, knocking around six of the plastic bottles of the stack onto the floor.

Instantly he looked up at Jemma, apologising for his stupidity. Jemma helped the man restack the fallen water bottles smiling. The last bottle, the man handed to Jemma as he thanked her for the help.

Jemma moved back to the counter and paid for her new bottle of mineral water. The shopkeeper was now back on his stool, mumbling words that Jemma could not understand. For a moment she thought he was complaining about her knocking over the water stack, but as the other man in the shop left behind her without buying anything at all, Jemma could see the shopkeeper's attention was purely on him and making sure this customer was not stealing anything.

For the next hour, Jemma was inside Fitness Now, working out as hard as she could. With her father coming for the weekend, she was sure that this would be the last time she would be able to train properly until Monday.

Walking back to her car, with sweat pouring from her head, the water bottle was already half empty.

Even driving the short distance home, Jemma was feeling unwell. The workout had been much harder than normal, and Jemma was now beginning to wonder if she had overdone it a little.

Walking into her flat, Jemma was feeling incredibly tired.

Opening the door with her keys, she moved into her flat. Jemma had barely got inside the door before a feeling of extreme nausea came over her. For the next thirty minutes, she could not move away from the toilet bowl.

Feeling completely terrible, she tried to call her father, but the phone was not answered. He probably had it on silent as normal.

Again, another bout of sickness hit her, this time making her worry. There was something wrong, this did not feel like a usual sickness bug.

Jemma felt a real desire to sleep. It was far too dangerous to try to leave the bathroom as her sickness was certainly unpredictable.

Still, in her Gym clothes, Jemma placed her head onto the soft pink rug that covered a good majority of the small bathroom floor.

Within seconds, Jemma was asleep.

Within the hour, Jemma Evans was dead.

Joshua Wright was in tears all the way home. After visiting the house where his request to have Jemma Evans show him around the Salisbury house, he would never buy was over, Joshua had driven away with a sense of sorrow and deep regret.

Finding Jemma Evans had been easy. Her name had popped

up in the first line of a search engine as the manager of Brymore Estate Agents, Salisbury Branch.

Joshua was no murderer, yet he was now being told to be.

Joshua remembered again the last lesson from the book of Charles Wyndham, which Mary wanted them all to understand and follow to the letter,

*"Sometimes, the small things He asks of us may seem unimportant or involve giving up things we think we enjoy. But to reach a level of intimacy with God where we hear His voice, we will know new places in the spirit, obedience must become a non-negotiable in our lives."*

Whilst the young woman, Jemma Evans, was upstairs in the vacant house taking the photo of the majestic bent spire of Salisbury Cathedral, Joshua had found his chance to commit murder. Joshua knew God had given him an opportunity.

Jemma Evans had left her bag and water bottle on the kitchen counter, which had made his murder plan very simple.

Moving quickly, Joshua had taken the water bottle and popped in five hundred milligram of Pentobarbital. Adding a little more water from the kitchen tap, he had needed to shake it up violently, for the tiny pills to dissolve quickly.

By the time Jemma came back downstairs, Joshua had returned the bottle into the lady's bag. Joshua would need to check on his work tomorrow, but he was sure that by nine p.m., God's work would be done. Joshua wanted to be very sure that Jemma Evans would not suffer after the pills were consumed.

She would just find peaceful sleep.

Why *He* had asked Joshua to choose this lovely, seemingly harmless woman was unknown to him. The woman, who seemed very normal and pleasant did not look to be threatening in any way.

Yet, Joshua was sure that this was the second person that He had told him to find,

*Find Jemma Evans. In Salisbury, you must look to buy what looks out at My Spire to Heaven.*

*This is the second wolf that must be culled.*

*You are chosen, Joshua. You are my shepherd.*

*You must Kill the three wolves of my flock, so the sheep can live in peace.*

*Do this Son of Adam, and Eden will welcome you home!"*

Why was Joshua asked to do these terrible things? It was against everything the Bible taught. Yet the voice was so real, so loving, so warm, so... commanding.

Mary could not answer him.

Mary would not answer him.

When Jemma Evans died, the voice in Joshua's head also faded a little more. There was only one wolf left for Joshua to be able to find his promised Eden.

# Chapter 16

## Ridley Goodman – The Last Hours

### Timeline—21 March 2018

The third square stanchion under the Tesco multi-storey car park in Yeovil town centre was a strange place to call home. But for the last nine months, it was the only home Ridley had known.

In the late summer, the ground had been soft, dry, and largely warm out of the rain. But as winter set in, the dark, damp, dirty area was altogether more uncomfortable.

Located away from the main public walkways, on the furthest side of the two-floored car park, most people kept their vehicles well away from the homeless cardboard tent's. Only at Christmas, when parking became an absolute premium, did anyone force themselves to park near to four men who slept under their concrete sky.

When the car park was full, the heat coming off one thousand engines sitting waiting for their owners to return was wonderful. When it emptied, the temperature dropped quickly, but it was still warmer than the open shop doorways within the town centre.

Ridley Goodman had grown up full of hope, with a real spirit to succeed. As an A grade student, from the age of eight, his parents had wanted nothing but the best for their middle son of three.

Ridley was given every opportunity to find his place in life.

Attending a good prep school, his family had easily been able to afford for Ridley to attend a large private school in North Somerset, which had prepared him well for Cambridge university.

Winning a full scholarship in molecular chemistry, Ridley's family were all expecting their son to pass through University earning the fully deserved letters after his name. Ridley was by far the cleverest of their three fine Christian boys, the family's pride, and joy.

This false hope and pride had all changed two Christmases ago, on the day Ridley walked back into his parents' home, with his new south African friend called Johannes. That dark day, the world of a parish vicar and his devote catholic WI wife had been shattered beyond any repair.

Forgiveness was beyond what doctrine dictated.

With the confession to his parents of coming out and being bisexual, the once loving vicar and his mother had not been able to allow this disgrace to fall upon the Goodman household.

Both Ridley and his then male lover were thrown out the same day, a disgrace to the family name.

A week later, Ridley received a letter from his mother asking him if he would consider conversion therapy. Offering to pay for the treatment, she said that Ridley had just lost his way and blamed Johannes for leading him astray.

Just six months later, Ridley and Johannes had also split up, especially when the money from Ridley's parents stopped them from keeping a roof over their heads.

As Ridley fell from his parent's grace, so did his attitude to learning and wanting success. Soon after the money stopped, Ridley became a victim of poverty, addicted to A-class drugs and the sweet taste of any alcohol, so much so that it got him thrown out of the university.

When the Dean discovered that Ridley was also working for a local Polish drug dealer, cutting, and mixing drugs for him using the universities lab facilities, it was instant dismissal.

Ridley was lucky he had not been arrested. When the drug dealer was unable to get his regular drug supply, Ridley was lucky he had not been killed.

With nothing more than the shirt on his back, Ridley Goodman walked out of his student life onto the streets, where he had been hiding ever since.

Having to learn the ropes and the way of the streets from others who had found their way to a homeless existence from similar experiences growing up, life was often lonely and difficult. Ridley could not remember how many times he had been beaten up, threatened, and even sexually abused.

But Ridley's story was tame compared to a few he had met. Some people on the streets preferred to be out in the cold, rather than constantly abused or beaten by families or past relationships. Ridley had seen both sides of the same coin.

Moving from town to town, Ridley finally came back to the southwest where he originally grew up. At first, he lived for a while in Bristol, where he had met a young girl called Karen Spicer. For weeks, they shared the same shop doorstep, where they became friends.

Ridley would help Karen when she needed to fill in forms or claim money at the job centres. Karen had never been shown how to read or write to any level, for she had taken to the streets since the age of eleven. Running away from two foster homes, Karen had never been allowed to succeed. Karen only knew of hardship and was in truth, never in any hurry to change it. All Karen lived for was the joy of a drink, a fix, and a packet of cigarettes. With a ruined nose from a life of minor drug abuse, the once pretty young girl looked twenty years older than her real twenty-one years revealed.

It was Karen who had convinced Ridley to follow her to Yeovil. Karen explained that life on the streets was "better" there, as there were not as many to share the spoils. There was also a very good soup kitchen that truly supported the homeless.

"If you going to be homeless, you might as well choose Yeovil. It is the Ritz compared to the streets of Southampton, Bristol and Swindon." Karen would state, knowing all of these places well.

Wednesdays were always good days on the streets, especially in Yeovil. Today, the little soup kitchen opened an hour earlier, and better still, the old woman who worked in the kitchen, who liked to wear her Salvation army uniform, always made her hot beef stew and apple cinnamon pie on Wednesdays.

For the first ten people through the door, they would be treated that evening to a delicious, cooked meal made by the hands of old Ethel. There was never enough apple pie to share with fifty, so first come was first served.

Ridley knew that Wednesdays were also the day where the community officers would come to chat to them all and try to offer work or look to speak about their abandoned families and ways back into modern life.

This was something Karen had rarely seen in any other town, but the joy of the food and drink from Ethel was such a pleasure, none minded the other people and pointless "do-gooders" around them.

Today, waking up from under an old sleeping bag, two cardboard boxes and a tattered checked blanket, had not been enough to keep out the biting frost of the morning. If it had not been for the warmth and shelter of the concrete car park, Ridley knew he would have half frozen to death last night.

Walking to the Lord's Pantry soup kitchen there was already a queue to the front door by the time Ridley arrived. The old woman Ethel was walking along the line handing out hot drinks for any who wanted them.

"Such a cold morning my dears. Take a hot drink and warm yourselves." the little old woman was telling the queue.

Ridley did not want coffee, he wanted lager, a strong wine, or the glowing heat that the only whiskey could muster inside.

Karen Spicer was in the queue. As she saw Ridley, she called him over, where for an hour they spoke about the cold of last night and where they were going to be sitting in the high street today. Begging was an art, where the best places needed early picketing to claim a spot for the day.

Karen made a kind offer for Ridley to join her, but he had politely declined as he already had plans.

Today, Ridley had offered to help the old caretaker of the Lord's Pantry with his tax return. For this service, John Mole had offered Ridley £50 cash in hand, no questions asked.

Ridley knew all too well that for John to get this sort of help from a professional, he would be paying five times this price, but £50 was more than Ridley could make in three days from working the streets, so this was a win-win for them both.

John Mole was an ex-con who had found God in prison during his later life. The man still had little to no time for policemen but had found a sense of peace in helping those less fortunate to him. A first, he was forced to serve here on the request of a community service order after he left prison. But, over time he had come to love this place, filled with people he could help, and in turn, some could help him.

As the so-called "manager" of the Lord's Pantry, John Mole was well-liked. More importantly, away from his earlier life of thuggery, armed robbery, and theft. John had come to the Lord's Pantry as a way of serving out his community service but had stayed on for the service it now gave back to him.

Now, anyone who came to know of John Mole was often offered to work for him on 'special' jobs, helping to serve the homeless and the darker trades of Yeovil. All this under God's blessing.

No questions asked.

After a simple breakfast, where Ethel served warm toast and tea, the homeless slowly dispersed to find their places of work.

Considering how cold it was outside today, Ridley was over the moon to be allowed to stay in the dining room of the Lord's Pantry for the day. John Mole had brought his tax folders over from home and kept Ridley supplied with cigarettes, warm coffee, biscuits and even a sausage sandwich he had managed to cook in the kitchen.

Ridley thought of poor Karen as she would probably be shivering outside of Boots. Pocketing a few of the biscuits, these he wanted to keep especially for her.

At noon on the dot, the old woman Ethel came in, carrying two huge pots of her stew. Placing them both into the ovens, there they would bubble gently until five p.m. tonight.

John Mole went out about mid-afternoon as he said he had to help out in the local nearby church. Ethel whispered to Ridley that he was probably going down the bookies, as some of his old habits were struggling to find God. At 3.55 p.m. John walked back into the soup kitchen, alongside a tall man, whose wide-brimmed hat did not suit his very bald head.

John introduced the man firstly to Ethel and then to Ridley.

The newcomer seemed to look familiar to Ridley, but it was Ethel who properly reminded him.

"Joshua has been coming here for a couple of weeks now. Helps me out in the kitchens. Such a lovely man. A true follower of our Lord. I don't know how we have coped without him." Ethel whispered.

Ridley had seen the man several times, but it was always from afar. Most of the time over the past two weeks, he was in the kitchen scrubbing plates and pans or tending over hot ovens. They had never spoken, but he could remember the man staring at him, with a cold, dark eyes.

John Mole seemed pleased that Joshua was back within the team again. As John sat watching Ridley finish his tax forms and submitting them on the only very old computer inside the dining hall, John seemed at complete ease as he smoked a cheap cigar,

"Joshua is such a good bloke. Like me, he has had a hard life, but God found him and showed him the way out. I think you can be like Joshua, my friend. You are a clever man Ridley, there is much a man like you can do in the world. There is plenty of work I can find you if you are up for it. I have a few people who could use men like you. Good money to be made for us both, no questions asked." John Mole told him winking.

Ridley nodded. The work today was good, and it had not been that hard to do. Perhaps it was now time he considered turning his world back around again. Living on the streets was not what he wanted. It had provided a means of escape.

"What kind of work John. I would not want to get back into anything too illegal. I was lucky to come out last time with my life." Ridley confessed, remembering the knife at his throat when the Polish drug dealer had found him high on the last of his drugs.

John shook his head, "Not at all Ridley. I have some friends who need someone with your particular skills. Chemistry, wasn't it?

They are looking to recruit clever people to help them on their... Mission to put the world right again." John Mole explained.

Ridley clicked the send button but was looking unsure. This did not sound at all above board, "Mission. You mean for the church?" Ridley asked, nodding as John gave him the £50 cash in five-pound notes. From under the table, he also produced a six pack of lager and two packets of twenty cigarettes.

John nodded his head.

"Of a sort. Sometimes, to do God's work, you need to try new things. Some do not wait before they act. Take nuclear power my boy, do you think God wants anyone to have that sort of destructive power. Some fight against this power and I for one, am with them, Ridley. My calling has brought me to find you. Joshua also thinks you are chosen. Do you see the way he looks at you? He knows a clever man when he sees one." John Mole whispered, nodding towards the man placing the large stew pots into the serving counters.

Ridley was curious, but as he opened the first can of lager, he soon forgot about John's offer. Behind him, Ethel had opened the soup kitchen, and people were already filing into the dining hall.

Karen Spicer was third in the queue. She looked frozen, with her once pretty mousey blond hair, bundled into a loosely tied ponytail.

As she saw Ridley sitting inside the hall, she quickly came over to him, "Got a spare fag, Ridley. I ran out this morning and I am gasping," she said, helping herself to one of the cans of lager.

Ridley gave her a whole packet of the cigarettes John Mole had awarded as a bonus,

"Take these Karen, I have another packet," Ridley said. Despite her rough nature and brash manners, he liked the woman, who still did not trust him. Ridley wondered if Karen would ever be in a place where she could trust anyone again. Ridley was doubtful.

Karen did not say thank you, but that was normal. On the streets, manners were not important.

*Take whatever was offered, take whatever was given.*

That was her motto.

Ethel called out to Ridley, "Come and get some food, Ridley. You have earned it today." the old woman said, serving the first of the queuing men at the counter.

Ridley was hungry and needed no invitation. Walking over to the counter, Ethel made sure both he and Karen had a huge portion of her bubbling stew. It was Joshua who was spooning the food into bowls. Moving over to Joshua, Ethel nudged his arm and winked. Whispering to the man in the brimmed hat, she spoke quietly to make sure the rest of the people in the queue did not hear her:

"Give them both a double portion Joshua," she said cheekily.

As Ethel moved back into the kitchen, Joshua smiled and asked something that Ridley did not hear.

"What did he say?" Ridley asked.

Karen chuckled, taking her stew over to a nearby table,

"The man in the hat asked if you wanted anything nice to drink with your meal?" Karen said, sitting down to eat and try to warm up a little.

Ridley looked back towards the man, who continued to just stare at him. Taking the sting out of this man's glare Ridley replied, "A fine wine to accompany this meal would be good. Maybe a White wine, not sparkling?" Ridley added.

Karen laughed and pretended to fold the paper towel the cutlery was wrapped in, onto her lap.

Ridley followed her lead by lifting a pinkie finger away from the can of lager that was nearly finished and drank it like a posh person drinking tea.

For a while, they chatted as they ate the stew.

Ten minutes later Joshua appeared at the tableside, with a small brown paper bag. Winking to Ridley, he put his finger on his lips to silence Ridley from saying anything.

Ridley opened the bag. It was a good white wine, just as he ordered.

Joshua was a good man, perhaps someone he would like to know more about. John Mole's offer came back to him again.

Tomorrow, he would return to the Lord's Pantry, ready to start his way back to a life away from living under Tesco's car park. Tomorrow his life would start again. Looking around the room, John Mole was gone so he could not tell him that his mind was made up. Tomorrow would be a good day, for he was going to accept John Mole's kind offer of employment and the strange mission the manager spoke of.

Karen looked at the paper bag and made a face, "I bloody hate wine. Never liked it as a kid. Makes me sick." Karen said honestly.

Ridley pulled off another can of lager and passed it across to his friend. Karen did not even look up but took the can and opened it.

Opening the bag, Ridley took a swig of the uncorked wine bottle. It was cold and good. The last time he had drunk wine was the day he had told his parents that he was bisexual. He had not even finished the glass that day before his father was showing him to the door.

For the next hour, they ate Ethel's warm apple pie, as Ridley finished most of the wine. Walking back to the car park, Karen said she would join him later, but first, she had an errand to do.

Ridley knew this probably meant she needed to get a fix. Karen was still an addict, which Ridley was slowly helping her through. But Ridley knew that Karen still had places where for a simple packet of cigarettes or a can of lager, she would get her daily drug fix.

By the time he reached his Tesco stanchion he was surprised with how tired he felt. Admittedly, he knew today had worked his brain more than it had been used for over a year, but he felt truly exhausted.

Taking his tattered sleeping bag out from a carrier bag, he took off his coat and found the biscuits he wanted to give to Karen. This would be a good early breakfast for both of them tomorrow.

Laying down, he could barely keep his eyes open. Perhaps it was the wine? It had been a while since he drank good wine.

Taking the last few gulps from the bottle, he finished the wine and placed the paper bag down next to him.

Pulling up the 75" TV cardboard box around him, he allowed his head to rest on his rolled-up jumper pillow.

Within seconds he was asleep, dreaming of his new life and the mission John Mole had promised him. Tomorrow he would accept John's offer in the search for a proper comfy bed.

When Karen Spicer came back, still high from her fix, Ridley Goodman was cold and dead.

***

Joshua watched as the two homeless people talked over their stew dinner. The wine bottle that was now being eagerly consumed by the man called Ridley Goodman was all he needed to see. Today, God's will be done and the voice inside his head was ever more silent.

Joshua had befriended John Mole only three weeks before, introduced by Frederick Bannister who had shared a cell with the soup kitchen manager for two years.

Joshua had helped serve inside the Lord's Pantry kitchens and enjoyed the work. He especially loved working with the little old woman Ethel, who had taken a bit of a shine to him. Working in the kitchen, he knew it was just a matter of time before he discovered the whereabouts of God's last wolf.

*Find Ridley Goodman.*

*In the Lord's Pantry, you will watch him feasting.*

*This is the final wolf that must be culled from my flock.*

*You are chosen, Joshua. You are my shepherd. You will answer the prayers of the future.*

*He who stops the slaughter of my lambs.*

*You must Kill the final wolf of my flock, so the lambs can live in peace.*

*Do this Son of Adam and Eden will welcome you home!"*

Joshua thought about coming back to help out in this soup kitchen again, for he liked Ethel Reading. This woman seemed to like him too, and she reminded him of his dead mother. Her kindness was pure, beautiful, and genuine. But with Ridley Goodman walking back to wherever he slept at night with a stomach full of his last three hundred and fifty milligram of Pentobarbital hidden within the white wine, the man would not see tomorrow.

God had told Joshua this was the last person he needed to kill. Joshua still did not know why these people were chosen to die. None of them looked to be evil or even able to do great harm to the world.

But Joshua knew that God was not to be questioned.

For *His* will to be done, Joshua needed to be obedient no matter how much he hated the tasks given.

Joshua knew he was now close to finding Eden.

But to find Eden, he had needed to act as the Serpent.

Three murders were a very high price to pay to find the road back to salvation.

# Chapter 17

## Conscience

### Timeline—24 April 2018

Nick Murray nearly jumped out of his skin when the phone on his desk started to ring out. For the past two days, his phone had been constantly in his hand, so it never had the chance to ring before he was on it again.

Lifting the receiver, PC Sally Gunel announced that a lady from a local religious order wanted to speak with him urgently. DS Nick knew this was already a filtered call, as both Sergeant Parson and PC Gunel were working tirelessly to find the small nugget of gold in the river of rubbish.

Nick asked Sally to put the woman through, "DS Nick Murray, how may I be of assistance?" Nick asked, his voice friendly and professional.

All he could hear was silence, apart from what Nick thought to be a choir singing in the background. He was about to ask again when a deep voice came onto the phone, quiet and unsure,

"Good Morning, DS Murray. My name is… Chaplin… Marina Gracely. I would very much like to speak to you, but I will not discuss what I have to say on the phone, I wish to speak in person sir." Mary Grace whispered from her balcony.

On her radio, the gentle sound of Christian song echoed out across the flat.

Two days before, Mary was feeling uncomfortable.

The was nothing physically wrong with her, but she could feel a weight on her heart that left her in turmoil.

It had started the previous day. Mary never liked to watch much TV, but always made sure she kept up with the local news. This six p.m. ritual was usually to understand if she needed to avoid certain city roads or know of God's weather to come.

The rest of the news was often depressing. Mary hated anything to do with politics, wars in foreign lands, and violence. Why people could not live-in peace was beyond her.

Tonight, Mary was eating alone.

Both Frederick and Barnaby were becoming regular visitors to this hour, which Mary did not mind, as she loved cooking for them both. As single bachelors, Mary liked to think that her friends had at least one good meal inside them a day.

Often the three of them would eat, before taking to the streets to try to sell her books. Whatever profits could be made by Mary's vain attempt to re-create how to speak with God, she would always put it back into funding Eden's Echo.

So far, the book had paid for the Chapel to be completely repainted, a new wooden lectern and most importantly, a huge tea urn for the after-sermon gatherings.

Mary was eating a cooked Haddock. Its strong distinct aroma had filled her flat, which she liked. It was not cooked to perfection like her mother would have done, but it was edible. With the door to the harbour facing balcony wide open, she knew that after the meal it would soon clear the smell.

Fish was the food for the soul. It always helped her think. It was rare she served fish when she had guests, but that was more out of the consideration for the lingering smells it left.

Bristol was filled with excellent fishmongers. Much of the fish was fresh. In her small congregation, two fishmongers liked to treat Mary with occasional gifts. This was very sweet of them, although she now had a freezer full of such gifts. It was surprising how many of her flock like to offer gifts. Mary did not like to turn anyone down when they felt their kindness was so well received. But the greengrocer, market seller, flower shop owner and milkman all liked to leave small tokens of thanks.

Finding God had helped them all become better people. This was something each of them felt needed rewarding.

Mary finished her fish and took the plate to the sink. Opening the large fridge there was still a half watermelon that she had shared and not finished with Frederick yesterday. It was already sliced and looked delicious. The market-trader had told her they were the best he had ever tasted, which Mary had thought was just market call talk, but the man had been good to his word. They were juicy and melted in the mouth.

Taking the watermelon and a spoon back to the wooden table, she sprinkled a little sugar over the bowl. This was always a sin to the waistline, but Mary already knew this was a battle she had lost long ago.

Reaching for the remote control, she switched on the news.

After several adverts telling people about extra strong toilet paper and cat food that was good enough for humans to eat, the familiar news theme tune started to play.

As per usual, Mary quickly whispered a word to God to pray that today's headlines were not of violence or poverty.

This was a prayer God rarely answered.

There had been so much news about horrific death of late, it was something that haunted her always. With the country also split right down the middle with talks of Brexit, there was no peace or tolerance given by either side. The country seemed to be on edge, with camps entrenched for a long war ahead. Civil war loomed where hatred blossomed.

Mary did not care about what any of the politics meant, all she wished was for people to understand that God wanted them all to hear Him, no matter who they were.

As Charles Wyndham had put it simply in his book,

*In God's name, men go off to war,*
*Take away war and God still remains.*
*God is calling, but we do not listen.*
*God is calling, but we do not hear Him,*
*God is so close, but we push Him away.*

Mary watched as the pretty newscaster appeared on the screen. The Scarlett red dress the lady was wearing instantly prepared Mary for a story of blood. In Mary's humble opinion, all women that read the news often colour coordinated to the stories they would read. This was probably sub-conscious and total nonsense, but Mary liked to listen and judge her thoughts on the first line the women delivered.

*"Good Evening.*

*The headlines tonight in the West Country.*

*Police release a photo image of a person of interest to them on the murders of three people across the west country.*

*Police would like to question this man before The Spiker has a chance to strike again.*

*The public is being urged not to approach this man."*

Mary was about to smile as her theory was proved right yet again when suddenly the sweet taste of sugared melon in her mouth felt bitter and sour. Dropping the spoon back onto her plate, she felt a cold inner wind blow through her soul.

On the TV screen, she could see the picture of a man in a

wide-brimmed hat. It was not an exact likeness, but Mary was almost certain she knew who this was.

The screen flicked back to the news presenter, as she gave out phone numbers and email address for anyone who recognised this man.

With her melon bowl still half-filled, Mary was in no mood to finish her dish. Instead, she felt as if she could faint.

Moving across the room, Mary sat down on a chair placed on her narrow balcony, to allow the fresh April air to breathe inside and calm her.

Mary was completely sure the man on the screen was Joshua Wright. If it was not him, it was someone who looked a lot like the man. Mary had not made a note of the phone number from the TV. All she could do was watch the ten p.m. broadcast to confirm her fears.

Since reading Joshua, Frederick, and Barnaby the final chapters of Charles Wyndham's teachings, Mary had seen very little of Joshua. Over the last year, Joshua was always the first person to arrive in the chapel hall and often the last to leave. But after that difficult night inside this flat, Joshua had only attended her services twice.

Mary had questioned him about it, but Joshua seemed to be at peace, stating his work was keeping him very busy. Frederick had tried to visit Joshua in the evenings, but both times he had just found an empty house. Mary was worried that the effect of whatever Joshua has heard the evening where God had finally spoken to him, was too much. This would not be a surprise, as the same had happened when Mary heard Him speak.

It had taken her several weeks to come to terms with the revealed Lord. Now she accepted His voice as she did with the TV newscaster, it was there when she needed it, and it gave her great comfort and hope.

Perhaps Mary needed to speak with Joshua, as this was probably her old mind showing her something that was not true.

Calming herself, she remembered when she has sat out on this very balcony the night after the last chapters. Joshua had been excited, but full of fear. As he spoke to Mary, it was as if he knew that his world had changed forever. Mary felt her heart leap when Joshua had spoken of the clear voice in his head. This was a rare event to hear so clearly, for most only ever heard vague whispers or moments on the wind.

But, as Joshua told her of the words he had heard from God's voice, Mary continued to smile, but could not help but feel a genuine worry, as she thought he must be mistaken.

On one hand, she was over the moon that with her help and hours of training, it had taken Joshua to this high level of Charles Wyndham's revelation. Teaching the talented Joshua Wright had been wonderful, as he was a sponge to everything Mary had to tell him.

Mary felt a huge sense of pride, that though her, this man was now in a direct commune to the Lord God.

But Joshua, through God's words and joyous revelation was also testing Mary on something she could not bring herself to believe.

Where did this leave her?

To deny him would be to deny her teaching.

To deny him, would dismiss her life's work.

Mary had not told either Frederick or Barnaby of what Joshua had told her that night. In truth, Mary still did not know how to interpret Joshua's message.

That same evening, Mary had written the message down, to read again when she was alone. Mary needed time to digest and understand what God was telling Joshua to do. If it was truly God he was hearing.

Mary took out the small scrap of paper she had written on. As she read the words again, it was difficult for her to comprehend. Mary knew that God spoke only of what he expected. God was to be obeyed, no matter how it tested to person. But these words now had a worrying relevance,

*Joshua, you are my shepherd and I love you for it.*

*You are my shepherd and he who will stop the wolves.*

*For the lambs to grow into sheep, you must kill these wolves for me.*

*For when the wolves gather, they will hunt in packs.*

*Do this for me, Son of Adam, and Eden will welcome you.*

Mary had tried her best to interpret what he had been told. Joshua had asked Mary several times about what killing the wolves meant. Was there a passage in the Bible this referred to? Was this a message for Joshua alone to know?

Mary did not know and could not answer him.

Mary wondered if God was trying to tell Joshua to be cautious about who was teaching him. Mary knew that Joshua had taken to listening to many American Evangelical pastors online who all spoke of God's words and ways to speak with the Lord. Looking through her huge biblical studies and countless texts and books, Mary did find one biblical reference that seemed to make sense of the words. It was from Matthew 7:15,

"Beware of the false prophets, who come to you in sheep's clothing, but inwardly are ravenous wolves."

This made good sense. Even Mary had seen her fill with false prophets over the years. Fundamental Christianism was becoming a pandemic across the world. Evangelical movements, especially across America were rife and full of preachers convincing their parishioners to give them money for God's holy cause. Why would God need money?

There was also another passage Mary found that spoke of Biblical references of lambs and sheep.

Isaiah 65:25,

"And the wolf with dwell with the lamb."

Matthew 10:16

"Behold, I send you out as sheep amid wolves."

All of these could be what God was referring to, but Mary was still unsure.

What was *he who stops the wolves?* and to ask Joshua to *kill the wolves for me* was breaking the fundamental rule to scripture, You Shall not murder.

Mary had spent days trying to understand Joshua's calling.

Only a week ago, Joshua had spoken to Mary on the phone. It was only a brief call, mainly for Joshua to thank Mary for showing him the path back to Eden. Mary was very happy that Joshua had found his peace and knew of God. But just before he hung up the phone, he had said something to Mary that again worried her.

Joshua told Mary that the message now made sense to him. Mary had wanted to ask why, but it was clear Joshua wanted to end the call.

Mary placed the small piece of paper back into her skirt pocket. Picking up the phone, she dialled Joshua's number.

It just rang and rang with no answer.

The following morning Mary did something that she had never done in her life before. Walking to a nearby local newsagent, Mary purchased a newspaper.

On the cover, the photo of the man she saw on the TV last night was staring back at her. This man was said to be linked to three murders, all seemingly innocent victims with no apparent links to each other.

Mary stared at the man on the photofit, in her heart she knew this was Joshua. When she read the line of an apple tree ring with a coiled snake, Mary was convinced.

As God had told her through the voice of Frederick Bannister, Mary had saved this man from suicide and eternal damnation. Through Mary, this man had not only learned how to hear God, but she had also given him a reason to live again.

But, if this man had committed the terrible crimes that were being reported, Mary had another calling. What would be the point in saving a man, for him only to kill others.

Only God knew this answer.

The following day, after a night of trying to speak and get answers from God, Mary had made her decision. With regret, as this was one of the hardest decisions she had ever made, Mary dialled the number of the police from the newspaper.

"Good Morning, Bath Police station. PC Sally Gunel speaking, how can I be of service today?" a friendly voice asked on the phone.

Mary could hear the well-trained customer service person at the end of the call. Just for the briefest of moments, she thought of dropping the phone again.

But a voice in her head changed her mind.

*"The lambs are all safe Marina. Bring Joshua home."*

Mary had never heard a voice like it before. It was as if she was on the phone with another person.

"Yes…my Name is Marina Gracely. May I please speak to DS Nick Murray." Mary said, knowing that even if the voice inside her head was her conscience talking to her, this was the right and only course of action to take.

# Chapter 18

## Deliver Us from Evil

### Timeline—24 April 2018

The roads into Bristol city centre were fully congested. DS Nick could not think of any other way to circumnavigate the city roads through the city without adding a huge number of miles to the journey. Sadly, he just needed to sit and put up with the rush hour traffic.

Nick's white Audi TT was air conditioned warm, and although the car was less than happy with the start/stop journey through the five p.m. commuters, it was fuel saving and comfortable.

After Marina Gracely's concerned call, DS Nick had gone straight to Sergeant Parsons for him to run a full check on her name. Immediately he found a picture of the Chaplain, who was shown to be a large black woman with a smile that simply pulled you in.

Marina's profile revealed she had worked in many places of worship over her lifetime, including several years inside the deepest Bible belt of evangelical America. Over the past ten years, Marina had authored three books, all of which were religiously based around a common theme. Working as Chaplain in her later life, she had found another calling to work inside prisons across the south-west, bringing the word of God to poor souls who were serving time. Marina stated in her books that she wanted all prisoners to find a righteous path away from the darkness that had delivered them too evil. This had led her to write her first book, titled, The Road back to God.

Marina Gracely's immediate family background check showed her to be the daughter of a village clergy, who in the 1970s had been working as the main vicar in the Stockton-on - Avon church.

Checking further police records and information searches, Sergeant Parsons discovered that the woman's father had also worked for a while inside the St Alfred's school, delivering sermons for religious studies. Marina's mother had worked in the school kitchens as head cook some years ago, retiring to live in Sussex. Both parents were now dead.

The whole family had lived for five years inside the Old Rectory, which just by coincidence happened to be the site where the first murder victim was discovered. DS Nick felt his heart beating again at the mention of the name of The Old Rectory. Why was this old house haunting him?

DS Nick was fascinated by what Sergeant Parsons investigations were telling him, as they all looked to be important leads on this case. The more DS Nick heard of King Alfred's school, Stockton-on-Avon, and The Old Rectory, the more he knew this must be significant to this case.

So far, Nick could not see the link. Marina Gracely did look to be another suspect, but Nick wanted to rule this out himself.

PC Sally walked over and joined them both.

Trying to impress the female officer, Sergeant Parsons quickly took control of the conversation, "I think I may have cracked this case boss. Do you want me to run her in? This link is certainly enough to get her in for questioning. If she is not involved, I think Marina Gracely must know our murderer. What do you think Sal?" Sergeant Parsons asked.

DS Nick looked at the screen. Although this did all seem to be linked to victims in the case, there was nothing that could bind this woman to any of the murders. It was Sally that convinced him to at least follow this up, "Boss, I have found something else on Chaplain Marina Gracely that may be of interest. Some years ago, as Mike says. Marina started working as the Chaplin in many of the smaller prisons within the area. Marina tried to help anyone who needed to find another direction in life. Marina made it her life's work to rehabilitate criminals and give them something other than the choice of falling back into crime."

"As Mike says, Marina is also a bit of an amateur author. She has written a couple of religious books about how to talk to God? I know. I thought that too before you say anything."

"Anyway, ten years ago she founded a small religious community in the area that has many ex-prisoners attending her small congregation. I suppose they all find a sort of comradeship after serving time together. But you are not going to believe what it is called Boss?" PC Sally Gunel, said, holding out a small printed off piece of paper from the printer.

DS Nick looked down at the picture on the paper. Smiling he took it off Sally and nodded his thanks, "Good work Mike. Good work PC Gunel. This is the link I needed." DS Nick said, heading to get his coat from the office.

Sergeant Parsons leant over to Sally and whispered into her ear, "Another Gold medal performance Sally. You will be looking for my job soon?" Mike Parsons told her.

Sally nodded, "That's the idea," she said, walking away to the shocked face of the sergeant.

On the passenger seat of the Audi TT, DS Nick looked over

at the small piece of paper Sally had printed out. It was only a small photo, but the picture on the pamphlet was enough for Nick to move quickly. This was too much of a coincidence not to take very seriously as it was a definite image of the ring Joshua was wearing, as described by Karen Spicer.

The paper copy of the printer pamphlet showed a community called:

*Eden's Echo – Come to Us and Hear God's Voice.*

At the foot of the pamphlet, similar to the one Nick had found in the entrance of the crematorium after DS Pete's funeral, there was a tiny logo of an apple tree. This time the logo on Sally's printout had a coiled snake wrapped around the tree trunk.

DS Nick had never really taken religion that seriously, apart from attending occasional weddings and funerals. These sorts of pamphlet were just words of recruiting evangelists. There was nothing illegal in claiming or printing what was shown in the title, the rights of religious claims were not in question. But the small logo on this pamphlet was an exact representation of what Ethel and Karen had tried to describe and draw. This organisation was run as the new pamphlet said, by Chaplain Mary Grace, it was the first real lead since find the name of Joshua, that made sense.

Sergeant Parsons was right.

This woman who had called Nick, knew something.

For a couple of days after the funeral, Nick had tried to call the phone number printed on the old red pamphlet he took from the crematorium, but it just went to a single dead tone. This number was long out of service, and the group called The Friends of Adam long since disbanded as far back as 2013. This lead seemed to be going nowhere fast, so Nick had quickly turned his attention back to Karen Spicer and Ethel's description of the man.

From what Sally had printed in her picture, this was a recently created pamphlet, showing a picture of Chaplain Mary Grace holding a copy of her printed book. What DS Nick must have picked up before, inside the crematorium was very old, which should have not surprised him considering how dusty the pamphlets were on the small table he found them on.

*"Who reads pamphlets at a funeral?"* Celia had asked him as he pushed it deep into this pocket.

The caller this morning had called herself Marina Gracely. This was no coincidence. Perhaps she likes to be known under a pseudonym for the books she wrote. Many authors of religion took this method of protection. A search on the police databases found the woman to have no previous criminal records. But a search on the databases also discovered that there was no such ordained Chaplin called Mary Grace on their records. How Marina had managed to get into prison without these checks was a problem for another day.

A quick search on Eden's Echo showed that a Miss Marina Gracely, lived on the Bristol Harbourside, in a new development where many of the flats were extremely expensive. Marina lived near a small community hall that was known to host a local prayer group twice a week, known as Eden's Echo.

PC Gunel had provided DS Nick with street map showing how to get to Miss Marina Gracely's flat, which looked to be right above the Eden's Echo community hall. Sally checks revealed that Marina not only owned the flat, but she was the sole owner of the community hall beneath. Marina also own six other houses across Bristol that she rented out to ex-prisoners at a very knocked down cost.

This woman was clearly not struggling for money.

Finally, a real breakthrough in the case.

With constant press coverage and Nick receiving heat from above to get "The Spiker" into custody as soon as possible, DS Nick needed a quick breakthrough. If this woman was nothing to do with the case, he was pretty sure she knew who was. The photo fit had caused her to lift the phone, and that had been enough to start the dominos falling as they fell towards whoever Joshua was.

DS Nick pulled up outside of the community hall at 5.23 p.m. Traffic had been awful. Nick had told Marina Gracely that he would be with her by five p.m. Nick now wished he had listened to Sally as she suggested DS Nick told Marina it would be closer to five thirty p.m. by the time, he crossed Bristol city centre at this time of the day.

Parking the Audi TT up on the dockside, it was a lovely evening. Several large boats bobbed up and down on the water, with the sun just seen setting behind the buildings on the far side of the docks. There was no doubt this was not a place for those without plenty of money.

All along the harbourside, new developments stood tall. Many of the higher-level apartments had shops below them, snaking their way around the dock's pathway. This place had been designed to be expensive and designer in looks. Several restaurants and exclusive bistros lined the walkway, many with customers sat outside enjoying the late sunny evening.

The short trek from the car park to the little community hall was off the main walkway. Most would have not even noticed the sign on the doorway unless you were specifically looking for it.

**Welcome to Eden's Echo.**

**All Are Welcome.**

**Meetings Tuesday and Thursday nights at six p.m. and**

**eight p.m.**

**In God's Grace with Hear Him**

**All Meetings Hosted by Chaplain Mary Grace**

DS Nick pressed the buzzer. Within seconds a voice replied,

"Please come up DS Murray. I was expecting you earlier." a female voice said.

The distinct click of a locked door sounded. Above him, a CCTV camera watched him enter.

DS Nick pushed the door open and walked inside. There was a small door leading off to what looks to be a large room lined with chairs and several benches. At the front of the room, a large cloth cross hung from hooks on a wall. Nick starred through the window of a door, into the room. This was the community hall made out to look like a small chapel. A table formed into a lectern at the front of the rows of chairs had a silver framed picture of Christ on the cross and another smaller picture Nick knew well. It showed God reaching out to Adam. It was the same picture Nick had on his fireplace at home.

In front of him, a set of steep stairs went upwards, where he knew Marina's flat to be. Walking up the stairs, the door at the top was wide open ready to receive him.

DS Nick called out before entering, "Hello, DS Nick Murray here to see Miss Marina Gracely." DS Nick stood patiently waiting.

A voice from inside the flat answered, "Please come in DS Murray. Come join me on the balcony, it is such a fine evening, and I do hate to be cramped up inside on such a beautiful day. I am afraid I have a prayer meeting at six p.m. tonight, so I am sorry to say our conversation will need to be brief." Mary Grace called out.

DS Nick walked through the flat and passed a huge wooden

table, covered in books at several burning candles. Behind the table, a huge bookcase was filled with dozens of books, nearly all looking to be of religious material. There were a few cookbooks, but these looked to be untouched for years. Nick could see a small kitchenette at the end of the room, with a lit-up oven purring with fan noise.

Walking across the room, he could see the large black woman in her late seventies or early eighties sat on an armchair, outside a pair of French windows on a narrow balcony.

As he reached the balcony, he took out his badge and spoke, "Good evening madam. I am DS Nick Murray. We spoke on the phone earlier today." DS Nick said, walking out into the brilliant sunlight. The view across the docks was stunning, somewhere he knew Celia would love to see.

Mary Grace stood and shook his hand, without asking, she began pouring a cup of tea as she spoke, "I like to sit in the sun DS Murray. it reminds me of South Africa when I was a very young girl. Most people call me Mary these days. I was born and christened Marina Gracely, but it was my father who first called me Mary. I never liked Marina, so I just kept it to Mary. I don't know why Gracely ever got shortened, but for a woman of God, DS-Murray, Mary Grace does fit the bill rather well, I hope you agree?" Mary told the man, offering him milk and sugar.

DS Nick thanked Mary for the tea. Although he was mainly a coffee man, he did not dislike the taste of heavily brewed tea from a proper china teapot.

"You wanted to talk to me about the photofit madam. As you are aware from the news reports, this is a dangerous man, any information leading to his arrest is very important to us." DS Nick told her, spotting the local newspaper of the West Chronicle resting on the arm of her chair, half-folded with the cover page showing the photofit picture.

Mary nodded.

"Yes, I can see that these crimes have been troubling. I am appalled at what I have seen. But, before I speak to you of this, I need to talk to you of faith and trust in what I do detective. I hope you will see Sir, that what I say to you tonight goes against everything I try to preach. My conscience to serve God is being tested against my need to serve the law." Mary added, sitting down with her teacup.

DS Nick felt the weight of her stare in his eyes. This was a woman who was feeling a sense of heavy guilt as she clearly knew the man in the photo.

"Do you know Joshua Madam? He must be found before he has a chance to strike again." DS Nick told her, with a sense of urgency in his voice.

Mary ignored him.

"Are you a religious man DS Murray?" Mary asked.

DS Nick was a little frustrated but did not want to lose her trust so decided to play along, "Not really. I was Christened, but I am no regular church goer." Nick confessed, taking a sip of the piping hot tea.

Mary nodded as if she knew the answer anyway.

"Many are like you, DS Murray. They only know of God when it suits them. But when I preach Sir, I try to help those discover a personal relationship with God. I have studied texts and written books for over fifty years, all showing me how God is closer to us all than anyone thinks." Mary told him.

DS Nick pressed again,

"Did you teach Joshua these skills to know God?" DS Murray asked.

Marry nodded.

"When I met the man, he was broken, in despair and on the brink of suicide. Through God, I have shown him another pathway. Through God's grace alone, he has changed his world around to become a good man sir. His faith in what I have shown him is absolute I am sure of this. Probably the best student I have ever known. He does so much good in the community and local area." Mary said, looking again at DS Nick's to read his expression.

Nick put down the tea.

"We are only looking to bring this man in for questioning. There is nothing to charge him on. But we do need to speak with him. Joshua cannot be charged for the religion he follows, but religion holds no shelter for murderers." DS Nick replied.

Mary just continued to stare.

"This DS Murray is my problem. At Eden's Echo, we show people how to speak with God and hear His words. This is a skill learned by only the best of my congregation. To achieve a personal relationship with God requires devotion and complete piety."

"So, with this thought sir, if I now tell you that Joshua did hear the voice of God, and He was told to kill for him, where does that leave me and my congregation. I am deeply struggling to come to terms with whatever has put Joshua on this dark pathway, but to deny that he did not hear His voice, means to contradict my very teaching.

Joshua is sure he heard the Lord's voice. Joshua claims that the Lord told him to kill for Him. Like Abraham in the Bible sir, Joshua was just following instruction."

"For me to dismiss this, is to rubbish my entire life." Mary Grace told the stunned Nick.

DS Nick needed to keep things down to earth and real,

"There is another possibility. What if Joshua was just using you as an excuse to kill. It is difficult to prove that a voice in his head was pushing him to murder innocent people. From what I know of God, this would not be tolerated in any way. Joshua is either very clever or deluded, both are dangerous." DS Nick said, regretting instantly using the word deluded.

Mary nodded.

"I thought I was deluded the first time I heard Him. For weeks I questioned what I was being told. God told me to help prisoners DS Murray. For fifteen years I have helped prisoners find a better way. I have provided them homes and a new pathway of good. God has always been the answer.

But I am now in a place where I should just dismiss all I have been teaching, as it has fuelled the actions of what you believe to be a deluded man."

Mary looked out over the water, "I will of course give you Joshua's address. I have no wish to see any more people killed. If Joshua is to blame for these terrible crimes, I am at a loss to how I must move on."

"It is a terrible problem for me, Sir.

You have heard of the garden of Eden, I am sure.

This is the place where God first spoke to mankind in the form of Adam.

Eden was a beautiful paradise. It was a place God had made on Earth for all the creatures of the world to live in peace with Him.

Adam was made as to the gardener of Eden, someone to watch over God's creation and protect it. Adam was able to speak with God as a son to a father, they were as a family. God saw that Adam was lonely so in His grace, he made Adam a mate, Eve, who loved him as a wife should. Together they lived in the harmony of God's voice as friends."

"All was wonderful until the day Adam took a bite from the forbidden apple. Eve was deceived by the temptation of the serpent's call. God cast him, and eventually Eve out of the harmony of Eden, into a world where God's voice was lost to him."

"This is a story I know you have heard before DS Murray. But the act of talking to God has been accepted completely throughout time.

Even today we try to speak to God through prayer and hope for a better life.

But what do we say to people, if they tell you God has answered their prayers or spoken to them?

Most are considered to be madmen or as you say...*deluded.*"

"But if I am to try to make sense of this problem Sir, I have come to only one conclusion.

For years I have tried to show people that it is God's voice calling out. Eden's Echo was how to find God again.

But, in the story of Eden, another voice is not spoken of. One that is commonly spoken through the voice of Eve, damning all women for eternity. I speak of the original sin Sir, where Eve presented Adam with the forbidden fruit of an apple."

"One bite cast mankind into the darkness forever. So, what is my point to all this?"

DS Nick listened, as he knew the woman was going to tell him who Joshua was and the location. If she needed to find some kind of justification of why Joshua has used her and the God she loved to kill, DS Nick thought it only fair to wait.

Mary Grace continued as Nick took up his tea again, "The other voice in Eden was that of the serpent. Who told Eve to give the apple to Adam? We later came to know the serpent as Satan."

"I teach people how to hear God calling them back to Eden. What if Joshua, like Eve, heard the voice of Satan? It is difficult for me to dismiss this, for the dark one is just as likely to talk to us, tempting us from finding God's Grace again. Perhaps Joshua heard the wrong voice and with this, he has found his way to sin?" Mary Grace said, shaking her head in sadness.

DS Nick placed the empty teacup back on the table.

"I can see this is difficult for you Madam, but whatever the truth, I want to make sure that nobody else gets hurt. That's all I want to do." DS Nick offered.

For a while Mary Grace said nothing, looking blankly out into the harbourside.

The ping alarm of her oven suddenly went off, snapping her back to life. Standing slowly, she made her way inside, followed by DS Nick. The clock on the oven was showing 5.50 p.m.

Mary opened the oven and took out what looked to be a quite burnt pastry topped pie.

"I was never much of a cook DS Murray. My mother tried hard to show me, but I never learned the true secrets of cooking. I must go downstairs soon as my parishioners will be starting to arrive for the Bible reading tonight."

DS Nick understood.

"Madam, anything you can give men to help with our investigations would be very useful. We are very concerned that this man may well strike again. No one deserves to die. Was it not a commandment, thou shalt not kill?" DS Nick said, trying to get this woman of God on his side.

Mary placed the pie onto the countertop to cool.

"A common misconception DS Murray. The actual Jewish translation in scripture is Do Not Murder. This is very clear and simple for all men to know. I know Joshua is a good man Sir. I am sure of it. Whatever voice he is hearing, it is not my God. Stop the murders, DS Murray, there should be no more killings in His name. Deliver us from evil." Mary Grace said.

Reaching deep into her skirt pocket, she withdrew a large, folded piece of paper. DS Nick opened it out.

On the paper was written an address just outside of Bristol and a full name.

### *Joshua Wright.*

DS Nick Murray thanked Mary and promised that he would make sure that this man was caught quickly and treated fairly.

As he left the flat and descended the steep stairs. Mary was waddling behind him.

People were coming into the door below and making their way into the community hall. DS Nick stopped to let a few people through the small doorway.

As he stood waiting, a man appeared and looked visibly white as he walked up towards DS Nick stood on the bottom stair.

Nick instantly recognised the man. The last time he had seen him, was the day a judge had passed the sentence of five years after killing his mother-in-law in a hit and run.

Barnaby Barnes had not been prepared at all. As he walked through the door to the community hall, the face of DS Nick Murray was stood staring at him. It was a face he would always remember, for it was the same man who had appeared at this door the night after he had run over the old woman on the street.

Mary had told Barnaby that if the old woman had not been killed that night, Barnaby would have committed a terrible crime killing up to five people with a shotgun. Mary was convinced that God had intervened that night, stating that he had judged what he thought to be the lesser of two evils or the greater good.

For the past six years, Barnaby had been looking for a way

to come to terms with his crime. Killing the old woman had been something he prayed to change ever since.

Mary Grace had always said that one day, God would grant Barnaby a chance to apologise for his crime.

Barnaby prayed each day for his chance to say sorry to the family he destroyed. In all Barnaby's training with Mary, he had still never managed to hear God's voice, but he knew that His will was channelled and one day he would get a chance to redeem himself.

DS Nick was shocked to see this man. As he approached, Nick wondered if he should just walk by without saying anything. How much pain had this man had brought to Celia over the last few years was impossible to gauge?

Celia was still in counselling.

The ability to just walk past was instantly made hopeless as Barnaby Barnes spoke to him, "Good evening DS Murray. It's good to see you again. I hope your wife is… coping." Barnaby said, offering out his hand.

DS Nick had no intention of shaking it,

"Barnaby Barnes. Has it been five years? They have passed by far too quickly, especially for my wife after losing her mother to your reckless driving." DS Nick replied as Mary Grace stepped around them.

Barnaby could not expect anything else. Taking a deep breath, he continued.

"Since that day, I have prayed so hard to bring peace to your wife. I have hoped for a chance to say sorry. I am deeply so sorry for what happened that night. I just wanted you and your wife to know this. I do not seek forgiveness from you. I only hope that God knows of my regret." Barnaby said, shaking his head.

Mary spoke.

"All men seek forgiveness. None of us is ever truly free of sin." Mary said, placing her hand on Barnaby's shoulder.

DS Nick felt anger, not forgiveness.

Pushing past Barnaby Barnes, DS Nick turned at the doorway and spoke, just before leaving the building, "Not all men are murderers. I appreciate your sentiment but knowing you have found peace after killing my mother-in-law, will not be enough to let my wife sleep at night. All men may seek forgiveness Miss Gracely, but there is no rule to say it will, or should be given.

Thank you, Miss Gracely, for your help today. My team will be in touch very soon."

DS Nick allowed the door to close behind him. Inside he could see Barnaby Barnes speaking with Mary.

# Chapter 19

## Seek and Ye Shall find

Timeline six fifteen p.m.—24 April 2018

By the time DS Nick reached the station, there was already a police car outside of Joshua Wright's house.

Sergeant Parsons and two officers knocked hard on the old wooden door.

After unsuccessfully pressing the doorbell button, the three officers were now looking for other options.

Sergeant Parsons decided to try the rear entrance, which was much more difficult than he first imagined. Behind the house a tall garden fence, bordered a small gravel pathway, allowing rear access into the six terraced homes. This was obviously not somewhere where any of the residents regularly walked, as it was stacked high with old, damaged furniture, several over spilling boxes, and piles of old chopped branches that had not been taken away to the dump.

Mike Parsons climbed over an old set of three drawers. The wood was wet and slimy, unpleasant to the touch. As he tried to vault the drawers, the wood gave away and his hand went through into the top drawer.

Feeling a sudden pain, Mike withdrew his hand and could see a long cut and a splinter in his palm. The splinter was easy to pull clear, but the cut was bleeding. Taking a tissue out from his trouser pocket, he did a rough job of patching the wound.

Continuing along the cluttered pathway, he found the gate that led into the rear garden of Joshua Wright's house.

It was six feet high and looked to be pretty sturdy to the push. It seemed to be bolted shut.

Reaching over the top of the gate, Mike found a rusty bolt in place. It was extremely stiff to move, but it did finally give way.

All this was good news, as the gate was locked from the inside. With the pathway so cluttered, it was pretty clear that nobody had tried to escape the house using this entrance.

Looking at the state of the overgrown garden beyond, the grass needed a manchette to clear as some of the bushes grew out wildly over the broken slabbed pathway, Sergeant Parsons knew that this was a place that no one came into often.

Climbing over brambles and doing his best to avoid the tall angry looking crop of nettles lining the pathway, Sergeant Parsons found his way to the top of three step s leading down to a plastic kitchen door.

The door was a typical two glass panel structure, with a figure of eight framework. It looked solid enough, newer than the windows of the house.

Knocking hard on the glass, Mike Parsons radioed back to his colleagues at the front of the house, "I am at the rear door. I don't think anyone has come out this way in years." Mike told his officers.

There was no answer after his second knock.

Looking through the kitchen window, Mike could see a tidy kitchen, but it needed modernisation. One of the cupboard doors looked to be hanging slightly, but it was not at all ragged. The worktops were clean and the sink empty of washing up. It all looked in order.

Looking along with the narrow galley kitchen, Mike could see a table, which seemed to be covered in paperwork. None of what was on the table was easy to see from his position.

Sadly, the only way to see the table properly was to look through the dining room window, which meant tackling the bed of nettles in front of it, some of which were four feet high.

Sometimes, police work was painful, he thought.

Moving back up the steps, he made his way slowly through the long grass and on towards the dining room window. Carefully Mike pushed the nettles back with a stick he found, but not without taking at least three stings to his hands and legs. Under the window, a huge bramble bush looked menacing. The green spring leaves were hiding the sharp thorns beneath. Mike pushed ever forward, leaning over the brambles as far as he could dare to peer into the window.

It was a difficult angle, but Mike could now see the table. Although the piles of papers and books were stacked high, they were neat. Mike read the titles of the first three books.

IS GOD SPEAKING TO ME? – Lyre Tennille

GODS VOICE – Michel Makleworth

THUS, SAITH TO LORD – John Beveren

Sergeant Parsons could see that all of the books looked to be along the same theme. To see the other end of the table, Mike needed to lean further towards the window.

Placing his still bleeding hand on the window ledge, he moved his body carefully into the brambles. It was not as bad as he first thought. The problem would be when he wanted to move away, as he could feel a thick bramble already gripping his leg.

Sometimes, police work needed to be painful, he thought.

Pressing his face up to the single pain window, he could now see the rest of the table clearly. One book was wedged open, at a specific page. Sergeant Parsons could see the title in bold at the foot of the page, but could not read the words above.

How to Hear God - Chaplain Mary Grace.

Mike's eyes moved across to the newspapers. The first was a local weekly journal, showing a picture of the face of the schoolboy Phillip Stevens. The next paper had no picture, but the story was about the estate agent in Salisbury who had been found dead inside her bathroom.

This was what they needed. This must be their man.

Mike needed to urgently get hold of a warrant to get in. If this man was hiding inside, Mike wanted him arrested immediately.

Pushing back from the brambles, Mike winced as the thorns cut deep into his legs. By the time he was fully upright again, Mike knew that at least three places on his legs were bleeding like the wound on his hand.

If anyone could see him, they would think he had tackled the man inside. Mike Parsons had suffered fewer injuries a week ago, and that day he had been holding a full riot shield facing two thousand Redemption Rebellion protestors in the centre Bristol.

Radioing back to the central station, Mike wanted to make sure nothing was misunderstood, "Mike Bravo 488, dispatch, are you receiving?"

A voice came back instantly, "Receiving you Mike Bravo 488. Go Ahead."

Mike spoke again, "Mike Bravo 488, we are at the home of suspect Joshua Wright. I have spotted evidence that needs further investigation. Request building entry warrant urgently. Over."

The voice came back again, "Mike Bravo 488 this is Despatch. Please wait while I escalate."

Mike Parsons made his way back up the overgrown garden.

Carefully he climbed over the drawers in the rear pathway and walked back down the side of the building, re-joining his waiting officers. The radio burst into life again.

"Mike Bravo 488, warrant pending. Please wait onsite. Can you confirm siting of a suspect?" the voice asked.

Mike lifted the radio again.

"Mike Bravo 488, no confirmed siting. We need to check the second floor, but the ground floor looks to be empty. Suggest full house search."

The despatch voice came back again.

"Mike Bravo 488, this is a condition five. Please remain onsite. We will send another team to you with the search warrant. It is vital that if the owner arrives home, he is brought in for questioning, do you receive?"

Sergeant Parsons replied, calling his officers back from the police car, "Mike Bravo 488 received clear, over," Mike answered.

For the next two hours, Mike and the two officers waited outside of the house. Around the street, several curtains were twitching as the police car remained parked in the street.

An old man who lived across the road came over and wanted to find out more, "Good evening officers. Can I help you at all?" the man said, holding out his hand to shake.

Mike Parsons walked over to the man, "Good evening Sir. Please can you return to your house? We are expecting another car to arrive soon. This is police business, there is no danger to the public." Mike said, turning the man towards his house.

The old man looked a little frustrated as he wanted to know more, "Are you looking for Mr Wright? I saw him this morning leaving with a large bag. He drives a blue van, he's a plumber, a good one too. He fixed my dripping bathroom tap last year, did not cost me a penny. I do hope he is not in any trouble. Mr Wright is well respected, like his parents who lived in that house before him. We recently gave him a place in the neighbourhood watch team." the man said, pointing to a sticker in his window.

Sergeant Parsons nodded.

"All this is very interesting Sir. But please can we ask you to remain inside your house until my team have gone. Do you know where Mr Wright was heading?" Mike asked, hoping to get a little more information.

The old man opened his door, seemingly put out that he was not able to remain speaking to the policeman on the street.

"I have no idea. Joshua comes and goes a lot. I know he attends a church in the city a few times a week. Mr Wright is a man of God Sergeant Parsons. I don't think that is a crime yet?" the old man stated.

Mike Parson smiled.

"It would be useful to have your name Sir, should we need your help later?" Mike asked, knowing the man wanted to ask more questions.

The old man seemed happier with this.

"My name is Clive Brightman. I am a retired schoolteacher. Taught history for thirty years, right across the country. I consider myself to be a good judge of character. Mr Wright is a good man. I can assure you of this officer."

Mike Parsons noted down the man's name in his book. Walking back towards the police car, he could see his colleagues talking to others who had come to question the police presence.

It took another hour before DS-Nick arrived with a signed search warrant. Walking to the door, they once more tried to ring the bell. With no reply, DS-Nick gave the order to get the door opened by force. Around the street, every window was filled with onlookers, who watched on in surprise.

With a simple crowbar, the latch of the door creaked and burst open.

DS Nick and Sergeant Parsons were the first inside the house.

A quick look around the three-bedroom house showed that as they thought the property was completely empty. Photos were quickly taken of the table.

In the living room, further religious material was scattered across the couch and two chairs. Moving up to the second floor, more books about speaking with God and a computer with a printer was filled with various printouts and screenshots of websites showing religious comments.

DS Nick put on his gloves and carefully began to search through papers. Most were just pages and boldly printed pictures of scripture. Mr Wright really was a man of God.

As Nick carefully found his way through the pile of neatly stacked papers, a shout from downstairs called him back down the lounge again.

Sergeant Parsons was also wearing gloves, "Check this out, boss. I think we can be sure this is our man." Sergeant Mike said, pointing towards a piece of paper.

DS Mike walked over to the small coffee table. Folded into a book, Mike Parsons had found a smoking gun of evidence.

Carefully he lifted what looked like a map up and opened it out across the table.

"What is it?" DS-Mike asked.

Kneeling down to the carpet, the lines on the paper were very fine, crisscrossing in blue. On closer inspection, it looked like a schematic or a photocopy of an old plan. DS Nick looked down into the bottom right-hand corner of the drawing. Some of what was written had been missed off the copy, but the name of the building this was from was solid.

Sergeant Mike seemed pleased with what he had found, "I think this is a plumbing drawing Boss. This is the pipe layout of a large building. What was the name of the school Phillip Stevens attended? I am sure it was King Alfred's." Mike said, pointing to the words in the corner.

DS Nick nodded. There was no need to reply. What Sergeant Parsons had found was damning evidence indeed. Mr Wright was known to be a plumber, but knowing he had access to the plumbing of King Alfred's school, would take some real explaining. DS Nick patted the sergeant on his back.

"Good work Sergeant Parsons, we have our man. Just need to find him quickly now. Put out an urgent call on the number plate of his vehicle. I want him caught." Nick said, pushing himself up again.

As Nick stood, he caught a glimpse of an empty box fallen under the huge leather armchair in the room. Carefully, still wearing the gloves, Nick bent and picked up to small cardboard box. It was empty.

On the side of the box, a tiny white label was half hanging off. DS Nick pressed his eyes closer to read the tiny writing.

*Pentobarbital 300mg tablets. Please read the instructions carefully before taking them.*

Taking the box, DS Nick walked over to pick up a plastic evidence bag. Placing the pillbox inside the bag, he asked the officer in the room to note down the discovery. Inside this one room alone, there was enough to not only call Joshua Wright in for questioning, but there was also enough to charge him for triple murder.

Murder rarely was easy to solve. Most people at least tried

to hide their tracks. This man had made no attempt to disguise anything. It was as if he knew that one day he would be found.

DS Nick had enough to at least put this man at the first murder scene. The drugs box was the same drug as Molly Symonds thought it to be. Joshua was the name of the man, which also put him as the prime suspect in murder three. If he could find something that could link this man to the murder in Salisbury, everything would fall into place.

DS Nick had no idea why each of these victims had been chosen. They did not seem to be linked in any way. But it now seemed very likely that this was the man responsible.

Did Joshua Wright have family or personal links to these people? Was there something that all these people had in common? Did any of them have something on Joshua?

Nothing yet made sense.

What DS Nick did not want was to charge the man for murder without any clear motive.

DS Nick walked into the kitchen and looked at the piles of religious books on the table.

Remembering Marina Gracely, Nick thought on her words, *"So, with this thought sir, if I now tell you that Joshua did hear the voice of God, and He was told to kill for him"*

If this were the motive to kill innocent people, there would be no doubt that when they caught Joshua Wright, the defence would have no choice but to look at pleas of insanity. Involving religion was never something DS Nick relished. It made everything three times more complicated and required treading very carefully. When dealing with religion, someone was always going to be offended somewhere.

Marina Gracely wanted DS Nick to think that Joshua Wright may have been told to kill by a voice inside his head.

DS Nick picked up a book titled, Talking to God.

Flicking through the pages, he could see various chapters all claiming how God could be heard.

DS Nick was no atheist, but this did all seem a little too far from reality. Chapter after chapter went on to say how the man could not only hear but talk with the almighty.

Putting the book down, DS Nick looked at the large, opened book on the table. The page was held down by two pebbles, on the chapter titled. "When God Speaks, You Must Obey Him, no matter your own thoughts."

It was truly worrying if people believed this to be the literal truth of it.

DS Nick knew that with religion there was a fine balance between madness and true belief. Only last week, he had watched a film with Celia about the two Popes. In the film, Anthony Hopkins was playing the Pope who decided to step down after he could no longer hear God's voice in his head.

Hearing God's voice was a huge part of what it was to be Pope.

The Pope was one of the most revered people on the planet with over a billion people following his every word. No man had ever called the Pope deluded.

So, with this thought, DS Nick wondered why most people who claimed to hear God were said to be mad? If Joshua Wright thought God had told him to kill, how the hell could this be proven in a court of law, where ironically God reigned supreme.

DS Nick moved the opened book to look at the cover. The author was Mary Grace, which did make sense. As he lifted the book up, something underneath it caught his eye.

Placing the book aside, Nick picked up an A4 sized piece of paper. The photo on the front was of a house for sale. It was a two-bedroom property, located in a small village outside of Salisbury in the village of Netheravon.

DS Nick turned the sales leaflet over. The photos on the back gave good clear images of two bedrooms a good-sized garden and a view from the main bedroom of the spire of Salisbury Cathedral. It was a truly breath-taking view.

DS Nick turned the leaflet over again to the front. The estate agent was a company called Brymore.

DS Nick could not believe his luck. He was about to bag the item when Nick caught sight of deep indents on the paper made by a hard-pressed pen. Someone had written something whilst pressing down on the sales leaflet. Nick took the leaflet over to the dining room window and angled it towards the dying light.

DS Nick could see a phone number written down. Below it was a name. Angling to the light again DS Nick now was convinced this was the man who had killed three people.

As the light shone over the pressed in letters, DS Nick could see the indented name with the date below,

*074.1 2851.*

*Jemma Evans*

*15.00 15 March*

# Chapter 20

## The Same Picture

### Timeline—27 April 2018

Somehow, as they always managed through contacts, leaks and occasional payments, the mainstream media got hold of Joshua Wright's name. The police ordered an immediate court order on publishing the name of "The Spiker" which most of the bigger outlets obeyed without too much of a fight.

The lack of policing on Social media was not so obedient to the law.

Within a day, the name of Joshua Wright was circulated across all regions of the UK. Air, Rail and Seaports, were given photos of the man the Bath police wanted, with explicit orders to make sure he did not travel abroad.

As PC Gunel sat behind the front desk of the Bath station, there had already been several calls in from other police stations, all claiming to have reports of the blue van owned by Joshua Wright. Some were just false sightings of light blue vans similar to what Joshua was said to drive. Once, Sally had called a team in Portsmouth to investigate a light blue van that was heading out onto a ferry, which was stopped. Another van was parked in a church car park, but when the police arrived, the vehicle proved to be a vehicle owned by a national electrician's group. Joshua's van was the same type and colour, and a trace on the number plate found that Mr Wright had purchased the van from the national business three years ago.

Today, there had been no trace of the van. CCTV cameras had seen Joshua driving south from Bath, but there was no trace of it once he reached the open countryside of mid-Dorset. It had just vanished off the face of the earth.

Where was Joshua Wright hiding?

The photofit of Joshua got a third-day press cover. If anyone did not know Joshua's face by now, it was only because they did not watch the news or read papers. Even the radio descriptions were good enough to know the man in question. The Spiker was now turning into a national manhunt, where PC Sally Gunel was the main hub of all calls.

Described as bald-headed, around 6'2" and often seen wearing a wide-brimmed green coloured hat, it was more than enough to keep the public interested.

PC Gunel, watched as DS Nick and his team convened for another briefing inside the incident room. Sergeant Parsons was totally invested in what DS Nick was telling the team, pointing towards several links on his whiteboard and possibilities of where the man could be hiding. The photo of Joshua Wright was now displayed clearly at the top of the pen lined pyramid, which was a copy of a photo they had found in the man's house.

Police were posted to watch Joshua's house and Eden's Echo community hall, just on the off chance he decided these were safe places to be, but with so much public interest, DS Nick was telling his team that Joshua was probably in hiding.

DS Nick had ordered a 24/7 watch on King Alfred's School and The Old Rectory, which were common places of interest within this investigation. Sergeant Mike had discovered that Joshua had been a privately paid plumber inside the school, having a free reign to wherever he wanted to go, whenever he wanted to go. The plans of the plumbing designs of the school found in his house had shown that Joshua was able to know every water outlet in the place. So far, they could not understand how he had managed to tamper with the water supply to only affect Phillip Stevens purple water bottle.

Over the past twenty-four hours, the officers outside Joshua's house had reported a delivery man bringing Joshua new boots, a postman with letters containing three sizeable cheques, and a small group of Jehovah's witnesses, approaching the doorway.

All had been watched, but each time the door remained closed. It did not seem likely that Joshua had up and left for good, as much of his clothing and possessions were still in the chests of drawers and two wardrobes. The police had even found his passport, which was good news. It was also four years out of date, so unless he had a fake passport, there was no way he could flee the country.

The only problem now was the media. The more news broadcasters spoke about and released images of Joshua, the more likely DS Nick thought that Joshua would see them and hunker down. If this man went into hiding, DS Nick did not know how long this manhunt would last.

The public and his superiors were calling for "The Spiker" to be off the streets. In the frenzy building up around this story, DS Nick worried that unless this man was caught soon, the public and his superiors would look to portion blame which would no doubt come to the lead investigator.

The phone on the front desk rang out again.

PC Sally was hungry, and it was now thirty-five minutes later than she usually broke off for a break. Picking up the phone, a man on the end of the line seemed nervous when he spoke.

"Hello, is this the Bath Police station?" a soft male voice asked.

Sally reached for a muesli bar Mike had given her earlier when he saw she had not left the desk all morning.

"Good Morning, PC Sally Gunel speaking. Can I help you?" she asked. Sally could feel another full day on the phone was taking its toll on her. Sally was tired, hungry and in need of a proper break.

The voice seemed unsure to speak again.

"I would like to speak to someone about The Spiker investigation, please. I have someone currently staying with me, who we think fits your description." the man said almost in a whisper, PC Gunel did not want to trouble DS Nick in mid flow of his morning briefing. The team were deep in debate, talking about the Sales literature from the house for sale in Salisbury.

All investigations into the second murder had changed from the idea Jemma Evans water was spiked after she left the newsagents on the way to the gym, over to a viewing she had with a man called Joshua in the late afternoon.

Sally had heard DS Nick talking about Molly Symonds description of Pentobarbital, and the potential for it not to overcome anyone for sometimes up to four hours after taking it. If it was caught quick enough, it was possible to revive many who had accidentally overdosed by pumping out stomachs. Joshua had made sure that each of his victims had taken enough to make them just go to sleep, their deaths painless and mercifully swift when it came.

The timeline in the Jemma Evans case, DS Nick had changed on his whiteboard. Originally, the time of death for Jemma was judged to be around 21.00. This was now being moved to around

00:10. As Jemma had been so violently sick before she eventually died, Molly now thought that if Jemma had been sick earlier and thrown up most of the pills, she would have possibly survived. For some reason, the drug had not worked as well with Jemma, which was still under chemical analysis. Molly Symonds said that one theory was to do with Jemma's birth control pills, countering the effect of the Pentobarbital. Obviously, neither of the men had this drug in their systems, which is why it worked as the murderer expected.

Molly was insistent that apart from Jemma's bout of sickness, she had not suffered in any way. Like the two male victims, they had all just fallen asleep and died soon after.

PC Sally loved hearing about the forensic analysis. If she had been a bit brighter, this would have been the way she would have liked to take her career. But Sally needed to be honest with herself. Science was never her strong point, as the three grade C's in triple science GCSE reminded her. Molly Symonds was a legend in the force, Sally was just a copper who could answer phone calls and make tea or coffee. PC Sally was loving her career in the police, but the rungs of the ladder were proving steep to climb.

The man on the phone spoke again.

"Hello, are you still there?" the man asked, as Sally had been miles away wondering if she should disturb DS Nick mid-stream.

Sally was polite, but a little confused as to what she should do if this call proved to be important, "Sorry sir, the investigation team are in a meeting here, can I help at all." PC Sally said, knowing this was probably above her paygrade.

The man was quiet for a while, as he was clearly thinking about if he should speak to the PC on the reception desk.

"I know you are looking for a man driving a blue van.

Baldhead, wide hat, quite tall. I have such a person sleeping in my B&B. Mr J Wright has been here a couple of day's now, missed breakfast twice. The van is parked in my underground garage, so the police would not see it from the street." the man explained.

Sally wrote down what the man told her.

"This is very interesting sir. Can you tell me the address please?" Sally asked, wishing she could put the call through to another senior policeman quickly.

The man grunted.

"That's my problem. If I give you my address you will come in swarms. I have a few other paying guests here. I do not want them spooked. Do you know how hard it is to get good paying customers these days? I have had six permanently empty rooms since Christmas." the man told her.

Sally wanted to say to the man that he had called her. But keeping it professional Sally spoke softly.

"I appreciate you taking the time to call us Sir. If this man is who you think he is, it is vital we get him into custody. We can send a couple of non-uniform policemen if you like. If he is the man, we are looking for, we will make the arrest outside of your house. Is this fair to you?" Sally asked, already finding the phone number in a simple lookup on the internet, linked to a bed and breakfast in Bournemouth.

*The Sunlight Guest House. Vacancies Available.*

The man on the phone was probably Melvin Otter, who was listed as the manager. Sally smiled, perhaps she would never be a forensic expert, but she had everything she needed to become a good copper.

Changing his tone slightly, the man spoke again.

"I will leave the garage open. You can check the van without having to come into our house. But please can you make sure my Guesthouse is kept out of any press or papers. I do not want this kind of publicity. It will attract the wrong sort of guests.

My wife and I run a B&B designed for those who appreciate and know of God. We have a small chapel next to us, and we run a nightly prayer group. I hope my wife has made a mistake, but she is sure we are harbouring the man you are seeking. My wife is scared to death." the owner stated, his voice now more concerned than angered.

Sally wrote down the number and the address. As she did the man told her the same information.

"I am at the Sunlight Guest House, Boscombe Road, Bournemouth. We are the last large white building that faces the sea before the road ends. Please be discreet. No flashing lights or sirens would very much be appreciated." the man told PC Sally.

Sally thanked the man, he was about to hang up when Sally thought of another important question, "Where is this man now. His room, your lounge, outside?" Sally asked the guest house owner.

Melvin Otter was speaking, covering the phone whilst talking to what Sally thought was probably his wife in the background. After a short, whispered conversation back and forth, the muffled phone cleared again and Melvin spoke: "This is the strange thing officer. It was what made my wife first think there was something odd about this gentleman."

"He is currently in our private chapel, deep in prayer. My wife says that he can often be heard speaking to himself. Last night we heard him talking inside his room, late into the night. I almost knocked on the door as he is meant to be single occupancy, but as we listened it was clear that he was the only person in the room."

"My wife says that he is talking to God. Some of what he says is complete gibberish, you know, talking in tongues I think they call it."

"We are Bible loving folk officer. But we are not into this type of religion. People have the right to know God in their own way, but this… it does not suit us, or my guests."

"When my wife saw the photofit on the TV news earlier today, and the radio said that you were looking for a light blue van, everything seemed to click into place."

"I have to say that the Mr Wright we have seen has been nothing but courteous towards us both. Charming to be honest with you. If it were not for his strange prayers last night, I may well have ignored the TV reports.

The man staying with us seems very pleasant. He even fixed a dripping tap in the room." Melvin Otter explained.

PC Sally scribbled down everything she was told. Her shorthand was rubbish, but there was now more than enough here to interrupt her boss.

"Thank you, Sir. You have been very helpful. We will send a team over to you from our Bournemouth station. I can assure you that they will be discreet." Sally re-assured the Welsh sounding man on the phone.

Melvin Otter thanked PC Sally and hung up.

PC Sally Gunel took her notepad and walked into the incident room. DS Nick was in full flow, discussing the plans of the water system at the private school. DS Nick was trying to say that he wanted to find a clear motive for the three killings. The private school was certainly a link to each of the victims. The schoolboy attended the school and Jemma Evans parents were cooks in the kitchen for a time.

It had been traced to find Ridley Goodman had also attended

the same school as a teenager for a short time, so the same private school was the only link to each of the three crimes.

DS Nick was telling his team that most murders were committed to people known by the murderer. Again, there was no evidence that Joshua Wright had ever met any of his victims until the day he poisoned them.

The motive was still eluding them all.

The method of death was also causing some confusion. Joshua Wright seemed to know that Pentobarbital pills could be used to bring on a painless death. Joshua had not intended any of his victims to suffer, but DS Nick wanted to make it clear that murder was still murder no matter if the victims suffered or not.

There must have been a motive, as picking three random strangers living some distance apart was extremely rare.

The public would tolerate who it was, given the evidence stacking up against Joshua Wright.

The public would not tolerate why he had done it, given the lack of any clue as to his reasons.

PC Sally walked up to the front of the room. The ten policemen in the room watched her moving around the tables.

It was unusual for PC Gunel to interrupt anything like this, this was obviously important.

DS Nick also knew that PC Gunel would not interrupt the meeting unless Sally had something she thought was important. Stopping the briefing, he smiled and sat on a small table, "What is it PC Gunel. Do you have new information for us?" DS Nick asked. The lack of Sally not carrying hot coffee was a sure sign his young police officer was concerned.

PC Sally handed the piece of paper to DS Nick.

Reading the paper, Nick read down and quickly jumped from his desk.

"Well done PC Gunel. I think we have him. Please ring the Bournemouth branch for me. Put them through to my car please, I am heading off to Bournemouth now."

"Tell them to not approach the suspect until I arrive. If he tries to leave the building, follow him. If he detects we are on to him, bring him in." DS Nick called for Sergeant Parsons to come with him.

As Nick grabbed his light black jacket from the back of his chair, he called across to PC Sally.

"As soon as I am through to the acting DS in Bournemouth PC Gunel, please can you brief the team here with what you have just told me. You can take the rest of the briefing for me. I want you all to concentrate on the motive. Why did Joshua Wright kill these people? If the only answer is that God told him to, we have a big problem ahead of us." DS Nick called out, as he left the building.

**17.23 p.m.**

DS Nick pulled into Boscombe road which was right on the pretty Dorset seafront. Two unmarked police vehicles were parked on the road, both with men waiting inside.

Pulling up behind the first car in his Audi TT, one of the men in the unmarked car got out.

The man looked to be annoyed until Nick flashed his badge.

"Sorry sir, I thought you were a member of the public. We have been quietly trying to keep the road clear until you arrived Sir. DS Whatley is in the car at the end of the street. We also have a team of officers hidden by the beach wall, another two are parked inside the guest house garage. There is a police van two streets away awaiting your orders." the plain-clothed officer told DS Nick.

DS Nick remained in his car, "That's great work officer. Is DS Whatley aware of the situation?" DS Nick asked, The officer turned as if he was staring out to sea, conducting the conversation with the men in the car as if looked across the bay.

"Completely sir. Your officer PC Gunel explained everything to him on the phone. We know how important this arrest is. We are all under instructions to take your orders Sir. Just make the call and we will move in." the officer told him.

DS Nick got out of the car. Next to him, Sergeant Parsons was sitting monitoring to police radio. His hand was still sore from the garden incident a few days ago. Clicking the mike, he radioed into despatch, "Mike Bravo 488, in position," Mike instructed the team.

Nick walked casually along the seafront pathway.

It was a beautiful evening with the sun gleaming off the sea in a million shimmered sparkles. Two jet skis skipped across the waves, expertly navigating around a dozen windsurfers.

Nick thought that Celia would love it here. Celia loved the sea, especially around the Dorset coast.

Once a year, they would both come down to Bournemouth and spend a weekend in a B&B very similar to the huge white house ahead of him. Hidden under a canopy of tall trees, the Sunlight guest house was certainly living up to its name. Even under the shelter of the trees, the sun was able to cover the white-painted house in early evening rays.

In the car park, a vehicle was moving around, looking for a place to park. The sound of the loose gravel under tyres, was louder than the sea lapping up the narrow sandy beach.

The tide was in, so much so that the concrete footpath which traversed the entire road, was only a matter of twenty feet away from the shoreline.

Nick could see another small building, about sixty feet away from the white guest house. On the door, a huge crucifix was painted, with tiny stained-glass windows along the sea side of the building.

This must be the Chapel Sally had described to him.

It would be easy to just rush all the policemen inside, but this was not what the owner of the guest house wanted. Bed and breakfast hotels like this were run without huge advertising. Many of the guests would probably be here from recommendations by others or the fact it was a religious place, known within the church.

You would not find this place on any standard good guest house list. The owners were all about who the guest was and not how many they could file through the doors.

DS Nick thought that the only way to do this discreetly was on his own.

Walking up the gravel driveway, two people were struggling to pull a large suitcase from the car they had just parked. The old woman was busy taking photos of the sea, whist and even older man struggled to pull the case forward. As Nick walked past them, he offered to carry the case to the front door. The old man was very grateful, "God bless you, sir. I would have still been here tomorrow." he chuckled.

DS Nick was pleased to get the two people out of the way.

Moving towards the single chapel door, Nick could see two of the officers from the unmarked car, walking along the pathway. DS Whatley was taking no chances at allowing the suspect to escape. These were purposely sent out to support Nick and more importantly, catch a murderer.

Casually they walked up to a short red brick wall and sat down, pointing as if in a discussion about the windsurfers on the sea.

DS Nick moved into the porchway to a single thick Chapel door. Pushing it forward, it swung back in silence.

Carefully Nick walked inside the long room, which looked to be empty of people, filled only with the bright evening sunlight that beamed through the multi-coloured windows.

There were three rows of eight chairs, which were staggered across the narrow room. At the front of the Chapel, a tall wooden cross stood centre stage on a solid wooden table, with two silver candlesticks on either side, both unlit.

Behind the narrow wooden table, two pictures were hanging on the wall in ornate frames. One was a classic painting of the virgin Mary holding the baby Jesus, the other was a picture of Adam touching the hand of God. This was a picture Nick had always loved and knew well.

He saw this same picture every day of his life.

The painting was a stunning copy, much larger than the first picture of the virgin Mary. It was very clear from every seat in the room.

DS Nick had often been lost in the same image many times before. There was something about the picture that had always captured his interest.

Nick had the same picture inside his home. It had been a mad sudden impulse purchase on a holiday with his wife Celia in Rome, Italy, eight years ago.

The day after Nick and Celia had looked around The Old Rectory in Stockton-on-Avon, they had taken a short weekend break, flying from Bristol on a trip with Celia's cancer recovering mother. With her cancer in remission, she had always wanted to see the Vatican before she died. As a means to try to think of something else other than Celia's father's untimely death, Nick thought the trip was good for them all to relax for a few days.

The picture on the wall and in his home was a copy of the painting by Michelangelo, painted magnificently on the ceiling of the Sistine Chapel inside the Vatican.

DS Nick had been completely captivated by it in Italy and had bought an expensive full print poster reproduction of it. Nick still had the picture to this day, stood in pride of place, framed above his fireplace in a thick silver frame.

Nick knew this picture was called The Creation of Adam. He never really understood why he loved it so for he was no art critic, but he would look at it every day as he sat in his front room.

Celia had wanted to move it many times, but Nick had always put it back up. Something about the picture always calmed him. Something about the picture called out to him. Something about the picture was important to him.

In the picture, God was reaching out to Adam. The picture always felt like it was also reaching out to Nick.

Moving into the Chapel, quietly looking for signs of anyone, he could not take his eyes off the picture on the front wall. Nick was about to turn and leave when a gentle voice behind him, made Nick turn quickly.

"It is a beautiful picture. Do you not agree?" a man said, sitting in the shadows at the far back of the room. Nick had been so lost in the picture at the front of the room, he had walked straight past a man sat in the dark shadows.

Nick turned and could see Joshua Wright sitting on a chair at the back of the room. The large wide-brimmed hat was on the seat next to him. Nick walked over to the man and sat in the chair in front of him. Keeping calm, he wanted to keep this peaceful tone to a man who was the lead suspect in three murders,

"I have this same picture in my house. I have always loved

it. It depicts God reaching out to Adam giving him the spark of life I am led to believe." Nick said, looking back at the picture.

Joshua smiled, his face was kind and not the face of a murderer, if there was such a face for this, "It is so much more than that. Everyone focuses on the two fingers nearly touching at the centre of the picture. The spark of life given to Adam by God, as you correctly say."

"But there is much more in this picture that most people miss. Like all the great artists of his age, Michelangelo used focus to hide what he was trying to depict.

If you look closely at the picture again, you will see that under God's left arm, He hides Eve away from Adam as she looks upon her man in what must be lost, love. The question this painting asks, is to wonder if Adam is reaching out to God or does his hand hope to find the woman he loves.

Is Adam reaching out for Eve?

To ignore God is the sin of man. Eve ignored God and fell to the temptation of the serpent, eternally damning mankind because of the taste of an apple."

"We know only through written scripture that Adam and Eve were both cast out of Eden, but I, like many others, do not think this was the first truth. Only Adam was cast out of Eden for eating the forbidden fruit, forcing him to leave everything he ever loved behind. God wanted Adam to know a life without love, teaching him a hard lesson, before he welcomed Adam home again."

"What Michelangelo was trying to show here, was that everything Adam loved was still held in Eden. God spent eternity reaching out to call him back inside. Adam's inability to hear God's voice has remained a sin throughout man's time on earth."

"But we also know that God is love. In Adams's sad fall from Grace, God still loved Adam enough to return Eve to him, where they married and had children, away from the paradise of their garden. God remained in Eden, some called it paradise, or heaven as we know it today, where he still calls to the sons of Adam for them all to come home."

Joshua Wright eyes were showing signs of tears as he explained the revealed truth of Eden's Echo.

DS Nick needed to get back on the topic of why he was there. It was clear Joshua was a very religious man, but Nick was not here to discuss what this picture meant. DS Nick refocused as he had enough of the stories and reached for his badge.

As he pulled it clear, ready to read the man his rights, Joshua spoke again.

"I knew you would come here. He told me where I had to be for you to find me. My task as His shepherd is finally complete. The Wolves are all dead, and the Lambs can walk free again.

I was expecting you yesterday, but I suppose a day is nothing when talking to one who knows of eternity."

"I will not struggle Sir. You and your men outside will have no problems in taking me in. I will honestly confess to the crimes you are here to charge me of. I have purposely taken three lives of this I cannot deny, nor will I pretend to hide." Joshua said, standing and holding out his hands expecting to be handcuffed.

DS Nick saw the door move as the two plain-clothed officers came inside. They were probably sent in by DS Whatley as DS Nick had been alone inside for a while with a murderer.

DS Nick signalled for the men to hold back.

Turning to Joshua, he pushed the man's hands down, "We will not use handcuffs, out of respect to the owners of this guest house. If you come with me peacefully, we will read your rights in the van outside. Is this acceptable to you or do I need to restrain you?" DS Nick asked.

Nodding, Joshua seemed content.

DS Nick pointed towards the two officers that stood waiting at the door. Outside, an unmarked van pulled up in the road. DS Colin Whatley was talking to the driver.

Joshua took one long last look at the picture of the Creation of Adam as he was escorted from the chapel. Nick followed close, making sure Joshua was not able to bolt. There was no attempt or even a sign that this was ever going to happen.

Climbing into the back of the van, DS Nick and DS Whatley entered the van behind Joshua. Nick read the man his rights as promised, before climbing out again.

DS Nick explained that he would now be taken to the Bristol police station for initial questioning. A solicitor would be present if Joshua wanted this, but this council was optional. Given the seriousness of the crimes Joshua was accused of, DS Nick recommended that he had a solicitor present.

Turning to leave the back of the police van, DS Nick could not help himself to ask the question that was burning on his mind, "Why did you kill them, Joshua. What were they all to you?" DS Nick asked.

Joshua Wright looking into Nick's eyes and just shook his head, "They were simply the wolves He told me to kill. That is all. Only God knows why these three were chosen, I was just His shepherd and His hunter of wolves." Joshua said as the doors of the van slowly closed.

# Chapter 21

## Confession

### Timeline—28 April 2018

DS Nick sat inside the quiet of the single tabled interrogation room. Sitting alone in the room to gather his thoughts, he was soon going to be joined by DI Kleverly from Salisbury station. Joshua Wright would be escorted into the room from his cell, as today they needed to formally charge the man with triple murder.

Over the past twenty-four hours, DS Nick had not really been home for any good length of time. Yesterday evening he had nipped back to kiss Celia and grab a shower, sleeping for no more than five hours before he was back at the station again.

Having Joshua Wright behind bars was only half the battle. His superiors wanted not only a written confession but just as he thought, a full motive of why Joshua had committed these three crimes.

It was pretty obvious that DI Kleverly was being brought in to manage the next few days before formally charging this man with triple murder. It was well known that DI Kleverly was much more adept in getting the right answers out of people in his custody. With one of the dead victims from his own town in Salisbury, he also had a vested interest in making sure the motive was found to fit the crime. But DS Nick still had the lead in this investigation. This was his suspect even though DI Kleverly formally outranked him.

DS Nick thumbed through his pile of investigation notes. Many of the papers were focused on Marina Gracely, Eden's Echo and the teachings she had given Joshua over the past couple of years.

As far as DS Nick could find, there were no legal cases ever charged for following a certain religion, especially when it involved teaching the bible. There was a tiny number of cases when brainwashing had led to prosecutions, but many of these were from forced learning and people held against their will. Marina had not forcibly asked Joshua to learn anything from her, in fact, it had been the complete opposite.

Joshua Wright had willingly listened and learned from her sermons and words. Evangelism was legal.

The danger that needed to be understood was a charge where religion forced Joshua to kill for another against his will. This certainly did not seem like the defence Joshua was looking to claim. Worryingly, Joshua Wright did not seem to be making any kind of defence, which did not help DS Nick at all.

In Nick's experience, those who tried to defend themselves often stumbled into allowing the police into knowing why they did it. Joshua Wright was freely admitting that he had killed the three young people. For these crimes, Joshua was openly sorry, but at the same time, he explained that his actions were all given to him from the words of God, and because of this, Joshua was totally convinced that the murders were divinely just.

DS Nick had spoken to Joshua Wright for a while when they arrived back at Bristol station late last night. Whilst he was duly processed and placed into a cell, Nick tried to question the man, who seemed completely calm, almost as if he were pleased to be caught and his life now in other people hands.

Nick had asked Joshua about Mary Grace, and the strange religion that Eden's Echo followed.

Joshua had just shrugged, telling him how wonderful Mary had been to him, "Mary saved me. Without Mary, I would have been dead two years ago, it is that simple. I was not brainwashed as you probably think. God choose me to be saved and to do His will. I have accepted this, which is why I do not feel any remorse for those I have killed. I just heard my calling and obeyed to His will." Joshua told the stunned officers around him.

It was now 09.50 a.m. DI Kleverly walked into the room. From the look on his face, Nick could see the man was clearly frustrated. Like Nick, DI Kleverly was probably getting heat from above to get this man formally charged. The media were crying out for a full confession, some had even printed Joshua's face and name in their papers today. The DI also needed a motive, preferably one that was not based on the actions of a religious nutcase.

DI Kleverly sat down next to Nick. Handing Nick, a hot coffee, he spoke.

"This coffee is from PC Gunel. She tells me it's still hot, and to get you to drink it, Nick. PC Gunel is a good copper, DS Murray. I would look to hang on to that one." DI Kleverly said, setting out his pen and notebook on the plain table.

DS Nick nodded. Sally was proving to be a real asset to the Bath station. After this case was done, DS Nick was already considering getting her name put up for possible promotion.

The door of the room opened again, and two policemen brought Joshua Wright into the room. One of the police constables unlocked the man's handcuffs before Joshua sat in a chair in front of the two detectives. Smiling, Joshua seemed relaxed and rested.

DI Kleverly was the first to react.

"Sleep well did you, Mr Wright. I would imagine a man who has confessed to his crimes as you have, would find sleep difficult to find." The DI said, staring at the bald man in front of him, for the very first time.

Joshua sighed.

"I always sleep well these days sir. It is the only time I cannot hear His voice inside my head. God fills me, sir, every minute of every day. It is both wonderful and sometimes very noisy. I sometimes need sleep to find peace." Joshua said, placing his hands on the small table.

Another knock on the door saw Joshua's legal representation appear. The suited man was very short, with a round face and circular spectacles. Hurrying into the room, he was carrying a briefcase that looked to be an exact replica of the red briefcase that the chancellor of the exchequer carried on every budget day. DS Nick wanted to chuckle, but this was not the place for amusement.

The man sat down next to Joshua Wright, and introduced himself, "Good morning, my name is Bill Gregory QC. I am Mr Wright's legal representative. Mr Wright has already told me that he does not wish to try to defend his actions. I am here to try to get the facts and offer legal guidance. As Mr Wright believes he was told to do these terrible things from a *higher power*, Mr Wright has asked me to make sure that his defence is only that he did these things because he was asked to do so. Mr Wright has also wanted me to state that he is of sound mind and is not looking for any type of insanity plea" Bill Gregory told the room.

DS Nick spoke quickly, cutting off Bill Gregory before he rattled on-again.

"For the record, I am now beginning the recording of this

interview. The time is 10.05 a.m. on the 28 of April 2018. We are in an interview room here at Bristol Police station. Present here today are DS Murray, DI Kleverly, Mr Bill Gregory QC and Mr Joshua Wright."

"I know you were cautioned at the time of the arrest yesterday, but I do need to caution you again now. You do not have to say anything that may harm your defence, but anything you do say maybe later given in evidence in a court of law. Do you understand this Mr Wright?" DS Nick asked, with the tape now running.

Joshua looked to his defence solicitor. Nodding, he understood completely what was being said to him.

DI Kleverly took immediate control.

"We are going to break this interview down today into three parts. In the first part, we will ask you a series of questions, which is your legal right should you choose not to answer."

"The second part is if this matter goes to court and anything you say with us today does not match the story you say in the court, this will go against you. The final part is this interview today can and will be used as evidence, so it is important to speak truthfully to help your later defence. Does this all make sense to you?" DI Kleverly said, looking Joshua directly into his eyes.

Joshua nodded and smiled.

DI Kleverly continued for a while asking a few questions about Joshua's date of birth, his general health condition and if he was happy with the legal representation in the room.

Joshua nodded to all he was asked without any question.

DS Nick this time spoke to Joshua, "Mr Wright, you have been arrested on three counts of murder by poisoning. These events took place between 28 February 2018 and 22 March 2018. During this time, we believe you purposely poisoned their water containers and bottles with a drug known as Pentobarbital. Each of the three young people, Phillip Stevens 16, Jemma Evans 27, and Ridley Goodman 21, was killed using the exact same method of a spiking their drinks.

I discovered an empty box of pills matching the Pentobarbital we believe were used in these murders at your house. This matches exactly to what our forensic teams have told us was used to kill these people."

"Added to this very damning evidence, we found a map of the plumbing in your house of King Alfred's private school in Stockton-on-Avon where Phillip Stevens was a pupil. You were positively witnessed at the school the day Phillip Stevens died of a huge drug overdose.

"In your house, we also discovered a sales leaflet showing the property in Netheravon outside of Salisbury, where you met Jemma Evans, just hours before she died of a huge drug overdose.

"We also have eyewitness accounts of a person called Joshua, very much matching your description, in the Lord's pantry kitchen in Yeovil town centre, just hours before Mr Ridley Goodman of no fixed abode spent his final hours, before dying under the multi-story car park of a huge drug overdose. We are accusing you of spiking their drinks deliberately with a purpose to kill Mr Wright."

DS Kleverly intervened, "All of this Joshua, is not looking good for you. Everything here that DS Murray has detailed, puts you in direct contact with each of the murder victims on the very day they died. It is clear to us that charging you today with three poisonings will be a simple case for any judge to prosecute."

Bill Gregory interrupted, "Mr Wright, you do not have to answer to anything being said here today. Each of this evidence

DS Murray had mentioned would need to be submitted before a court. They are placing you with these three strangers but have not yet offered anything in the way of a motive to why you did what they are saying."

Joshua took a deep breath. Shaking his head, he almost looked sorry for a moment.

"The reason why these good policemen have put me at the places they state is because I was there. I am not looking to hide any of this. I told you, I am guilty of all these charges. There is really nothing more to say. I will plead guilty in any court, for to hide my crimes is to deny my God." Joshua told the men.

Bill Gregory noted down what Joshua was saying. It looked like any defence would be almost impossible.

DI Kleverly spoke.

"So, for the tape, you are telling the room you murdered these people knowingly? You are freely admitting your guilt. A word of caution Joshua, we will charge you formally for these crimes if you continue to admit your guilt here today." DI Kleverly added.

Joshua looked at Bill Gregory, who offered the same words of caution to the legal case.

Joshua leaned back on his chair and looked upwards,

"As I serve God, I am telling you the truth. I am guilty of these crimes DI Kleverly. I confess to you and my God."

DS Nick made a statement into the tape verifying that all in the room had heard Joshua's confession. Bill Gregory put his pen back into his red briefcase as he could not offer any more advice to a man who was determined to confess the truth of what he had done.

DI Kleverly was not yet done, "So, we now have a murderer for these crimes, what we need is a why Mr Wright. Why did you choose three seemingly random people to murder by poison? What had any of them ever done to you?" the DI asked, as this was the crux of what he needed today.

Joshua looked at the two detectives for some time before he answered. Joshua knew that they would not understand what Eden's Echo had taught him to hear. They would certainly never believe that his God had told him exactly who He wanted dead.

In honesty, Joshua did not know why these three young people God had called the wolves were chosen to die. Joshua was just the hands that did God's work. Three were dead by his hands alone, but Joshua could not give any reason apart from God told him they must die.

"Do you believe in God? I mean really believe. I know you DS Murray has some interest in faith. You told me you keep a picture in your house on the Creation of Adam. It is not the picture that fascinates you, it is the spark of life. Did God really make Adam and then Eve?

It is a wonderful story, one that I believe to be the truth." Joshua told them all.

DS Nick tried to steer Joshua away from where he had hoped the conversation would not travel. But hopelessly, Joshua continued, "I only came to know of my deep faith last year. When it hit me, it was like a huge weight was lifted from my burdened soul. I was shown how to hear God's voice and when I heard him, it was as if it was the first day of my life." Joshua said, remembering the night at Mary Grace's dinner.

DI Kleverly could also see where this was going,

"Please don't try to convince us Joshua that God told you both who and where to kill these people. God does not ask anyone to kill for him. What is the rule, oh yes, thou shalt not kill?" DI Kleverly said, his voice slightly agitated.

Joshua corrected the DI before continuing.

"Thou shall not murder is the correct words of this holy commandment DI Kleverly. It is a common mistake."

"But I must agree with you. God's makes the rules very clear that murder is abhorrent. But in that commandment, he was making rules and instructions for the people he loved so. This was not a command from Him to Moses.

God makes it very clear that obedience to what He says is above all other rules. When God asks anyone a direct commandment, who are we to deny Him." Joshua explained, knowing they would never understand the voice he still heard every day, every hour, every minute.

DS Kleverly spoke up.

"You are stating for the record that you believe God told you to murder three innocent people. God told you alone to do this. God spoke to you... Joshua Wright, a plumber from Bath and said, go forth Joshua and kill innocent people for me." DI Kleverly said, with a lot of sarcasm.

DI Nick added "You have to admit Joshua, it does not sound very likely that God chose you to kill for him. There is no church or religious group in the land that would ever agree with what you are telling us. God is all-merciful; he does not ask people to kill for him. That's even if we are to believe you do actually hear him?" DS Nick had to agree with the DI.

Joshua knew that it was impossible to convince anyone of God's grace with the training he had. God was there with him now, telling Joshua that it was now time he told the truth.

Joshua knew his salvation was close. There was no point in trying to deny anything.

Joshua tried one last time.

"I have learned to hear Him, and He speaks to me. If the

Pope were sat here in front of you and told you that God speaks to him every day, how would you react to this? If a priest hears his calling, what or who do you think he hears? When a man kneels to pray and God answers him, do we call the man mad?"

"I can only speak the truth to you, for I have made my peace with God and He has told me to be honest with you.

To answer your questions, Honestly, I do not know why these people were chosen to die, that is for God alone to understand. I have asked this question many times to try to clear my conscience, but God does not answer me this question.

All I hear is that the Lambs are safe again and the wolves are dead. I am sorry this is not what you want me to say, but it is the truth, which is what this interview is about today is it not?" Joshua told the men around the table.

DS Kleverly shook his head.

"You are using God to try to cover your actions for three murders. This is not the reason Joshua, and you know it. When we find the link, we hope your confession will be just as honest with us. Can you tell us if this has anything to do with Mr Frederick Banister and the death of your parents? Is Mr Bannister involved in these crimes and you are trying to cover for him?" the DI asked.

Joshua seemed totally thrown by the introduction of his friend Frederick's name. DS Nick was also unaware of why DI Kleverly was bringing the name of Frederick Bannister to the table.

Joshua spoke, still calm but intrigued, "Frederick is my good friend. He does know of what Eden's Echo can bring to a man, but he has nothing to do with these crimes. The culling of these people from God was my task alone. Frederick knew nothing of this. Frederick is a good man, another true man of God. Yes, he has served time in prison, but it was there he found God." Joshua said, knowing the story well of where Mary found this man.

DI Kleverly was trying to find another angle to get Joshua away from his confession that God had told him to do these murders. He had only just discovered some new information about Eden's Echo that had recently crossed his desk, which he thought was worth testing.

Opening his notebook to an old newspaper cutting, he produced a story and a photo of a crashed bus, with a car underneath, almost flattened. The newspaper clipping was seven years ago, in 2011.

"For the record on the tape, I am about to show Mr Wright a newspaper clipping that I believe he will recognise." DI Kleverly stated to the tape.

From the expression on Joshua's face, he recognised it immediately and needed to turn away.

"That is the crash my parents were both killed in. That was the bus my father drove during the daytime. Why are you showing me this?" Joshua asked, his voice for the first-time wavering.

DI Kleverly said nothing for a moment whilst Joshua looked at the terrible photo. He then spoke softly.

"Do you know who the bus driver was that night, Joshua? It was Mr Frederick Bannister, the man you know to call a friend. It seems very strange to me that the person who killed your parents is the same man you now call a friend. This man went to prison for the crime of killing your patents through dangerous driving. Six years later, you and He are friends. Did Frederick Bannister have anything to do with these murders Joshua?" DI Kleverly asked, knowing that he had found no link, but hoped that involving this man would change Joshua's story.

Joshua looked at DI Kleverly.

"This cannot be the same man. The person who killed my parents was twenty-five stone and had a full head of hair. He could not be the same man? I would have recognised him." Joshua said, openly.

Joshua racked his memory to the man he had watched in the court dock after his parents were both killed. In truth, he did not really recall anything about the year after his parent's accident. Wrestling with a desire to commit suicide and taking many drugs, Joshua had never been angry with who had caused the crash, for they could never bring them back.

Joshua could remember a huge man, long-haired with a full beard. The man had pleaded guilty and gone to prison.

At the time, that was enough.

But Frederick Bannister was now a lean man, balding and clean-shaven. It was Frederick who had first brought Mary to his door. Frederick had done everything he could to make sure Joshua was accepted into Eden's Echo. Over the last two years, how many times had they both attended Christian projects, soup kitchens and helped the homeless together?

Frederick had been a true friend and passionate Christian.

As he looked at the picture, he suddenly remembered Mary talking about everyone finding God for different reasons. Joshua knew both Frederick and Barnaby had been recruited by Mary in prison. Both had their own reasons for coming to God.

Frederick had wanted to help Joshua so much.

Joshua sighed.

He now understood none of this was out of friendship towards Joshua. Frederick was trying to make amends for what he had *done* to Joshua.

Frederick's salvation was finding a way to pay for the crime of killing Joshua's parents. What better than helping their son back from the brink of death.

Joshua looked back to DI Kleverly,

"Thank you, DI Kleverly. I did not know this.

We all have our ways of finding peace with God. Frederick never told me who he really was. I knew he had been in prison, but I never asked what for. I just accepted his friendship, as I still do. Without Frederick, I would have never found God. Like Mary Grace, Frederick Bannister saved me and for this, he will always have my thanks. The death of my parents was terrible, but this was an accident, not a crime. I forgive Frederick, I still value his friendship.

"For this, I will always be grateful.

Everyone has a past they need to present before God. Some ask for their sins to be washed away and to do this God can offer a pathway to freedom. Only God has the true power of forgiveness, no matter the crime.

Frederick Bannister is his own man with his own road to Eden. I can promise you that he is not involved in helping me find my path back to Eden and God's grace." Joshua said.

DI Kleverly looked frustrated. They would need to come back again and find the true reason why Joshua Wright chose to kill these people. Nothing this man was saying made any sense, but he was totally admitting to the murders without a shred of remorse or trying to cover his crimes. Joshua was calm, collected and far from the nutcase, he thought he was going to be.

DI Kleverly shook his head and looked over to DS Nick.

DS Nick was ready.

"Joshua Wright. In the presence of the people in this room today, I am formally charging you for the murders of Phil…"

DS Nick read the formal charges and asked Joshua to read a

statement he had written during the interview. Joshua seemed happy with the charges and what DS Nick had transcribed. Signing the paper, DS Nick terminated the interview.

Joshua Wright was properly handcuffed and taken back into custody.

To a fanfare of press and media teams, Joshua Wright was formally charged with the murders of three young people. The Spiker was behind bars.

With the only motive announced that Joshua was hearing voices in his head that he thought was God telling him to kill, for the next fifteen months, there was a whole host of debate from religious groups and sceptics alike, trying to distance themselves from Joshua's claims.

Only Mary Grace believed Joshua had heard a voice. But Mary's dilemma was to try to work out whose voice Joshua heard.

DS Nick and DI Kleverly tried everything they could to discover another more plausible motive, but there was just nothing that ever-made sense to cause these pointless deaths.

The public seemed to finally settle on the randomness of these murders, and the press moved on to their next big story.

DS Nick was not convinced.

Whatever voice Joshua Wright thought he was hearing inside, the man never faltered on his story. Nick was sure that it had something to do with the private school in Stockton-on-Avon, but the more he tried to find the missing piece of the puzzle, the more it just left him at another dead end.

\*\*\*

Seventeen months later, on the day when Joshua Wright was

sentenced to a whole life term, PC Sally Gunel had watched the families and spectators sitting high up in the courtroom.

That day, three priests, two vicars and several religious group leaders had attended the final summaries from the legal QC's. The media buzz was again huge, as so many of them were keen to know how this case would finally conclude.

As she listened to the religious leaders outside whilst they waited for the judge to deliver his final sentence, they were talking together.

All of them were convinced that Joshua Wright was a complete madman, deluded in the voices he was hearing in his head.

As they stood in their dog collars, tunics, and religious costume, each of them was quick to dismiss Joshua's claim to hear God.

"God would not speak to ordinary men like this."

"God would not tell anyone to kill for him."

"God is merciful. He does not speak to murderers."

PC Sally Gunel shook her head. All of the men here were meant to be men of God. If any one of them said that God had spoken to them, none would have batted an eyelid.

Sally made her way across the corridor, over to Marina Gracely, who was sat in the courtroom with Frederick Bannister and Barnaby Barnes.

PC Gunel found a seat next to Marina who was sitting holding what Sally thought to be a large Bible.

Leaning across to the large lady's ear, Sally whispered, "Do you think Joshua was told by God to do murder?"

Mary looked at the police officer and smiled, "I have had nearly two years to think about this. I have spoken to Joshua five times in person to ask him.

All that I know is that Joshua Wright is a good man officer. There is nothing that I have heard to make me think that the Lord did not choose him, whatever his strange reasons." Mary whispered back, making the sign of the cross over her breast.

# Chapter 22

## A Moral Compass

### Timeline—5 September, 2019

The van with blacked out windows arrived at Bristol prison just before eight p.m.

Joshua Wright, the newly sentenced prisoner given a whole life term was taken out from the rear of the vehicle into a processing room.

Outside the gates of the prison, a huge group of press photographers had tried in vain to snap into a dark window as the van passed by.

On the tv and radio, reporters were alive with the story of the whole life sentence given to Joshua Wright, aka 'The Spiker'.

DS Nick Murray and DI Kleverly were stood in front of the courtrooms, taking questions from the reporters, who had again given this story front-page ink.

Many of the questions were the same as what DS Nick had been getting since first charging Joshua. Just as Nick had thought, everyone was happy that this murderer was securely behind prison bars, but it was still a huge topic of debate as to the real motive.

DS Nick stood back allowing DI Kleverly to take questions about his part in the case. The DI had never come to terms that Joshua had confessed his real truth. As he stood before the crowd of the press, he assured them all that over time, Joshua Wright would change his story of why these random strangers were chosen to die. Until then, the police would not rest until a motive was properly discovered.

Molly Symonds was questioned at some length about her analysis of the drug which was used. Molly assured the press that none of the victims had suffered or even known they were dying. Molly told the media that each of the three victims would have just gone to sleep, painless and without any fear they had ever been targets on Joshua's Holy kill list.

When DS Nick Murray took the podium, mercifully, many of the questions the reporters had in their notebooks had already been asked. DS Nick just needed to field anything that had been said from inconclusive answers from his colleagues.

The lead investigator looked out across the crowd. Tomorrow they would be just as frenzied over another breaking story. Like a pack of wolves, they pounced on corpses, stripped them bare of flesh before moving on to the next kill.

DS Nick stated his name into the microphone. For a second, there were no questions. Nick thought his luck was in.

But it was a woman, in the front of the group who called up with a question he was hoping would never be asked, "Emma Giles, The West Chronicle. DS Murray, can I ask if you believe in God sir? If you do, then do you believe Joshua Wright was telling you the truth? Does the police have the power over God's will?" the woman said, forcing the attention and every camera towards Nick.

Nick had thought about this question for nearly seventeen months. Since the day he had first met Joshua Wright, Nick had never found him anything other than courteous, friendly, and even helpful.

As the months in custody passed, Nick had needed to speak with Joshua often, trying the narrow down a reason why he had committed these murders.

During this time, Joshua would often talk about God to him. The man was a true believer, there was no denying this.

Joshua confessed that Mary had told him about Barnaby Barnes and his link to the hit and run killing of Nick's mother-in-law. Joshua was convinced that God had put them on a path where they were destined to meet.

Nick believed this to be just a pure coincidence.

In one of these meetings, Joshua had said something to him that even Nick had struggled to fully put aside as co-incidence.

"The day you found me inside the chapel DS Murray, I was told by the Lord who would be saving me. God told me that the man who will help me find salvation would know and speak of Eden.

You came in looking for me but found yourself lost in Michael Angelo's majesty of the picture of Eden, The Creation of Adam. This was the sign I needed."

"Did you not say to me that you had always found this picture wonderful. It was a sure sign to me that I should not struggle and followed you peacefully.

You may find this hard to believe, but we have spoken before DS Murray, although it was only a brief meeting. I am sure this was also a sign that God had our destinies aligned. Our paths were predestined to cross." Joshua said out of the blue.

Nick could not recall this meeting, "I think you may be mistaken, Joshua. I have a good memory of faces. This is what makes me a good policeman." Nick said quickly, trying to change the conversation.

Joshua continued, "I must confess it took me a while to remember where I had seen your face before, but I too rarely forget a face. It was only brief, but it was you, I am sure of it, although I spoke to your wife more than I spoke with you that day." Joshua replied.

Nick raised his hands, clearly feeling concerned, stating he could not remember.

Joshua smiled again before telling him, "It was about nine or ten years ago. At the time I was looking for a new home as I wanted to get out of my parents' house. You and what I assume was your wife were about to look at the same property in the village of Stock-upon-Avon, where King Alfred's school resides on the hill. I had just been shown around a house called The Old Rectory.

You were to be the house viewing after mine. Can you remember a man advising you not to buy this house because the young girl with the lead estate agent, let it slip that the garden flooded twice a year?

It has been plaguing me where I saw you before. This was the time. I am sure this was you stood next to the gate with the broken sign of The Old Rectory.

God brought us together long before we had any reason to know our paths would cross again." Joshua revealed.

Nick was stunned. He could remember the man at the gate, who Celia had said was a really lovely guy. It was only a brief meeting, but Joshua was correct.

Nick thought about the day. Something else came to him.

In cold reality, Nick spoke in a dark tone to Joshua.

"Did you know that was the house Phillip Stevens died in? The young girl you are speaking of is Jemma Evans. This was her first job before she moved into Salisbury.

Your second victim Joshua, the person who you would later murder.

Since your trial Joshua, we have discovered that The Old Rectory was previously owned by Ridley Goodman's parents for a time. This cannot be a mere coincidence.

All three of your victims are linked to that one house Joshua.

All three of them have been inside The Old Rectory.

How does that make you feel?" Nick asked, wondering if there was any more of a link to this house as a possible motive.

Joshua just shook his head, "God certainly moves in mysterious ways, DS Murray. Who are we to question his methods? This house must have been important to God. When prayers are answered, they often leave us puzzled to the truth of it all." Joshua had told him.

DS Nick Murray stood before the crowded press group who were silently awaiting his answer to reporter's question. The young woman Emma Giles stood impatiently waiting for an answer. Emma's profile as an investigative journalist in the press world had risen hugely since revealing Nick's whiteboard to the world.

Sally had told Nick about the incident and how his board had possibly been leaked.

DS Murray was not angry with Sally. But his distaste for Emma Giles methods was certain. He did not want to give her anything here today.

DS Murray finally moved towards the microphone to answer the woman who was relishing the other reporters admiring her awkward question.

"Thank you for the question, Ms Giles.

What Joshua Wright's version of the truth is, should never be important to the outcome of this case. What is important is that the man who killed these innocent people will tonight begin a whole life sentence, which brings little comfort for the families they leave behind."

"You asked me If I believe in God Ms Giles.

I believe religion is and should always be a very personal thing.

We all can sometimes do things that we later come to regret.

When we make a mistake or we are surprised by an outcome, we often use the Lord's name in vain.

Oh, God! Oh my God! For God's sake!

It is easy to blame God. Did Joshua use this method to hide his crimes? We may never know."

"What makes us do anything in the world is a topic for moral debate way beyond my pay-grade. You would be better asking these men of the cloth here, than a mere policeman to answer this moral question. I am just a policeman."

"Police work often tests our morals and the things we are told to do to bring justice.

We serve the public to the best of our ability and follow the strict written laws. Our Bible in a way."

"Take last week, I was asked to help break up a disordered crowd, who were all passionate anti-nuclear bomb protestors."

"Morally, let us be honest, none of us seriously want a nuclear bomb to explode in the world, these people were right to be protesting this topic. Yet, the law told me that I had to force some of these angry people to the ground and make arrests for disturbing the public order.

Did I personally believe what I was doing was just? Honestly, no, but the law only allows for peaceful protest no matter how emotive the subject or my personal views."

DS Nick had the crowd listening. He had not meant to speak for very long but felt that before the press went to print tomorrow, the police were represented properly, and Joshua Wright was condemned for his crimes and not his believes. With the TV cameras and radio teams broadcasting life, there was no way he could be miss quoted. DS Murray continued, "Knowing right from wrong is not written Ms Giles, it is taught to us all from a very young age.

"Joshua Wright believes in God, I am sure of this, but this belief led to him to kill three innocent people? Will he come to regret this? I personally very much hope so. But currently, he blames his actions on God alone."

"Your second question about if I think the police have powers over God's will?

Just look where you are standing today. Anyone who gives evidence in the courtroom behind me is given the option to swear upon the Bible or a preferred religious text.

This is used as a moral marker of people speaking the truth. This is their right the rules of the land have no argument to this sworn oath.

For people with no faith, this is not done, but ultimately God does reside over in many places of law.

God is the higher power here. God guides us and acts as the moral compass for us to follow the law. Gods true will is unknown, but one thing I can tell you for certain today."

"In the story of Joshua Wright, I believe that God moved in a very mysterious way." DS Murray concluded.

Mary Grace had tried to get a prison visit sorted to see Joshua, but so far this had been denied. Mary had not given up on Joshua no matter how far from the path he had fallen. Mary was certain that the voice Joshua was hearing has been that of the Serpent, not God.

The story of Joshua had been an important lesson for her. Eden's Echo not only taught her students how to hear God, but it also gave an open frequency to the serpent or Satan. Both God and Satan had spoken to Adam and Eve in Eden, as it was the very birthplace of original sin.

Mary knew all too well about the dark temptation of sin.

It was what lead her father, a once-popular vicar in the village of Stockton-upon-Avon, into leaving the parish after stories were proved of his involvement with young boys in King Alfred's school.

Mary was allowed to stay with Emerald Down-Lacey to continue her education after her parents fled back to Africa. Emerald had treated Mary like a daughter, eventually leaving her great fortune to Mary alone when she died.

Soon after her parents fled England, on the advice of Emerald Down-Lacey, Marina changed her name by deed-poll.

Marina Gracely, became Mary Grace Down-Lacey, the sole heir to the Down Lacey estate, which included The Old Rectory house, which Mary later sold to Ridley Goodman's parents.

It was much later on, after Emerald died, when Mary was tracing the Wyndham family tree that she made a discovery which seemed to make sense why Charles Wyndham had always been so kind to Emerald.

A scandal at the turn of the twentieth century reveal that Emerald Down-Lacey was the secret daughter of Charles Wyndham, who was born out of wedlock to a servant girl when he was no more than sixteen years of age.

Charles, parents had sent their son off around the world to hide from this disgrace. When Charles returned, he never forgot his responsibilities of taking care his only illegitimate daughter, taking her in as one of his own.

Only a few had ever known the truth of who Emerald really was to him. It was why he had shown her the secrets to Eden's Echo, it was why his sister had given Emerald the book.

# Chapter 23

## Flash Before Your Eyes

### Timeline—1 October, 2019

Joshua Wright had been in prison for three weeks.

The prison guards did not consider him a high risk, especially now all the media hype was beginning to die down and moving onto something else. Joshua had a cell to himself, for a while at least. They would soon be moving him to another block, where peace would be almost impossible to find. In his short time behind bars, Joshua had been calm, helpful, and not shown any signs of aggression.

Sat alone inside his prison cell with a tattered copy of an old Bible he had been given from the prison library, Joshua closed his eyes to pray.

Since the end of the trial, the voice inside Joshua's head had almost faded. It was as if God had deserted him, as His will was done.

As Joshua silently sat on the floor of his cell, using his known techniques he called out for God to hear his call. Like a wave of rushing water, a voice returned again, strong, full of love and commanding. This time the message was a simple one, showing that God had not yet abandoned him.

*"Come home Joshua, Eden awaits a true Son of Adam."*

Joshua snapped opened his eyes.

Faced with a lifetime of imprisonment and with no possibility of parole, there would be plenty of other chances to find a means of ending his life over the coming years. But what was the point in waiting? Today, God was asking Joshua to come home, which obediently Joshua would follow.

Taking the single bedsheet, Joshua wound it tightly into a long rope shape. The bunkbed inside his cell was made of a solid steel frame, with a long, tube bar across the width at each end.

Carefully, Joshua tied one end of the rope sheet to the bed bar. The other end he wrapped around his neck tightly as he was standing.

Lowering his body weight to sit on the floor, the sheet wrapped around his neck and would not allow him to reach the cold concrete seated. As the sheet tightened, it started choking him, crushing his windpipe.

With the noose ever tightening from just his body weight, Joshua closed his eyes and waited for God to take him back to Eden.

As Joshua lost consciousness, his mind was filled with a strong clear vision. Joshua had heard and read of this before, where a man's life flashed before his eyes before for God took them onwards.

But this was something else. This was something *different.*

These visions were far stronger, far more vivid, and more importantly, it was not his life flashing before his eyes.

*Joshua could see an old townhouse, located at the end of a block of terraced houses, all identical to each other. Alongside the house, a huge black iron fence ran around what looked to be a large primary school.*

*Outside in the playground, hundreds of children were playing happily as the sun shone down on them. Joshua felt a feeling of complete happiness as the children all played together.*

*Beyond the playground, the sports pitch of an upper school backed onto the primary school. Here the fields were filled with boys playing football and girls clashing hockey sticks together.*

*Joshua recognised this place.*

*This was the school he happily attended growing up. Much had changed, but he definitely knew where he was. The townhouse was that of his grandmothers, or at least it used to be.*

*There was a sign on a wall with the street name, Eden Grove. Now he was sure this was the road where he had once lived as a boy before his parents could afford to buy their own place.*

*Drifting into the door of the townhouse, Joshua was shown to a wide kitchen. Every worktop, table and surface were filled with handmade signs and posters, some of which made no sense to him. There were pictures on the walls about climate change and banning the bomb. Many were set with wooden posts making them easy to carry into protest rallies or marches.*

*Joshua could see the extinction rebellion symbol on a new poster, but the date on the sign made no sense.*

*!!Time has run out!! Join us on our March 28.11.30.*

*He could remember his grandmother making jam in this room. The smell was incredible. But not today.*

*Joshua's view was changed to face the large table in the centre of the room.*

*Sitting at one of six wooden chairs, a man was busy drawing what looked to be another poster, similar to the Extinction Rebellion signs. Joshua thought the man looked familiar.*

*He was thin, with unkempt braided hair. The narrow black beard he supported was also braided, with several coloured beads threaded at the bottom.*

*Resting against the table, a single metal crutch was propped* up nearby, within easy reach for the man to grab, as Joshua could see this man only had one leg.

On the table, the stub of a roll-up cigarette was smoking in an ashtray, as the man was too busy designing his artwork to think about it.

From another door in the room, a woman entered. Joshua recognised the red-haired woman immediately, although she looked older than the last time, he had seen her.

Joshua watched the two people in the room.

It was as if he were a ghost, watching down on a scene from above.

The woman walked over to the man and put her hand on his shoulder. As she looked at the poster, he was drawing she smiled and patted him supportively, pointing at the nuclear symbol.

There was no doubt in his mind, this was Jemma Evans. From her swollen stomach, she looked to be about six months pregnant.

The man at the table nodded and reached for a dented purple water container. Taking a long drink, Joshua could see by the three empty wrappers on the table, this man was addicted to eating healthy protein bars.

Joshua watched the man, as he reached for an apple in a bowl. Taking a bite from the forbidden fruit, he pulled another poster out from the pile on the table and gave it to Jemma.

The man was talking to her, but Joshua could not hear him.

In fact, everything was silent.

Joshua suddenly felt cold as he recognised the man at the table. It was Phillip Stevens. Much older than the boy he killed, but Joshua was sure this was the same person, in his late 20's.

Was God trying to show him something?

The huge poster Jemma received from Phillip was made

specifically for a protest on the newly completed Hinckley Point Nuclear Power Station. It was a simple and effective campaign poster,

**Join Us – Nuclear Power WILL Kill the World!**
**It is time we acted.**
**Blow them up, before they blow us all up.**
**Stop the switch on.**
**Vision, not Fusion.**

More people started coming into the kitchen. None of these were people Joshua recognised, but he knew the type. Most of them looking like rejects from the hippy days of the 1960s.

The newcomers started picking up various signs and were talking excitedly. Jemma was leading the conversation, pointing, and showing plans of the Hinckley point site.

Joshua could see that she looked to be in charge of this small group of activists. They were all about to embark on a protest rally, using Phillip's homemade signs.

Joshua looked over to the calendar stuck on a large fridge. It was covered in handwritten messages against various dates.

Some were showing recent rallies, other dates giving specifics of protests marches, but one date was circled heavily.

Joshua moved closer. This could not be right!

The date today was showing 28/11/30.

The date circled in black pen on the calendar was 30.11.30.

The words against this date were worrying.

**Hinckley Point Switch On. The Big Bang!!!**

Joshua wanted to wake up from this dream. He wanted to warn someone about these activists. But if these were all just peaceful protestors that had no real power, their cries and voices would just drift on the wind, until the power switch moved to the **on** position.

But how could this be? In 2030 both Philip Stevens and Jemma Evans were long dead. This was something he knew for sure, as Joshua was the one who poisoned them both.

The vision of the kitchen slowly faded to white.

Joshua could see he was now upstairs inside the same house, once more looking out across the playground of the school filled with children shouting and laughing.

Parents were beginning to gather around the entrance gates as it was close to finishing time.

In the distance, a whistle echoed as a football match got underway, with parents stood on the side lines cheering on their sons.

Joshua turned around from the single window. The bedroom he was stood inside was small. When Joshua was a child, this had been his room. The black mark on the ceiling was still there, caused by his accident with matches and a deodorant can. But today, it was not being used as a bedroom at all.

Jemma Evans walked in carrying the large protest poster Phillip Stevens had created for her. Walking over to a man, hunched over a high wooden bench which had been built across the entire wall of the room, his back was turned to Joshua.

Jemma moved over to him and put her arms around the man, kissing the back of his shaved head. The man sat up for a second and reached out to touch Jemma's bump. Just as quickly, he returned to his work.

For a while they spoke together, with Jemma taking the lead in the conversation, talking about the plans today and tomorrow.

The man was clearly busy, looking to be mixing something in what Joshua thought to be a homemade chemistry set.

As Joshua continued to watch the man working, Jemma stood back and closed the bedroom door.

The man handed Jemma a pair of goggles, which she put on, looking a little apprehensive. Tying back her long red hair, she moved to the other side of the room near the window, next to where Joshua was watching from.

The man turned towards her. Even though he was wearing a black face mask and plastic goggles, Joshua recognised Ridley Goodman instantly.

Over the last ten years, if this was what he was witnessing, Ridley had risen up from his homeless position in Yeovil, where Joshua had first found him.

Ridley now had grade two short tidy hair, clean-shaven and the most expensive watch Joshua had ever seen on his wrist. With a thick gold chain around his neck, and two gold rings on his fingers, Joshua was sure that Ridley's sudden rise into money had been lucrative and quick.

Perhaps Ridley had taken up John Mole's offers of employment?

John Mole had made the same offer to Joshua, but he politely refused. Frederick Bannister told Joshua that even though John Mole was a born-again Christian, his links with the Polish drugs trade were still bringing the old man a tidy profit. The Lord's Pantry provided John Mole with excellent cover.

The only other real difference from what Joshua could remember of Ridgely Goodman was the number of tattoos that now dominated his arms and neck.

Many were symbols of defiance. Ban the Bomb, Extinction Rebellion and anti-abortion all had been placed on each arm, but there were several others symbols that Joshua did not recognise.

There was a symbol on Ridley's neck that looked to be a religious cross, but it was circled with a huge drop of what Joshua thought to be a blood coloured teardrop.

*This was not a symbol known to Joshua. It did not look peaceful, it looked rebellious, even violent.*

*Suddenly the visions of what was happening came to Joshua.*

*God was showing him a vision of the future.*

*But it was not the future from Joshua's world.*

*God was showing him his victim's world if Joshua had not killed them as instructed.*

*Was this to be his penance?*

*Did God want to make him feel remorse for what he had done?*

*Why was God wanting to torture him this way?*

*Joshua moved across to the high bench Ridley Goodman was working against.*

*It was completely covered in what looked to be mixtures of dozens of chemicals, some of which had toxic symbols on labels, others with danger written on dark frosted bottles.*

*Carefully, Ridley was pouring them into what looked like a sealed plastic ball, with a tiny opening in one end.*

*Wearing thick purple safety gloves and a full pharmaceutical mask, Joshua now wondered what the hell was going on inside this room.*

*Jemma was not taking any notice of Ridley working. Instead, she was stood at the window, writing text messages on her mobile phone.*

*Joshua tried to see what she was writing.*

*It was difficult, but from what he could see, it was a warning to someone.*

*It was a bomb threat.*

*Who were these people?*

*Joshua was familiar with activists. Some of their causes he had openly supported from afar. But whatever had happened to the three people God had chosen him to kill, was a step above anything he had ever seen before. These were the real deal, activists who meant business.*

*Ridley reached down under the bench. Carefully he lifted up a small cardboard box, containing an electrical device. It was not large, but from the digital timer led screen and the wires poking in and out of it, Joshua knew he was looking at a homemade improvised bomb.*

*What were these people planning to do?*

*Phillip Stevens opened the bedroom door and hobbled into the room. Placing his crutch down against the bench, he moved awkwardly onto an empty stool next to the Ridley.*

*Putting on another pharmaceutical mask, Phillip helped himself to a spare set of goggles hanging on a hook behind the bench. Ridley carefully took the device out from the box, and gently placed it down to the bench.*

*Checking the device by sight alone, Joshua was no expert, but it was pretty clear what it was.*

*Joshua looked back at Jemma's phone again and caught the sight of just two words on the mobile phone before she sent the message.*

*Hinckley Point.*

*Joshua panicked but was unable to do a thing. Were these people stupid enough to attempt to blow up a new nuclear power station? Surely not?*

*Peaceful Activists! No! These people were Terrorists!*

*Jemma moved across to the bedroom window and looked out over the school playground. Flicking up a photo on her phone, there was an image of a beautiful red-headed five-year-old girl smiling at her whilst sitting upon a swing. Behind the swing, Ridley Goodman was pushing the little girl, who looked just like* him.

The next image was of Jemma and Ridley embracing a tiny baby in a hospital.

Joshua now understood that sometime in the near future, Ridley and Jemma would come together and form a family.

But what sort of family dealt in chemicals and bombs?

Jemma opened the window and leaned out. Waving down towards the playground, a little red-haired girl in the schoolyard was waving back up at her. It was the same girl as in the photograph on the mobile phone.

Did this little girl have any idea that her parents were terrorists!

Joshua changed his attention back to the two men on the high bench.

How long did God want him to see these images?

Was he trying to show Joshua that killing these three people was a good thing?

With extreme care, Ridley lifted the sealed red plastic ball, now filled with a chemical cocktail, lowering it into a specially designed clip holder on the device. Locking the ball into the chamber, Ridley turned to Jemma and said something clearly funny as Ridley was laughing. Jemma did not laugh.

Phillip Stevens clicked open the lid of a laptop. Plugging a lead from the improvised device into a port on the side of the laptop, a schematic of the device appeared on the screen.

For a while, Phillip appeared to be checking and running diagnostics on the device. Joshua could see this man was now an expert in such things.

Joshua watched as the LED timer on the device changed from 00:00:00 to 24:00:00.

With an agreed nod from Jemma, Phillip pressed a green

*button on the laptop and the timer began to start counting down, second by second. 23:59:59.58.57.*

*How Phillip had fallen into following such a dark path was unknown.*

*But a tattoo of what looked to be a military emblem was proudly displayed on Phillips's forearm.*

*Joshua had seen this emblem before.*

*In the early years before his father had driven buses, John Wright had served for fifteen proud years inside the British army.*

*Eight of them in bomb disposal.*

*It was the same tattoo his father had shown him, Joshua was sure of it. The honoured badge of Explosive Ordnance Disposal. This tattoo was earned out of merit, not just given to anyone who walked into a tattoo parlour.*

*Had Phillip Stevens served in the army, he must of?*

*Did this explain the crutch and his one leg?*

*Was Phillips Stevens set on a path of revenge?*

*With the device configured and set, Phillip turned around on the stool and spoke for a while to Jemma and Ridley. Spinning back to the laptop, he accidentally clicked, over what looked to be a flashing red timing button.*

*This was clearly a clumsy mistake.*

*The LED lights on the device flickered and within seconds, changed to show 00:00 on the display.*

*In complete panic, Phillip tried to pull the connecting lead clear from the homemade explosive device.*

*Joshua's vision went an instant brilliant shade of white.*

*As the white faded, Joshua was aware of another vision unfolding before him.*

*This time he was looking at what looked to be the ruins of a scene in Syria. Bombed husks of totally destroyed buildings were no more than hollow shells and piles of concrete rubble.*

*Joshua immediately realised this was not Syria.*

*Dozens of ambulances, fire crews and police cars were parked along the entire length of Eden's Grove road. Everything was pulsing with a heartbeat of blue light.*

*Along the city road, the smouldering remains of six terraced houses, plus what had once been a busy primary school, was still smoking, with occasional bursts of flame from ruptured gas pipes. Without any thought of the danger around them, heroes wearing the helmeted uniform were still climbed through the rubble, many already carrying tiny black body bags.*

*A short distance away, medical heroes worked in vain to try to save children who had been happily playing sports, when the wave of death rolled in, dressed in white light.*

*In a rough circle of what looks to be hundreds of metres wide, Joshua could see the bomb accidentally set off by Phillip Stevens had been devastating. There was little to nothing left of the building or human life.*

*How many had died?*

*100? 200? 500? All of them innocent, all of them, lambs.*

*It was difficult to imagine what the emergency services had arrived to find. The primary school alone was alive with children and parents when the chemically enhanced bomb detonated. This did not take account of the apple juice factory on the other side of the street, which was also laying in fallen ruins.*

*Joshua felt his heart die. What had they done?*

*What had driven decent people to become so evil?*

*Surely God was not involved with this?*

*A newspaper blew down the street in front of him.*

*The paper was dated one day on from the blast.*

*Its headline was clear.*

**Terrorist Plot Kills 500+**

*Joshua could see a picture of the lead policeman in charge of the investigation for this tragedy new.*

*DI Nicholas Murray. This would make sense.*

*The story on the cover of the newspaper was from a journalist Joshua had never heard of. Emma Giles was amongst the first of the news teams said to have reached the terrible cornered off scenes.*

*Joshua knew that he was being shown the words on the newspaper, as all around him, people were desperately searching the rubble for any further signs of life.*

**As my eyes first focused on the death and destruction before me, I could no longer hear the screams of the dying, nor the wailing sirens of another emergency vehicle arriving.**

**I was deaf to it all.**

**My mother, you will know as the famous Catherine Giles, once wrote a report of a story she covered in Beirut, the day after a huge bomb exploded near to a hospital.**

**The following morning, after the area was deemed safe enough to visit, my mother was taken into the ruined hospital which was already overflowing with casualties.**

**These are her words from that day:**

**As we entered the hospital doors, Doctors were pleading with the camera teams, begging for people to bring fresh blood supplies and generators just to keep the lights on.**

**Six operating theatres were lined up with patients supporting wounds I could not bear to witness. At any moment, the roof looked as if it could collapse on us all. But the doctors continued to work, most of them telling me that God would protect us.**

*The heart-wrenching cries of bereaved men and women broke me, as families searched for missing loved ones or learned of those who were already gone.*

*One little boy sat alone in a corridor. He could not have been more than eleven years old. Across his face, blood had splattered in thick red clumps, and he looked to have several deep cuts on both his arms.*

*I approached the boy and asked him if he was alone.*

*He nodded and looked at me with the biggest saddest eyes I had ever seen. There were no tears, he was beyond that.*

*The little boy said his mother and father were both killed in the bomb. He said it was like an earthquake, then he felt something hit him and everything turned red. The boy told me that his father had jumped on him to stop the noise.*

*When the boy awoke, he said his father was still there, but only some of him.*

*I never found my mother the boy said calmly.*

*She went straight to God.*

*My mother's harrowing story has stayed with me to this day.*

*Anyone who can actively set a bomb off intentionally, especially where innocent children are in the line of fire, these are the worst type of murderers.*

*They have no equal.*

*They are the wolves of the world.*

*Today, what I have witnessed is something near to what my mother saw in Beirut. No words from a journalist or pictures from a camera can possibly describe the sense of hopelessness and despair I am currently witnessing.*

*If God is watching from above, then I hope he can show us justice.*

*As I stand here watching men of God deep in prayer, united in their faiths condemning the destruction this has caused, I can't help feeling that they are all too late, as death beat them to their prayers.*

*If there is a God above, why would He allow such horrific acts to befall the lambs of the world.*

*Like the little boy in Beirut, I stand here lost, alone and beyond tears.*

*Surely, God has the power to hunt out the Wolves.*

*I pray for a miracle. I pray for hope. I pray for justice.*

*Hear my prayer God as only you have the power that could have stopped this tragedy.*

*God bless every single person who was slaughtered here today. Some papers are calling this story,*

*The slaughter of the Easter lambs.*

*God, my written prayer is to you alone.*

*I pray you to find a way to seek out and kill these wolves.*

*Save the lambs, for they are all your sons and daughters.*

*Emma Giles.*

Joshua could feel the air in his lungs now completely starved. As he drifted back into the consciousness of his cell, he knew he did not have long.

*God had shown him why. Joshua had killed the wolves.*

Joshua could now die in peace.

A voice inside Joshua's head was a welcome return. Only moments before death allowed him the peace he wanted, Joshua now understood why His God had shown him these terrible visions of a future, that would mercifully now never come to be.

*Joshua. It is time to come home to Eden.*

*I have shown you the wolves, and the lambs you have saved.*

*The lambs are all safe Joshua. You have served me well.*

*Come home, son of Adam. Eden welcomes you.*

Joshua Wright felt at complete peace.

As darkness swallowed him, Joshua could see a brilliant light.

Mary had once told him that sometimes God's pathway only became clear at the very end of a person's life.

From the moment he had first heard God's voice, Joshua had not understood why he was chosen to kill three innocent people.

It was completely at odds with everything he was taught by Mary. Many times, he had flatly refused to carry out God's instruction, but the voice inside his head had driven him ever onwards, ever louder, ever stronger, until only these murders could allow him to find some sort of peace again.

In his final moments, God in His divine grace had revealed to Joshua why he had given him this grim holy mission of murder. Joshua had died knowing why he was the hunter of wolves and what he had saved from the world to come.

As Joshua stepped into Eden, only he would ever truly know of his place in this story. Emily Giles would never know that her prayers had been answered.

Joshua died alone in the comforting knowledge that his murders had ultimately led to *The Greater Good.*

# Epilogue.

DS Nick Murray was promoted within a year after the murder charge was given to Joshua Wright, aka The Spiker.

As the new Bristol DI, Nick made sure his two sergeants Mike Parsons and Sally Gunel were posted to his station with him. They were both fine officers who he trusted completely.

Sergeant Parsons continued to be a regular pain to Sally's everyday life, even after she got married to a local bricklayer. Sally Gunel learned to live with Mike Parsons and his stupid comments, for under his persistent chauvinist ways, he was a very good policeman.

This tolerance was her gold medal performance.

DI Murray had hoped to retire, but Celia knew that it would be a few more years before her husband picked up his carriage clock and settled for an easier life. DI Murray was married to the job.

It was as if he felt some divine calling to serve.

Mary Grace wrote the second copy of her book, only a year after she learned of Joshua's sad suicide in prison.

Mary was permitted to speak at Joshua's funeral, which both Frederick Bannister and Barnaby Barnes had also attended.

They were the only people to say goodbye to the man, who the world still called evil.

Mary still believed that Joshua had been tricked by Satan. This was covered heavily inside her new book.

Eden's Echo part two, Mary had called 'The Serpents Call'.

'The Spiker' murders were never fully solved.

Why Joshua Wright had killed three randomly innocent young people was never fully understood. For years after, this case was studied by students in law, but no evidence was ever produced to create another plausible motive.

Joshua was labelled an insane murderer who cold-bloodedly killed without remorse or motive, apart from his strange unproven claim that God had chosen him to do it. The randomness of these deaths was rare for murder, but so was the painless method Joshua had chosen as his weapon.

No faith leader ever believed Joshua's claim of talking to the divine. All of them stating the commandment of "Thou shall not murder" was one of God's fundamental rules.

The ability to learn to speak to God from a book or tape was also branded dangerous unless of course, you were from the cloth or clergy. Yet, hundreds of books remained freely available online and in book shops on the topic of "How to Speak with God.".

In 2013, Pope Benedict XVI announced that God had stopped talking to him directly, deciding amongst other reasons to step down as the vicar of Christ on earth.

There had been a huge outcry at the time, as Pope's were not supposed to retire.

When the Pope announced to the world that God's voice was gone from him, he revealed to the - soon to become - Pope Francis, that it was no longer right for him to be God's vicar when His voice was silent.

One Billion plus Catholics freely accepted that Pope's could speak directly to God.

Joshua Wright was labelled insane.

# Other Books Available from Steve Wilkinson

Blood Moon Prophecies Book One: Blood Raven
Blood Moon Prophecies Book Two: Rise of the Serpent
Blood Moon Prophecies Book Three: The Last Serenade
Swords of the Pious: Red Wolf
Kindred – Part 1: Blood and Sweat
Kindred – Part 2: Hope & Fear
Kindred – Part 3: Trust & Loss
You X Two: Fiat Lux
Rare: Beyond the Great Spirit
Sleeping Through
Memories of Ancient Futures